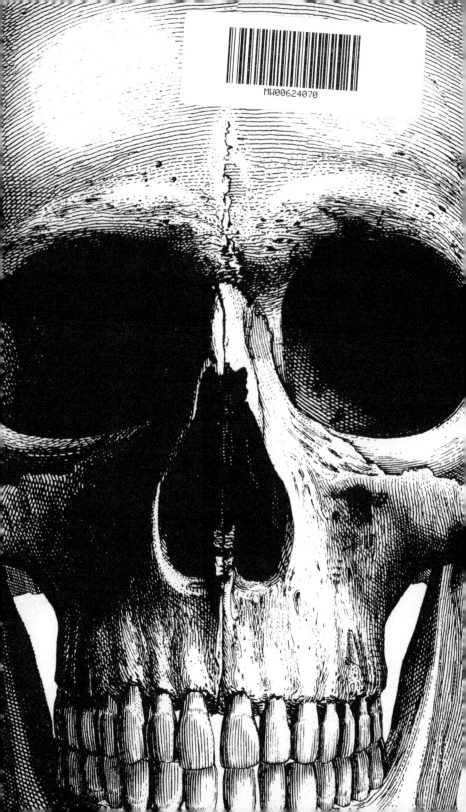

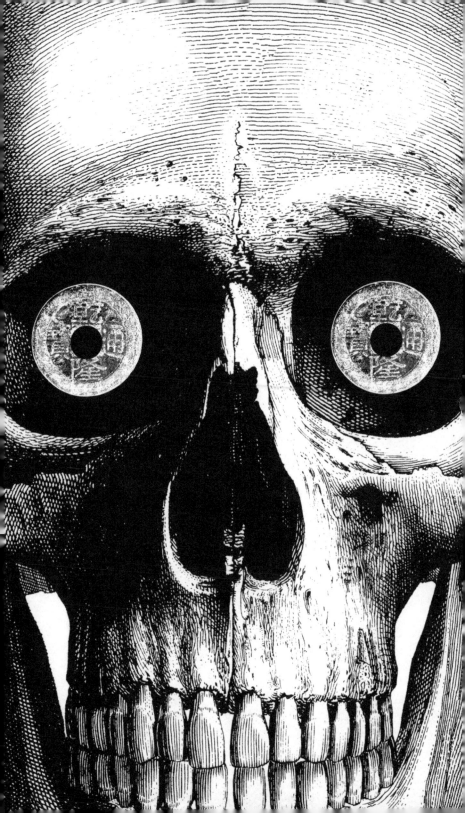

PENNIES FROM HEAVEN

A NOVEL BY

James P.
Blaylock

DIP

2022

Book design by Pedro Marques.
On the cover: *Sunset glow on Mount Tamalpais* by William Keith, 1896
and a detail of *A vanitas still life with a skull atop a book,*
an hourglass and two glass vases of fl owers by Guercino, 1619-20.
Text set in Caslon.

Printed in England by T.J. Books
on Munken Premium Cream 80 gsm stock.

PS Publishing Ltd
Grosvenor House
1 New Road
Hornsea, HU18 1PG
England
editor@pspublishing.co.uk

WWW.PSPUBLISHING.CO.UK

"What if the elephant in the room
is the skeleton in the closet?"
— William Ashbless, "Destinations 1958"

With love for Viki, John, Danny, and Jodi Blaylock. And especially for the amazing Duke Buchanan Blaylock.

I would like to thank a number of knowledgeable friends and early readers whose information and suggestions made this a better book. (Anything in the book that's less-than-better is my own doing.)

∞

Jessie Weiland, Betsy Elliot, John Blaylock, Danny Blaylock, Paul Buchanan, Lew Shiner, Mark Duncan, Lynn Jones, Doug Dechow, Tim Powers, and my friend Paul Apodaca, who has a profound and arcane knowledge of Orange County history. And also Jerry Simms, who years ago gave me a beautiful copy of *Caminos Viejos* by Terry E. Stephenson—a book that turned out to be inspirational.

And, as ever, I'll point out that my wife Viki tirelessly read and corrected early and late drafts of this book.

PENNIES FROM HEAVEN

Friday

1.

JANE LARKIN RESTED against piled up pillows, working in the glow of her tiny bedside lamp. She was adding up budget numbers in a spiral notebook for the second time and not much liking what she saw. The clock read four in the morning, but she knew that she was through sleeping, just like she knew there was nothing wrong with her arithmetic.

She listened to the sound of October rain gurgling out of the downpipe into the flowerbed, and now and then a gust of wind drove raindrops against the windowpanes. Summer had abruptly turned into fall at the end of August this year, and there had been an unending succession of cool days and cooler nights throughout September, with unseasonable rain two or three times a week, often heavy. She wished that a fire was burning in the bedroom fireplace—one of the nicely quaint elements of the old Spanish-style house that she and Jerry had bought six months ago in Old Orange, the downtown historical district of the City of Orange.

A year ago Jane had been awarded a MacArthur Foundation grant and had found herself director of a project she had named the Old Orange Co-op. She had been happily shocked to receive the funding she had asked for, enough to pay limited salaries and expenses for three years, by which time the Co-op was intended to be self-perpetuating. That would be possible only with help from the city and elusive private money. The months, however, were flying fast, and the perpetual rain was literally drowning the Co-op's activities.

Jerry breathed evenly on the opposite side of the bed, half-out of the covers, his legs stippled with the glow of the streetlamp slanting through the blinds. She discovered when they were married that sleeping was one of Jerry's talents. His black hair was bed-raggled, as Jane's mother used to say, and his face wore a serene expression. He was tall enough to take up the length of the mattress, and even in sleep his muscles were clearly defined, which came from years of swimming. Jane envied his ability to eat anything and not gain weight. She thought about waking him up, accidentally-on-purpose, so that she had someone to talk numbers with. He was good at convincing her not to worry.

The melody from "Pennies from Heaven" came into her mind, along with the memory of her father singing it to her when she was a little girl, afraid of thunder. She had loved the idea of carrying her umbrella upside-down when it rained in order to catch heavenly pennies. She would have hummed the tune, but not at this ungodly hour of the morning. Pennies weren't going to cut it anyway.

Their dog Peewee, a cross between a shih tzu and a pug and maybe a French bulldog, lay on his back between them snoring, resting against Jerry's side, his feet pointing toward the ceiling. Peewee's face was perfectly flat—a moon-like, two-dimensional face that made him appear self-satisfied and contributed to a noisy night's sleep. Jerry shifted, rolling slightly closer to the edge of the bed, and Peewee did the same, crowding up against him, as if shrinking Jerry's available space in a bold effort to tip him off onto the floor.

Jane set her notebook aside and picked up the collection of ghost stories she'd been reading before bed last night. She had put it down when it became particularly nightmarish, but it would probably be safe now that her mind had no interest in sleep. She had just started to read when Peewee abruptly woke up, stared wide-eyed at Jane for a frozen moment, and then heaved himself to his feet, jumped to the floor, and ran out through the doorway.

Someone on the porch? Jane thought, but now she saw that the ceiling lamp was swaying on its chains. Part of her mind associated it with Peewee's hitting the floor, but now the ground gave a lurch and the entire house shook and bounced on its foundation, the blinds clacking against the window frame and a cloud of black soot whooshing out of the fireplace. She heard a rumbling sound, or perhaps imagined it, and she pushed Jerry's shoulder hard, shouting his name as she clambered out of bed. Awakening instantly, Jerry followed her into the doorway where they jammed themselves in, holding on as the shaking increased.

The door started to swing shut, and Jerry threw out his hand to catch it, banging it open again, taking another second to flip on the light switch, a small relief that lasted about a second before there was a cracking noise beneath their feet followed by what sounded like a small avalanche. The floor slumped directly beneath them, and both of them gasped, Jane certain that they were going through. The floor jarred to a stop even as she thought it, but the house continued to lurch and roll. Something hit the ground out in the living room, and the picture hanging over the bed—a dancing woman in a flowered dress—slid downward along its wire but didn't fall.

"Hold on!" Jerry shouted unnecessarily, and Jane squeezed his arm in reply, since she was already holding onto him as well as onto the doorjamb. She felt the waves of energy moving beneath her feet—actual waves, not the jolting any longer, but more evenly as the 'quake slowly faded. The night grew silent and still, but the hanging lamp over the bed continued to sway on its chains.

They stood for a few more moments, still holding onto each other and waiting for it to start up again. Jane had the weird feeling that the whole world was swaying, and she looked away from the lamp, which made her seasick.

"That was unpleasant," Jerry said.

"My heart's beating like a hammer," Jane said, releasing his arm. "I thought the house was coming down."

Jerry stepped out of the doorway and got down on his hands and knees to look at the crack that had opened in the floor. Two tongue-and-groove oak slats had puckered open along Jane's side of the bed, the ends of the slats still miraculously closed and flat. There was white dust in the air, and small chunks of plaster lay on the floor from a crack in the ceiling.

Jane picked up her robe from the chair and put it on. The clock read 4:19. There was no possibility of more sleep. She looked closely at the tiled fireplace now, thinking about damage. The grout was still tight and clean, which was close to miraculous. The Arts and Crafts tiles, hand-made in the 1920s, would be hard to replace if they could be replaced at all, especially the four oddball tiles with Chinese motifs laid in among the rest. They were seriously old, with pastoral paintings of trees and distant mountains in blues and greens.

A brass-framed mirror was set into the center of the top row of tiles, which was peculiar. The man who had built the house had evidently been eccentric. When she sat in bed she could sometimes see the shadow of her face in the faded old mirror, and she saw now that the mirror was cracked, the only apparent 'quake damage besides the floor and ceiling. Maybe she would talk Jerry into moving the bed. She had no desire to look into her own cracked face.

"Can the floor be fixed?" she asked Jerry.

"Anything can be fixed." He smiled at her as if there was

nothing to it, clearly more worried about Jane's worrying than about the problem with the floor. He pulled on the chinos he'd been wearing yesterday and slipped on a pair of shoes. "Step back into the doorway another second, just for the fun of it." When Jane had pinned herself in again, he stood over the crack in the floor and bounced up and down.

"Is that wise?" Jane asked.

"It depends on how you define wisdom. According to Socrates it's a squishy word."

"Like the floor," Jane said. "Let's not dance on it until it's put back together, okay?"

Peewee wandered back into the room now and hopped up onto the bed, settling on Jerry's pillow and staring roundabout with an accusatory look.

"Peewee woke up ten seconds before it started and ran away," Jane said. "He knew it was coming."

"Just like the Chinese earthquake pigs," Jerry said. "Maybe we can put a cow bell around his neck and hire him out. I'm pretty sure everything's fine with the floor. A support post probably shifted and a beam slumped a little before it settled again. The nice thing about wooden houses is that everything is tied into everything else and it holds itself together. I'll head down to the cellar to take a look. Probably I can fix it myself."

They walked through the living room into the kitchen, Jane turning on the lights as they went. Half a dozen books had fallen onto the floor, jolted off the small table next to the couch. Jane put them back in their place and looked around, astonished to see that there was no other apparent damage, no other cracks in the ceiling, nothing broken. It didn't seem possible, the way the house had rolled with the 'quake and yet held together, everything riding along like a boat in a storm.

In the kitchen she dumped water into the electric kettle and plugged it in. "Coffee?" she asked, as Jerry dug the big flashlight out of the cupboard.

"Thanks," he said. "I just want to check out the cellar. Shouldn't take ten minutes."

He went out through the back door, and after a moment Jane heard the cellar hatch creak open. She poured hot water over a bag of green tea for herself and then made Jerry a cup of coffee with the filter cone, leaving the cone on top of the mug to keep it warm.

She fetched her laptop computer and went back out into the living room, where she opened the blinds and looked out at the rainy street and the camphor tree on the parkway, half-expecting to see buckled pavement or tilted phone poles, but there was no sign of any trouble at all in the misty glow of the streetlamps. Old Orange had shaken itself out like a big rug and then settled back into place.

Mrs. Collins, across the street, stood on the sidewalk in her bathrobe and slippers looking at her house, an ornate old half-timbered place with gables and a steep roof that neighbors referred to as the Snow White house. Jane was tempted to stroll across the street for a chat, but Mrs. Collins waved at someone unseen, who was out and about farther on down, and then headed back up the walk.

Peewee had already hopped up onto the big chair by the window, so Jane shifted him sideways and squeezed in next to him. She scratched him behind the ears and sipped her tea, thinking about the Saturday morning bookmobile that she was planning as an addition to the Co-op's farmers market. Part of her mind was waiting for the 'quake to start up again, and she thought of Jerry crawling around in the cellar, the house collapsing on him.

"Quit it," she said, and Peewee looked up at her, obviously assuming that she was talking to him.

She had a breakfast meeting this morning with a Mrs. Lettie Phibbs from the Antiquity Center in order to discuss the bookmobile project. The Center had deep pockets, which wasn't a bad thing. But she found now that she dreaded the meeting just a little bit. She had met Mrs. Phibbs a couple of times in the past, and the woman had struck her as being slightly off-kilter. But an off-kilter ally with funds was better than no ally, and how many people were entirely *on*-kilter when you thought about it, except perhaps sociopaths, who had no kilter at all.

On the internet she found a number of used food trucks for sale moderately cheap—the old ones, anyway—although it might cost as much again to repurpose one, not to mention potential repairs to the engine or transmission. She looked at several photos, trying to get a sense of what was being offered, wanting to have a picture in mind when she talked to Lettie Phibbs about money. She could fake the rest.

Her mind went back to the 'quake again, and she searched the internet for some mention of it, finding it instantly, posted just a couple of minutes ago. It had been a slip in the Newport-Inglewood fault, the same fault that had triggered the Long Beach 'quake in 1933. That one had been a 6.4 magnitude roller that killed 115 people, most of them crushed by falling brick from unreinforced walls and chimneys when they ran out-side. The fault had been quiet until this morning's 5.4 shaker, according to the brief report. It was a modern miracle that the information had appeared online so quickly, and also that there was nothing in it that was the least bit useful.

"I won't let Jerry hire you out as an earthquake pig," she said to Peewee, who had a small sense of humor and who was sound asleep now and breathing heavily. Jerry, on the other hand, had a double dose when it came to a sense of humor, which sometimes got him into trouble with people who had little or none at all.

2.

JERRY DESCENDED the several concrete stairs into the cellar, switched on the bare bulb overhead, and then shut the hatch in order to keep the rain out. The place smelled of dusty stone, old lumber, and dead air. The light bulb was dusty and threw a feeble light, and the maze-like cellar was a place of deep shadows. In the six months they'd owned the house he had meant to hook up better lighting and clean the cellar out, but the task had been easy to put off over the summer, which he and Jane had spent fixing up the house and yard.

The cellar was a big one by southern California standards, with a section of concrete floor and a considerable space dug out beyond where the floor ended. The house's old gravity heater was down here, the burners surrounded by a heavy concrete box. He could see light from the kitchen through the register in the floor above the heater box. The water heater stood nearby, alongside an open plywood cabinet. Inside the cabinet lay a box of wooden matches, no doubt for lighting the water heater pilot a decade or two ago. There was a dead flashlight, too. He decided to leave his live flashlight in the cabinet when he closed up.

Another thing occupying the considerable cellar space was a wrought-iron log rack, still heaped with sawn limbs and wedges of stumps. It was a good place to keep firewood dry, although it was also a spider palace. He could see the spiky egg sacs of brown widows, which beat black widows, although he preferred no widows at all, at least living in the cellar. The logs would have to go. Alongside the log rack were three wooden packing crates sized like nesting dolls, with the lids removed and set diagonally into the crates. The crates were keepers.

He saw now that there was more earthquake damage than the crack in the bedroom floor. An even wider crack had opened up in a brick foundation wall that stretched from the base of the fireplace across to the concrete perimeter foundation under the east wall of the house. The top-to-bottom crack in the brick hadn't been there when he had last been in the cellar, so it was obviously 'quake damage. The wall was a little over six feet high, built of burnt clay bricks that ran along under a big beam, as if the brick wall was meant to support it. But that seemed unnecessary given the hefty size of the beam. Surely it could support itself. And why brick rather than concrete like the rest of the foundation?

What looked like white sand had leaked out of the crack, which was another strange thing. Why on earth would anyone build a wall of hollow brick and fill the voids with sand? Mortar would make sense, but there was no virtue in sand.

He shined his flashlight into the maze of posts and beams beneath the distant bedroom. Someone had dug out a path in that direction as well as excavating other random areas, a half-finished attempt at carving out useful space, probably. He could just make out the brick base of the back-to-back fireplace in the distance, each side with its own chimney-pipe and damper. To the left of it lay the crawlspace beneath the bedroom, his destination as soon as he lit the place up.

He had been right about the bedroom floor: a vertical support post appeared to have shifted and now stood at a wonky angle. The beam it supported had bowed beneath the weight of the house, just enough to open the crack. The beam didn't appear to be in any danger of failing, however, at least not from this distance. He could lift it straight with a bottle-jack at a civilized hour, stand the post up straight again, and lower the beam back onto it, tying the pieces together with steel plates to prevent the same thing happening again.

The top-to-bottom crack in the brick wall was more interesting—an opportunity, to be sure. He could simply knock a three-foot width of the bricks out entirely, opening up a passageway to the most useful part of the cellar. He would set posts on either side of the door, just in case the brick wall had some structural purpose after all. The posts would further support the beam.

He could excavate the cellar to his heart's content after that. It wouldn't take much digging to open up enough square footage for a brick-walled wine cellar. Although he and Jane weren't wine connoisseurs, he'd be a fool not to put one in. Even a cheap bottle of wine tasted better if it was hauled out of a wine cellar. The thought of wine reminded him that it was his and Jane's anniversary in a few days and that he needed to buy champagne and a present—something nice. And he would make her dinner—steak Diane, maybe, with garlic mashed potatoes. Ten years!

He looked more carefully at the delta of white sand on the floor and spotted what looked like a big coin standing on edge, half-buried. Clearly it had fallen out of the crack along with the sand. It appeared to be an old Chinese coin, brown-black with age and with a square hole in the center of it—a lucky coin if he ever saw one. The raised pictographs on it were strangely intricate, although they didn't suggest pictures to him.

The sand on his fingers was the bright white of coral sand rather than silica, although it appeared to be made up of tiny crystals. He put his tongue to it. It was salt, not sand. Someone—a lunatic, maybe—had filled the hollow spaces in the bricks with salt. He stood thinking about this for a moment, coming up with nothing to explain it. It was time to return to the waking world, to his coffee getting cold on the kitchen counter and to Jane, who was drinking her tea alone. A fire in the fireplace would be a good thing to restore a sense of home-liness to the unsettling morning.

He pushed open the hatch, switched off the light, and climbed out. The rain had stopped, but water was dripping from the eaves, and the air smelled of rain on concrete, wet mulch, and night-blooming jasmine. There was dawn light in the east-ern sky now. He flipped his lucky coin into the air, caught it in his palm, and put it into his pocket.

3.

SCOTTY'S DRUGSTORE and Soda Fountain was busy for breakfast, this being a Friday morning. Jane found an empty table near the back, with red and white leatherette booths on either side of a Formica-topped table with a blue and pink pattern of stovetop percolators and old toasters. There was a cheerful clattering of plates and glasses and porcelain coffee mugs along with the chatter of conversation, the people behind her talking about the earthquake. She sipped her coffee, looking out at the street through the windows, watching for the arrival of Mrs. Phibbs, now ten minutes late.

Servers brought plates of hot food out from the kitchen through a nearby swing door, and Jane contemplated snatching the bacon off the next plate that came past the table. She could eat the evidence and deny the crime. But here was Mrs. Phibbs coming in through the door. Apparently spotting Jane, she pushed her way through the activity between the long counter and adjacent tables. She was wearing a voluminous scarf decorated with pictures of books, several pieces of silver jewelry with big turquoise stones, and a pair of half-glasses with heavy blue frames beneath a bubble hairdo and bangs that gave her an odd, little-girl look. Jane guessed she was in her mid-sixties. She wasn't a big woman, but there was something sturdy about her, what Jane's father would have called hearty peasant stock.

She squeezed into the booth and said, "It's high time that you and I had a real confab, Jane. I'm *so* happy you agreed to meet with me."

"The pleasure is mine," Jane said, smiling broadly. "I . . ."

"Hold that thought!" Mrs. Phibbs gestured at a passing waitress in a red apron and said, "We'd like to order breakfast, young lady, if you have the time. We're *ravenous*, so you'd best take our order if you want a real tip rather than a penny in the bottom of a water glass." She winked at Jane, as if this was intended to be a harmless variety of teasing. "I'll have the special, with the toast *golden* brown. Tell the cook that if the toast is too dark he'll hear from me. The eggs over medium, lacy around the edges, but *not* browned. The bacon crisp. I cannot abide flaccid bacon."

"Yes, ma'am," the waitress said, and looked at Jane, who ordered fried eggs, bacon and rye toast as simply and clearly as she could. It struck her that it would be necessary to double-check the tip.

"Now, let's introduce ourselves properly," Mrs. Phibbs said when the waitress had gone off.

"Yes," Jane said. "You go first."

"All right. People call me Lettie, which is short for Leticia. You are hereby directed to do the same. I earned my master's degree in library science from the University of Southern California. This was a *long* time ago to be sure. I specialized in southern California history. I grew up in Orange County, you know. I'm *from* here, if you take my meaning. *Know thyself*, Jane. That has always been my motto—*know thyself!* And one cannot know oneself unless one knows one's roots."

"Very sensible," Jane said. "And you decided to work as a private librarian in a non-profit library? That was an adventurous decision."

"I opened the Antiquity Center as a *real* library and museum, Jane. Not the modern-day delirium tremens that calls itself a library but sheds books like a dog sheds fleas. I've always gone my own old-fashioned way." She nodded sharply and said, "Now, it's your turn."

"Okay," Jane said. "I graduated with a degree in zoology from U. C. Riverside, worked at the Orange County Zoo for a few years, taught at Fullerton College for a few more, and then went back to Riverside for a degree in urban planning."

"Because you dreamt the dream of the Co-op!"

"Exactly."

"Most inspiring book?"

"Maybe . . . *The Death and Life of Great American Cities*."

"I can't recall having read it, although I'm certain it was an inspiration. Your dream is a *good* dream, Jane, and I'm happy to find that we're both dreamers. We were destined to fall in with each other—two women in charge of burgeoning non-profit enterprises. I'll tell you that I very much like this notion of a book caravan in your Co-op's farmers market. I've been giving it *serious* thought. But first tell me what you envision. We'll see if we're on the same *page*." She covered her mouth and tittered through her fingers, and it came to Jane that Lettie had made a librarian's joke.

"I'd like it to appeal particularly to children," Jane said, "with readings on Saturday mornings, storytellers, chalk artists, maybe puppet shows."

"No *real* books? No literature? No local history?"

"Oh, yes, of course real books. Mainly real books. But an interactive sort of a place—*fun*, if you see what I mean."

"I believe I do," she said skeptically. "I was thinking about the problem of babysitting loose children."

"Students from the college could take that on. I've got two of them interning with the Co-op."

Mrs. Phibbs gave her a skeptical look. "*Paid* interns?"

"No, not yet, although I'm considering hiring them at the end of the term. At the moment they earn three units of credit."

"*Good*. Keep it that way. Don't waste money when you can find free labor. That's rule number one. When their term is done, send them packing and advertise for newbies. Do *not* confuse business with sentimentality, Jane. A penny saved, after all. What else do you envision?"

"I believe we could set up the . . . caravan . . . in a disused food truck once we removed the interior of the truck and put in bookshelves. I've got volunteer help for that and a design in mind."

"A city-approved craftsman?"

"My husband, actually."

Lettie frowned and began to speak but was distracted when their food appeared. She inspected her toast and seemed satisfied, although the eggs, she told the waitress, appeared to have been in cold storage for a month or two, given the color of the yolk.

"I could . . ." the waitress began.

"What *good* would it do?" Lettie said. "They're bought in wholesale lots, no doubt. The cooler is full of last month's eggs. I'll just hold my nose when I eat them."

Lettie turned to Jane and said, "I believe I met your husband at the City Sociable in February. I'm embarrassed to say that I can't recall his name."

"Jerry," Jane said, watching the confused waitress drift away.

"Ah! Named after St. Jerome of Wales, no doubt."

"He's Irish, mainly. But I might start calling him St. Jerome when I'm angry with him."

"Which I hope is rarely, Jane. I was always unlucky in love. I had a husband many years back, but he. . . passed away." She sat for a silent moment before asking, "What does your Jerry do for a living? Is he on the Co-op payroll? An officer?"

"No, he has independent means, actually. He studied literature at the university, didn't want to teach, and so he stuck with carpentry, which he was good at. Not long ago he sold his business." It occurred to her that she might have said too much, but there was no taking it back.

"Independent means? Isn't that lovely. I don't mean to pry, but if you have access to . . ."

"I decided that I wouldn't lean on Jerry for money," Jane said, anticipating her next question. "Nor my friends, unless they offer it."

"You're a self-reliant woman! That's good for your soul but not for your bank account, if you take my meaning. Would you *lean* on your husband's money if the Co-op were bound to fail?"

"Maybe, but I'd rather fail on my own terms. We're a community property household in all other ways."

"And yet despite your independent soul you took your husband's family name?"

"I wasn't fond of a hyphenated name, and I like the name Larkin. I guess I'm old-fashioned."

"More jam, please!" Lettie demanded when the waitress came into view. "Well! I admire your pluck, Jane. And I like it that you've got a rose-tinted Pollyanna streak in you. Now give me a quick rundown of finances. How does the Co-op survive?"

"It's complicated, and we haven't reached sustainability yet, but member families pay fifty dollars in annual fees, thereby accruing shares in the Co-op. City residents are entitled to a twenty percent discount on shares. Any member can claim a plot in the community garden, but a booth at the farmer's market costs $120 per month, which is thirty dollars every Saturday morning. Booths or garden plots that aren't maintained return to the Co-op after three months."

"My heavens. I don't wonder that you're worried about sustainability. Fifty dollars here and thirty dollars there! Can a serious supporter buy multiple annual memberships?"

"Yes. A voting member needs ten."

"Then put the Center down for fifty. If we're in league

together, the Center will want a loud voice when it comes to decision-making, and that'll get you an immediate transfusion of funds. But *surely* you have donors who offer real help?"

"We do, several generous patrons actually, and we're always on the lookout for more." *A loud voice?* Jane wondered how she could slow Lettie down without shutting her down completely.

"I can help you find real donors," she said, pulling the plastic top from a jam container and spreading jam on her toast. "Generous patrons are a rare breed and hard to get at. I'm on friendly terms with some of the wealthiest families in the area, however. Can I tell you a bit about how we do it at the Antiquity Center? You might find it educational."

"Please," Jane said.

"First, I hold an endowed Chair. That's vital, do you see. It secures your income into perpetuity, *and* you dictate your own salary, which can be a trap for the greedy, but it's an avoidable trap."

"Someone must have been very generous to endow a chair."

"Professor Arthur Johnston from Tidwell College, whom I married. He was well off, although not what anyone would call rich. But even a small amount of wealth can make good things happen if it's handled correctly, and I assure you that I had no scruples about leaning on his money to promote the Antiquity Center. It was not *me* who profited, do you see. He envisioned the Center and I brought his dream into being. He left a significant sum to keep the Center going, including his collection of books, artifacts, and memorabilia, mostly historical Californiana. He gave me *complete* control, and when he passed away the Center became my own by right of inheritance. I was damned if a Johnny-come-lately, know-nothing, managerial type was going to sit in my chair. The point being that we should be looking for *long-term* funding."

We . . . Jane wondered whether Lettie's little speech had something to do with Jerry's money being off-limits. "You're something of a tiger," she said, smiling at Lettie.

"I'm proud to say that I am—a rare breed. A private librarian has no master. I'm at the behest neither of the city nor the county, and in that regard I serve as a watchdog—an historical watchdog. And I have *teeth*. I can be quite useful to my friends, Jane, and a woeful enemy to my foes. I say that in the interests of plain speaking. I can see that you and I will be the *best* of friends."

She sat smiling, waiting for Jane to respond.

"I hope so," Jane said, at a loss for anything better and wondering what foes a librarian might be an enemy to.

"I'll consider these book caravan ideas of yours," Lettie said. "We'll cuss and discuss it, as I like to say, along with the issue of patrons. In fact, I might go one better. I have a contact who can secure vehicles at the best prices, so if you have a particular truck in mind, text me the particulars. Meanwhile, I have to dash. My clerk will be counting the minutes until he's off work. Ach! I've left my purse behind! I could run for it, if..."

"Don't do any such thing," Jane said, and she took $30 out of her wallet, handed it to the waitress, and told her to keep the change. Lettie widened her eyes, which Jane found satisfying. The two of them made their way out of the café, which was half-empty now that the breakfast rush had throttled down. On the sidewalk Lettie took Jane's hand into her fingers and shook it as if she was ringing a small bell. A horn honked out on Chapman Avenue, and Jane saw that it was Jerry driving past, waving out the window of his old pickup truck, a wide grin on his face, the wind blowing his hair.

"Who on earth was *that* leering creature?" Mrs. Phibbs asked.

"That would be St. Jerome," Jane said.

"I didn't recognize him. He had the visage of a ... He had an odd sort of look on his face. I'll bid you adieu, then." With that she turned away and headed east down Chapman Avenue at a determined clip.

Jane reminded herself not to be judgmental. It would be easy enough to drift into eccentricity living alone throughout one's life, mourning a dead husband. But she would have to think hard about how much leeway to allow Lettie Phibbs, even if the woman turned out to be serious about finding financial supporters for the Co-op. Aside from Jerry, Jane neither wanted nor needed a partner. It was a conundrum, though. Money was never free, even when it was given away.

4.

AT ACE HARDWARE Jerry had bought odds and ends to shore up the foundation of the house: a brick hammer, a four-ton bottle-jack and a concrete slab to set it on, metal plates and screws, and a pair of cotton coveralls with handy pockets that had put him back nearly forty bucks. Working under a house was a dirty business. The sky was a deep, clear blue, thank God, but the radio had just reported a flood watch to go along with the approaching storm—another worry for Jane and the Co-op garden and farmer's market, which sat on the flood plain along Santiago Creek.

He turned down Shaffer Street past the Holy Spirit Church with its bell tower and stained glass windows and old brick, and then west again on Chapman Avenue, heading toward the Plaza now, the heart of Old Orange. As he was passing Scotty's Drugstore and Soda Fountain, he saw Jane coming out onto the sidewalk behind a woman with hair like a silver orb and oddly short bangs—the librarian, Mrs. Phibbs. She looked well-fed and well-to-do. He tapped on the horn and waved broadly out the window, Jane waving back, Mrs. Phibbs frowning at him, probably thinking he was ogling the two of them. She was half-right. He was ogling *one* of them, given that it was okay these days to ogle one's wife.

Jane had always reminded him favorably of Wilma Flintstone, although the red in her dark hair was mainly visible in sunlight. She wore it the same way as Wilma, though, piled on top of her head. When he first met her at a Halloween party she was barefoot, wearing a cavewoman dress and Wilma's signature stone necklace. He'd tripped over a low table gawking at her when he walked in—something she reminded him of from time to time.

He saw his barber crossing the street toward the bank, and he waved as he swung past into the traffic circle, stopping at the crosswalk for a woman walking two chihuahuas and a bulldog. Across the way, near the fountain in the Plaza, fifteen or twenty people were chanting slogans, holding signs that read, "It's the Plaza, not the Circle!"

He waved cheerfully at them, too, feeling as if he were living on Penny Lane, and then he drove entirely around the Circle, or maybe the Plaza, a second time, looking at the sycamore and magnolia trees, and at the tiled fountain that was flinging sunlit water into the air. The Continental Café was busy out at the sidewalk tables, and the drive-through at Rod's Liquor had a line waiting. Maybe the earthquake had put people in the mood to drink. He turned into the Omega Burger parking lot, considered stopping for a pastrami and egg burrito, reconsidered, and turned back onto Chapman, heading back east in the direction of home.

When he passed Scotty's the second time Jane was nowhere to be seen. She would hear about the flood watch soon enough. Probably she'd already been alerted. She was a slave to weather and water, tracking stream gauge and rainfall data like other people tracked sports statistics. He thought about the doll-like Mrs. Phibbs now and what she might know about the Chinese coin in his pocket. Work on the cellar could wait for the half-hour it would take to chat with her.

He turned into the parking lot behind the old two-story craftsman bungalow that housed the Orange County Antiquity Center, a place he never before had a reason to visit. There were two other cars in the small lot—a black Cadillac Escalade and a battered Toyota Prius with a bicycle rack on the back. He pulled in next to the Prius, which left two spaces open for history buffs.

∞

Jerry was met with a pervasive silence when he entered the wood-paneled vestibule. He stood still, simply getting a sense of the place. Either the interior had been carefully restored or was lucky enough to have been preserved over the past century. The oak floors were bordered with a walnut inlay and were scattered with area rugs that muffled the sound of footsteps. He looked into a nearby glass case with a display of art pottery and Depression glass and old jewelry—lots of silver and turquoise. Framed photographs hung on the walls above the display case, depicting the city when it was incorporated in 1888—a crowd of founding fathers in top hats and mustaches and black clothing, but very few city mothers in evidence.

Out beyond the vestibule lay what must have been the living room of the house when it was still functioning as a house. A carpeted stairway led away to the second story. Mahogany bookcases lined the walls of the room along with more display cases, and in the center stood three mission-style oak library desks and chairs, with another waist-high display case along the wall with a Navajo rug hanging above it. There were a dozen plein-air paintings on the walls—very nice paintings, it seemed to him. If he were a thief he could fill a wheelbarrow with prime antiques and art objects and haul them away.

"Mr. Larkin, I believe," a woman said from behind him, and he turned toward the voice. It was the upper half of Mrs. Phibbs herself, smiling at him now from behind a long counter.

He dipped his head in a small bow and said, "Mrs. Phibbs!"

"Indeed. I've just been breakfasting with your beautiful wife. Jane is doing some interesting work—*very* interesting work. You're lucky to have such a woman by your side. I hope you appreciate her."

"Every day," Jerry said.

"What brings you to my Antiquity Center, Mr. Larkin?"

"Call me Jerry. What *brings* me here? Curiosity mostly. We bought a Spanish-style home over on Water Street six months ago, and . . ."

"The old Clemens residence. I know it well. It's got quite a history."

"Does it? That's what I was led to believe by the realtor, who . . ."

"That would be Kat Winkle, as I recall? She and her husband Perry are *very* good friends of mine. I've known them for years."

"Yes, Kat Winkle. Anyway, she mentioned that the house had a lot of history, like you said. I'm just curious about it. Nothing specific, really. I woke up this morning and realized that I didn't know much about the house I lived in. Am I making sense?"

"Indeed you are. You've come to the right shop if it's information you're looking for, Mr. Larkin. You're from elsewhere, aren't you? Jane tells me that you moved into Old Orange only a short time ago."

"Both of us grew up in Anaheim. That qualifies as elsewhere, I suppose—four miles as the crow flies—and we've been leasing a house on Lemon Street for the two years before we bought the Water Street house."

"Newcomers, then! You'll find that Old Orange is a world unto itself. Some of our residents go back *seven generations*. We value our history, unlike Anaheim, which bulldozed theirs forty-five years ago."

"I wasn't around then," Jerry said, "but I remember it as clear as yesterday. What sort of history, then? Our house, I mean."

"The past is always a long story, Mr. Larkin, but I'll give you the sound-bite version. The land that the city occupies was granted to Jose Antonio Yorba in 1809, a Spanish land grant. In later years it became the Rancho Santiago de Santa Ana, over 60,000 acres. The Yorbas were one of the first families."

"Those were the days," Jerry said. "I wish our quarter of an acre had been granted to us instead of costing close to a million bucks."

Mrs. Phibbs frowned at him again, as if he was making light of serious things. He told himself to cut it out. This was the sort of thing Jane warned him about.

"As I was attempting to say, the land between Cambridge and Water Street, where your house lies, was the site of the Flores Adobe. There was a well on the property dug by Estancio Flores in the middle of the century. He was the brother of the infamous bandit Juan Flores. You've heard of the Flores gang?"

Jerry shook his head. "No, ma'am."

"It's a fascinating piece of local history, at least for someone with a healthy curiosity. One theory has it that the bandit Juan Flores murdered his brother over a woman and stolen gold. Estancio Flores simply disappeared one day, and the old adobe sat empty. There was uneaten food on the table, the door left open, the animals untended. It's quite a mystery."

"He didn't return?"

"He did not. And Juan Flores was hanged in Los Angeles not long after that, which ended the story of the two brothers. It was because of Estancio's well that your own Water Street became the first real street in the area. The city still taps into the aquifer beneath the surface of the Flores land. By the time Water Street was laid down, the adobe was long demolished. The area was planted in oranges in those days. Some years after the First World War there was sub-division, and your house, if I'm not mistaken, was built in 1926, one of the earliest in the tract."

"I'll be darned," Jerry said to her. "Jane will be fascinated to hear all this."

"I'm fairly certain that Jane is already aware of much of it. Her Co-op was founded on historical principles, I believe. We don't trifle with history here in Orange. We relish it."

A hot dog joke came into his mind, but he swallowed it. "You're right, of course. I didn't mean to trifle."

"Here's something closer to home for you, Mr. Larkin. The man who built your home was a Mr. Maxwell Clemens, a stonemason, who harbored a Chinese woman in the house. A woman from *the old country*. Her name was Ling Jiao, and she spoke no English."

"Kat Winkle mentioned this when we were first looking at the house, but I don't know the particulars. So you say he *harbored* this woman? Like a boat?"

"If you wish. Certainly she was safe from storms as long as she remained indoors. She was said to be a servant whom he had brought along from San Francisco. There was a cabin at the rear of the property back then where she lived, or where the man Clemens *claimed* she lived. Popular suspicion was that they secretly co-habited. In those days, of course, there could have been no marriage. People would have made them miserable."

"And that went on in our very house?"

"The point is, we had a *mixed-race* couple right here in Old Orange, and, yes, they lived in your very house. That's something you can be proud of, even if their lives were carried on in secret."

Jerry nodded, although he couldn't quite see her point. *Proud* though? "So the house has a story of its very own."

"*Every* house has a story of its own, Mr. Larkin. Houses are living things, until they're destroyed. They outlive people if we take care of them. Ling Jiao died at a young age, and is thought to have been buried in the immigrant plot at the Anaheim Cemetery. Oh, there's a story there, to be sure, and with elements of tragedy."

"There is," Jerry said, nodding politely. "Part of the reason I stopped in to see you is that I was wondering if you know anything about coins—*old* coins? I found one, and I wonder what it is, historically speaking. Coincidentally, it appears to be Chinese."

She stared at him for a long moment as if taking his measure and then smiled. "Coins are not my area of expertise, Mr. Larkin, but a librarian is not trained simply to be a repository of information. She is trained to find what she doesn't know. If you brought an old coin with you, trot it out."

5.

JANE WALKED UPHILL toward the highest elevation of Hart Park in Old Orange. The day was almost hot by now, the sun shining as if making up for lost time. The muddy park was nearly deserted, the tennis courts and playgrounds still puddled with water. She took off her green Co-op windbreaker, tied it around her waist, and looked out over the freeway, ugly and loud along the south edge of the park. The open space provided a gorgeous view of the Santa Ana Mountains, however, which were spectacularly clear this morning.

There were storm clouds lingering over Old Saddleback, the local name for Santiago and Modjeska peaks, which appeared to run together as if they formed a single mountain. Dark washes of falling rain curtained some of the slopes, which were still bright green, a wonderful thing after three years of drought. Another storm was lurking out over the ocean—a big one, given the satellite images on last night's news, with potentially heavy onshore winds starting tonight.

She hated to cancel the Saturday morning market, but blown-down awnings and a market empty of patrons were worse than a cancellation. The farmers, many of them driving what amounted to jalopies, came into town from as far away as Ventura, San Diego, and the Inland Empire, so an early cancellation was better than a last-minute one.

She decided to wait for Mother Nature to decide, and set off along the walkway that led to the east bridge over Santiago Creek, beyond the Co-op garden. The creek descended from the high slopes of the Santa Ana Mountains, pooled at the Santiago Creek Dam where it formed Irvine Lake, and then, in heavy storms when the Lake overflowed, pooled again at the Villa Park Dam before flowing down into the flatlands.

The creek's upper reaches were still essentially wild, but over time the lower reaches had been channelized and largely covered in concrete in the interests of flood control. Twenty-odd years ago, however, the channelizing had been reversed with the implementation of the Santiago Creek Revitalization Plan, and now long stretches of the creek were shaded by oak, white alder, and sycamore trees, and there were biking and walking trails where there used to be concrete, chain link, and graffiti.

To Jane's way of thinking, the word "channelized" meant pretty much the same thing as "imprisoned", and she was looking forward to the day when the creek would be entirely free. Contrarily, the Hart Park parking lot was a quarter-mile-long section of paved creek bed that was heavily used by park goers and by the Co-op, with high, stone retaining walls on either side. In rainy seasons the creek occasionally rose to the top of the eight-foot-high stone walls, rushing through the park in a torrent, carrying driftwood and flotsam along on its journey to the ocean. Jane preferred the restored wild creek to the tamed creek, but the word "wild" had real meaning—meaning that had to do with floods.

On Saturday mornings the Co-op farmer's market stretched along the south wall of the creek, a circus of white nylon awnings, and the parking lot and adjacent neighborhoods were full of cars. A stream of water ran along the depression at the bottom of the parking area now, which meant that water was flowing over the spillway at Irvine Lake. If the stream got much deeper, the city would close the parking lot barriers along the north side of the park.

The Co-op garden stood on the heights above the creek to her left, terraced with old railroad ties and with stairs built of railroad ties up the center of its four acres. The land had been set aside by the city for public use. Part of it was a small orchard of orange and avocado and persimmon trees, and on the lower, steeper slope, there was a head-high forest of California juniper trees and banks of creeping juniper to ward off erosion. There was no one working any of the garden plots this morning, the ground being too muddy. The unseasonal storms had brought the Co-op to a near-standstill, which was bad for business.

She stood for a moment looking at the garden shed, which was overdue to be moved to a higher elevation before a determined storm could wash it away. It had once been a concession stand and storage shed for the baseball diamonds, but the baseball diamonds had long ago been moved up the hill. The city had given the shed to the Co-op under the condition that it be moved to higher ground. Moving it meant dismantling and rebuilding it, which Jerry had volunteered to accomplish as soon as the weather had regained its senses.

She walked along the creek-side path toward the weir now, shaded by oaks and sycamores. She secretly thought of the wild little kingdom that surrounded her as her own domain, especially on an empty, cloudy morning like this one. And yet she knew that the thought was contrary to the very idea of a Co-op, which was communal by definition. Without the community there could be no Co-op. Her nightmare was that one day she'd be relegated to her office downtown, taking meetings and phone calls, removed from the creek and the garden and the activities of the market, her life having become channelized by success.

She came out of the shade and into the sunlight at the edge of the weir now, where a stone wall had been built across the creek, forming a pond. Water was flowing out from under the weir, although there were check-gates that would close off the flow to maintain the depth of the pond in the summer months. Two weeks ago she had spotted a rare, western pond turtle a few feet from shore, and it was common enough these days to see newts and crayfish and small catfish in the shallows.

She skirted the pond and headed upriver, under the bridge at Cambridge Street and past the willow- and sycamore-shaded flats to the edge of Tustin Street, where the creek became an ugly concrete culvert. She pictured what it might be some day in the distant future. Dreaming about the future, however, was frustrating when her mind was on the present, and she turned around and headed back the way she'd come.

6.

IN THE SILENCE of the Antiquity Center, Mrs. Phibbs stood considering the coin. She looked hard at Jerry, and then turned her head and shouted, "Mr. Carmody!"

"I figured the coin was Chinese because of the pictograms," Jerry said, "if that's the correct term."

A weedy-looking, youngish man came out of the back now, from an area that looked as if it might be a kitchen and workroom. He peered out through frameless glasses, and his hair was shaved on the sides and stood up on top as if a wind was blowing up out of his ears. Possibly he was older than he looked. He didn't appear to be happy, and perhaps never had been, and he evidently didn't give much of a damn about food, because he was skinny as a cadaver. "The word for the symbols is *logograms*," he said in a bored voice.

"Mr. Larkin, meet our own Mr. Carmody, who works for us part-time restoring books and doing the financials. Mr. Carmody is also a coin man, and is employed part time by the Dutchman. Do you know Dutch, Mr. Larkin?"

"Sad to say, I do *not* know the Dutchman. Did he run with the Flores gang?"

"I'm not sure I ... Ah! I see that you're making a joke again. His actual name is Hyink, Mr. Donald Hyink. His friends call him Dutch. He has operated a numismatic enterprise out of his house on Prospect Street for most of fifty years—*very* well known in the area. An *international* reputation."

"I look forward to meeting him some day. And I'm happy to meet you, Mr. Carmody. I'm Jerry Larkin." He held out his hand but the man simply stared at it, so he gestured at the coin in order to give his hand something useful to do.

Mr. Carmody didn't bother to pick the coin up, but looked at it for a solid three seconds, shook his head, and said, "It's worthless. It's not a real coin."

"It quacks like a coin," Jerry said, smiling at him.

"What?"

"Like a duck. I mean to say that it *looks* something like a coin. It's round, and ..."

"It's a Yansheng charm, not actual money. It's also referred to as a Chinese numismatic charm, and is worth exactly its weight in bronze, somewhere near a dollar a pound currently, so let's call it ten cents real money to be generous."

"A *charm*? That's interesting. What sort of charm?"

Carmody shrugged theatrically, as if he couldn't be bothered. "*Any* kind. It's all crap anyway, so you can make up whatever you want." Then he said to Mrs. Phibbs, "I'm off work in ten minutes, and I have to put things away."

"Then you'd best get a wiggle on," she said, and Carmody disappeared back into the kitchen.

"I hope you'll forgive Mr. Carmody for his lack of the social graces," Mrs. Phibbs whispered.

"My own social graces aren't stellar, or so Jane tells me now and then, especially when I use my thumb to push food onto my fork."

She blinked at him in response and said, "Now that we know the nature of the object, we can delve into its mysteries."

"You're speaking of the coin now?"

"Of course I am—the charm, that is to say. It *is* coinciden- tal that it's a Chinese artifact."

"I guess it is, sure."

"The historian in me wonders where you found it. Digging in the back yard, I'd warrant. Do you own a metal detector?"

"I do not," Jerry said. "I like the idea, though."

"They're great fun. I've got a first-rate detector, not a mere bottle cap magnet, as we like to say. I'm a relic hunter for the most part. My greed has entirely to do with historical knowledge."

She paused now to let that soak in, as if she was fairly sure that Jerry's greed was the common variety, which it was, for the most part. "In the old days homeowners buried refuse in back yards if they couldn't burn it," she said. "People often bring us items that turn up when they're gardening—old bottles, porce- lain dolls, crockery items—all of them pieces of history. I'll bet you found this in your own back yard."

Her comment struck Jerry as a question disguised as a com- ment, which was a little too pushy for his taste. He suppressed the desire to tell her that it was none of her business, which would be unfriendly. "I found it down along Santiago Creek in the park," he lied, "not far above the weir. I was out walking with Peewee on the trail and spotted it lying there with some other coins, no detecting necessary, just luck. I figure that it washed out of the sand because of the storms."

"Peewee? Who is Peewee?"

"Our dog. Peewee is in charge of the animal babysitting center at the Saturday farmer's market. That and sniffing out earthquakes is his life's work. He's not an ambitious dog."

She narrowed her eyes. "What other coins did you find if I might ask? Anything interesting?"

"No. Just quarters and dimes washed up in the high water. I was hoping for silver coins, but no such luck. This charm was the only interesting thing."

"I see. So there's actually nothing coincidental about it?"

"Not really," Jerry said. "Tiny little coincidence, maybe."

She stared at him for a long moment and then winked at him, as if she had his number. "We might be able to discover something about the charm if you'll allow me to take a photo of it." She produced a cell phone and, without waiting for Jerry to agree, aimed it at the charm, snapping photos of both sides before sitting down in a wooden desk chair in front of a desktop computer. The keyboard was visible to Jerry, but not the screen.

"We'll have an electronic treasure hunt," she said cheerily, fiddling with her phone. "I'll just send this photo through." She started in on the computer keyboard now and in no time said, "Voilà! Here's an identification site for Yansheng Charms."

Jerry restrained himself from walking around to the other side of the counter and looking over her shoulder.

"And here's yours, high-lighted. Let's see." She stared down her nose at the screen for a time, and Jerry had the odd feeling that she was figuring out what to tell him, or was coming to some private conclusion. She smiled broadly now and said, "It's apparently known as a 'Laid to Rest' charm, having to do with burials. It's meant to *lay the spirit*, if you take my meaning, and was either inserted between the front teeth of the corpse or left exposed in the crypt. It almost gives you the horrors, doesn't it, to think where this coin might have been in its time. Ah! Here's a link to a *valuation* site!"

She tapped on the keys again, staring intently at the screen. "It's a *collectible* object, I'm happy to say. Here's one very like your own offered at a *whopping six dollars!*" She stood up out of the chair now, smiling broadly, her work done.

"That *is* a whopper," Jerry said, "but for six bucks I'll keep it. Thanks for the treasure hunt, Mrs. Phibbs."

"One of many possible treasure hunts. Take a word of advice from a well-meaning librarian, Mr. Larkin. We recommend what is commonly called *lifelong learning*. Exercising one's mind wards off dementia, broadens one's outlook, and makes the world a far more vital place as one comes to understand it better. One learns to tell the difference between truth and nonsense." She paused for a moment to stare at him. "We have *fascinating* historical information in our archives, which you are welcome to browse through at any time. Are you a reader at all?"

"Billboards, racing sheets, cereal boxes, that sort of thing."

"You're *jesting* with me again. I *do* have a sense of humor, Mr. Larkin. I like a good giggle."

She reached under the counter, drew out several old books, sorted through them, and handed one to him. "This is *Caminos Viejos*—'Old Roads,'" she told him needlessly, the title being embossed on the leather cover. "The author, Mr. Stephenson, was a local historian in the early part of the past century. You'll be particularly interested in the later chapters, which chronicle the depredations of the Flores gang. Their story makes exciting reading, a Cain and Abel saga right in your own back yard. Be so kind as to wash your hands before you open the book. Do not bend the spine back or crease the pages or eat while you're handling the book. And be sure to return it to me tomorrow."

"Thanks," he said. "I'll do that. No greasy thumbs."

"We have an extensive collection of esoteric documents on the second floor—particularly rare items including several pamphlets concerning the Flores gang written by Mr. Stephenson. If this book piques your interest, you can take a look. Or a *peek*!"

"I can pick a peck of pickled peeks," he said.

She nodded and said, "If you'd like to return the favor, please consider donating your very interesting Yansheng charm to our collection. You can take a nice tax write-off! Have a good day, Mr. Larkin."

She went off toward the kitchen now, leaving him to loot the Antiquity Center at his leisure if he was so inclined. It occurred to him that the Center perhaps didn't get a lot of visitors. It had the air of a private sanctuary, a miniature Hearst's Castle—Phibbs's personal hideaway.

He went back out through the vestibule, wondering how she had managed to vacuum away most of his energy and why she gave two damns where he had found the coin. She was a nosy old gastropod, but maybe that came with the territory, hiding in a historical center and all.

She had reacted hard to the Yansheng coin, though— something more than a six-dollar reaction.

7.

LETTIE PHIBBS WATCHED through the window as Jerry ambled toward his ratty old truck and climbed in. The man had money and a smart wife, and yet he was scarcely better than a wisecracking bum. He drove out to the street now, turning in the direction of the Water Street house. She couldn't think of it as the Larkin house. The Larkins hadn't lived in it long enough to possess it, so to speak, and in any event it was an historical structure, outside common definitions of ownership.

She turned away from the window and went back to the work she'd been doing when Larkin had walked into her life: two more screws to put into the new microwave shelf over the kitchen counter. She zipped them in with her cordless drill and then wiped the wallboard bits off the counter with a damp paper towel.

"Some people would have a man in to do a little job like that," she said.

"That's true," Peter said. "And some people would just set the damned microwave on the counter." He began shoving things into his backpack now, as if making it clear that he had no time for her.

"I'm not *some people*, and you aren't either, Peter. What did you think of Mr. Jerry Larkin?"

"I didn't think of him at all."

"I think the man has the face of a liar. Poor Jane Larkin, to be married to such a man. I don't admire flippancy, and flippancy combined with falseness is . . ."

"Flippity-falsity?" Peter said.

"If the term amuses you. What did you think of his coin?"

"That it wasn't a coin."

"What does it *mean*, Peter—that he *found* this particular coin?"

"It means that someone bought it at a junkshop downtown for a dollar and then lost it. His lucky day."

"Your negativity is not always an asset to you, Peter, nor to me. You miss the subtleties. The man was on the verge of revealing that he found the coin on his own property, and then he lied and said he had found it in the creek. Why would he do that? What is he *hiding* and why is he hiding it?"

"Because you were coming on like the Inquisition, Lettie. Talk about subtlety!"

"Nonsense. I was stirring the man up. Planting seeds. I mean to take a closer look at Mr. Jerry Larkin, and to start today. Can I entice you into putting your backpack down and working for another hour? Call Dutch and tell him you're detained."

"Why?"

"I want you to create an old document. There's no need to go overboard with the artistry. This should be from a century ago. A single page, I should think. Folded and carried in a pocket. Rough and ready will do the trick."

"Who does it have to fool?"

"Jerry Larkin. He'll be happy to be fooled."

Peter slid open a narrow drawer in his desk and took out several sheets of paper—blank end-pages removed from old books. "I'll use tea to age it. It's amateur, but it'll do. Handwritten?"

"Yes, in an ignorant scrawl. And put a torn edge on the paper, I should think, as if someone tore it out of a book in haste. I'll just dash something off and you can copy it out."

"You haven't mentioned paying me," Peter said.

"You'd demand a fee from the good Lord himself, Peter. How much do you want? Will $100 satisfy you?"

"Not quite. Let's say $300, if there's anything like real forgery about it."

"I assure you it's a mere prank. We'll call it $150, since you're giving up your pittance from the Dutchman."

8.

JERRY CHIPPED AWAY at the bricks and mortar with the chisel end of the brick-hammer, stopping now and then to shovel up salt and broken pieces of brick and dump it into a five-gallon bucket. Many of the bricks had come out whole, and these he put into a pile. He could score and break them later to fill the crenellations around the perimeter of the door.

Old man Clemens evidently did good work. Just *why* he did the work was another matter, especially since his wall was an impediment to getting at the underside of half the house. He must have known that, so maybe it was purposeful, although it made no obvious sense.

Another brick slid out now, and when he bent over to stack it on the pile of keepers, he saw that it had a pressed-in date and the name of the brickyard where it was cast—H. Garber, 1933. So the house was built well before the wall went up, which was interesting but didn't solve any mysteries. Jane would want the brick as a souvenir. Either that or he could give it to Lettie Phibbs and claim the donation on his taxes.

After clearing away the debris, he pulled on his coveralls and a pair of work gloves. Today's fair weather had warmed the world up, and the coveralls were sweat-producers, but filthy coveralls beat filthy clothing. He ducked through what he was already thinking of as "the door", wearing a miner's headlamp, which cast a glow immediately ahead of him, although the light dissipated in the twilight beyond.

He hunched along the upward sloping ground toward the eighteen-inch-high crawl space beneath the bedroom, towing the bottle-jack and other tools and hardware in a big canvas bag with a zipper. His miner's lamp picked out the problematic post beneath the bedroom floor now—a short support post that was merely dangling there, pulled loose from the bottom. Some sort of sinkhole had opened up beneath whatever had supported the post, collapsing bricks and debris making the avalanche of noise that he and Jane had heard during the 'quake.

He crept forward on his stomach now, dragging the canvas bag behind him, crawling past sections of salt-filled bricks stacked into little walls, two bricks high. These weren't mortared together and couldn't possibly serve any structural function—the beginning of an abandoned project, maybe, or evidence of insanity.

His headlamp revealed the cave-in now, a sizeable hole in the ground. The dislodged post dangled in front of his face, bent nails protruding from either side where they'd been yanked out of whatever it had been tied in to below. He grabbed the post, levered it back and forth until it came loose, and then tossed it aside before pulling himself forward on his chest until he could see down into the hole—a chamber some three feet square lined with adobe brick and now half-full of the dirt and stones that must have covered it.

It was obviously old, pre-Clemens, unless Clemens had made his own adobe bricks. That wasn't likely, given that he had a slew of manufactured bricks lying around. Jerry wondered what the chamber might have been—ideally not a septic tank. A small cistern, maybe, big enough to hold a hundred gallons for watering stock, back when this had been ranchland.

Rough-cut pieces of plank had fallen into the hole and were half-buried. A small concrete pier that had supported the post lay canted over on top of the debris. The wooden block fixed to the pier was solid and firmly attached, so he could reuse the pier, which would save him a trip back to the hardware store. He reached in with both hands and hefted out the pier, setting it out of the way.

The mortar between the adobe bricks was mostly intact, and there was a ledge around the top perimeter where the boards had been set into the brick as a lid. There was no way around the obvious: he would have to clean the debris out of the pit in order to have a level place to put the concrete slab and the bottle-jack, and then re-position the pier and the post—a pain in the neck, but not complicated.

He leaned into the hole again and grabbed a piece of the wooden plank, working it loose from the rubble and tossing it away. Another plank followed, and then a third and a fourth, leaving the square, open hole full of soft dirt and pebbles. He wondered if he could simply level out the dirt, tamp it down, and set the stepping-stone right down on it, the lazy man's way of getting the job done. The energetic alternative was to scoop out the dirt until he found solid ground and then back-fill the hole with sand or concrete or both.

He lay there on his stomach, looking down into the illuminated chamber, taking a rest. What if this wasn't a cistern at all, he wondered, but a filled-in well? They were living on Water Street, after all, and Phibbs had yammered about there being a well. The house stood maybe a quarter mile from Santiago Creek, without much elevation between the two. The last thing he wanted to do was to burrow down toward underground water, especially in a wet year like this one. The water table might be just a few feet below, and the aquifer below that.

The dirt appeared to be settling of its own accord now

that he had disturbed it, filtering downward, and he wondered whether there was a hollow space underneath. He imagined a sudden collapse, water gushing up out of the ground, their driveway turned into a tributary of Santiago Creek. But the settling slowed and stopped, revealing what looked like the end of a broken-off tree limb. He reached down and grabbed it, yanking it free.

Not a tree limb at all, but what appeared to be a human femur.

He dropped it back into the hole and found himself gasping for breath. The dark space beneath the floor closed in around his little island of light, and the weight of the house seemed to compress the air. He shifted his head back to open his throat and breathed deeply, making an effort to calm himself and fighting a senseless revulsion. There was little difference between a dry bone and a dry stick. They were both dead things. Maybe it was a bone from the leg of a dog—a big dog, for sure.

He pulled the bone out again and set it aside, then shifted the soil with his gloved hand. He saw the top of another bone, broad and flat, and he plucked that out too, trying to maintain a scientific perspective despite knowing now that this wasn't the remains of a dog. What he saw was a human pelvis, the old bone hacked and splintered as if the legs had been chopped off with an axe or a sharp spade.

9.

JANE MADE SLOW PROGRESS back to the park, taking the time to pick up particularly ugly pieces of litter and stuff it into a black plastic yard bag. The high water had washed down all sorts of trash and debris—old shoes and clothing, beer bottles, a paperback book with the cover gone, turned into a dirty sponge. The sack was quickly heavy, and so she tied the top and slung it over her back, making a mental note to organize a creek cleanup after the weather settled down.

She heard a cough from farther down the creek, and she looked up to see Lettie Phibbs, of all people, working the bank with a metal detector. Lettie had changed into khaki pants and rubber boots and wore a floppy sun hat and an apron with cargo pockets. She was studiously sweeping the detector back and forth, stopping now to scoop up sand and shake it out again through the sifter at the bottom of the scoop.

Jane was struck by the coincidence of seeing Lettie twice in the same morning, but it was a pleasant surprise. This Lettie Phibbs was much more interesting than the Lettie she had eaten breakfast with. Jane headed toward her, stepping over muddy depressions in the bank and going around tangles of brush.

Lettie looked up, saw her, and waved cheerfully, shouting, "Why if it isn't Jane Larkin carrying a Santa Claus bag."

"I thought I'd pick up trash on my little hike," Jane said. "I'm afraid it's futile until these storms pass."

"And scarcely a fitting pastime for a woman of your stature."

Jane ignored the statement and said, "I had no idea you were a detective."

"A detective of the secrets of the past! I like that. Lost objects can tell us as much as the stories in old books. Look at this. I've just now unearthed it." She showed Jane an age-blackened pocket watch with the name *Jasper* etched into the top of the case. She opened it carefully and exposed the interior, a broken crystal and a ragged hole rusted through the painted face of the watch, the frozen gears visible beneath.

"Makes you wonder who Jasper was and how he lost his watch," Jane said.

"Exactly. My instincts tell me that he lost it right here. Watches don't float, after all, and are unlikely to have been swept down the river. I intend to put it on the website to see whether someone can help identify it. Pocket watches were out of fashion by World War I, you know. So I'll guess that this was lost a century ago, when men were actually named Jasper. I'll see what Mr. Nguyen at the jewelry store downtown has to say about it, and then put together a story for the Antiquity Center blog."

"Any other finds?" Jane asked.

"The sand is a little bit damp for sifting, but so far I've found two wheat pennies, and a buffalo nickel." She reached into her pocket and took out the nickel, which she handed to Jane. "My gift to you."

"It might be valuable," Jane said, trying to make out a date.

"Then it's your lucky day. This is my first donation to the Co-op. If it's worth a fortune, you'll be out of the woods."

"Thank you," Jane said, thinking that it would be best simply to take the coin, although for some reason it made her uneasy, as if taking it would seal her fate. But refusing to take it would insult Lettie's good intentions.

There was a movement near a stand of willow scrub nearby, and Jane spotted a big toad looking out of a clump of weeds. It was mottled black and white, as if chiseled out of granite. "Look at that fellow!" she said happily.

"What fellow?" Lettie glanced around, apparently mystified.

"The toad," Jane said, pointing. "There in the grass."

"Toad! Is it *venomous?*" She removed her glasses and squinted in that direction. "I've heard they kill dogs."

"Not this kind," Jane said. "It's an arroyo toad, *Bufo californicus.* They disappeared from this part of the creek years ago, but they're back now, which is a good sign. It's the third one I've seen. Do you want to hold it? You'd run a small risk of being peed on, but it's not poisonous pee."

"Oh my God *no,*" Lettie said. "How can you say such a thing? Ugly, warty monster."

It came into Jane's mind that Lettie was the ugly, warty monster, which was unkind. But she had turned back into the woman who had threatened the waitress at Scotty's with a penny tip in a water glass.

"Let's hope the nickel is worth a fortune," Lettie said. "And if you're worried about being indebted to me, get the notion out of your head. I'm indebted to *you.* If it weren't for you, I wouldn't be out searching the creek this morning."

"Is that so?" Jane asked.

"Indeed it is. No sooner had I returned to the Antiquity Center this morning, but who should walk in? Guess!"

"Guess? I don't have any idea."

"Your own Jerry."

"Jerry dropped into the Center? Whatever for?"

"That's what I asked myself. He doesn't seem the type. In fact I find him quite baffling. I refer to his manner of speaking. He *meant* well, no doubt. You're already aware of this, of course, but he had found an old Chinese coin this morning—not really a coin, actually, but a variety of charm, *shaped* like a big coin, very popular in Chinese culture over the centuries. It's interesting to look at, but nearly worthless, unfortunately. *Surely* he showed it to you."

"No, he didn't," Jane said, but then regretted saying so. It wasn't Lettie's business.

"Perhaps that's not *all* that strange. No doubt married couples keep small things from each other for reasons of their own."

"Jerry and I aren't fond of keeping secrets, actually. It's more likely that he found it this morning after I left the house."

"To the contrary, he told me that he found it right here along the creek, entirely by chance. He had been out walking the dog Peewee."

"He was walking Peewee along the creek?" This didn't seem likely to her, but she kept it to herself.

"Yes, and it's a bad idea, if you ask me. There are coyotes here, you know, as well as raccoons. A dog is no match for a determined raccoon attack. I lent him a book, by the way—something you might be interested in."

Jane nodded. "Thanks," she said. "I'll have a look at it. Peewee's not all that small, though. He has a lot of heft to him. So you're out looking for more of these coin charms that Jerry found?"

"Well, I suppose I am. You might say that I'm digging for clues. This particular charm of Jerry's, we discovered, is associated with the *burying of the dead*."

"Maybe Jasper is buried out here."

"He's no doubt buried *somewhere*," Mrs. Phibbs said. "We're all creatures of the earth. Dust to dust."

"Ideally not soon," Jane said. "It's been good chatting again, Lettie, but I should get back to the office. Happy hunting."

And with that she turned back down the creek, wondering what it was about the Chinese coin that had prompted Jerry to keep it a secret from her, and how it was that Mrs. Phibbs had developed such an impressive talent for being irritating.

10.

THE EARTHQUAKE HAD OPENED up a crypt beneath the house, not a cistern or a septic tank or a filled-in farmhouse well. It came to Jerry that he should let sleeping dogs lie, as the saying went. A few buckets full of tamped-down dirt would cover the bones. There was no need to tell Jane that there was a graveyard under the floor of the bedroom.

But he knew it wouldn't do. The sleeping dog was already awake, and it had to be removed. He pushed more dirt aside, recoiling again when he unearthed a tilted-upward human skull, staring at him through empty eye sockets, the age-darkened brain case broken like the shell of an egg hit with a spoon. There were fragments of old brown material, probably a decomposed shirt, mixed into the soil around it along with pieces of vertebrae.

He rolled onto his back and stared at the underside of the floor, simply breathing, contemplating the small slashes of light showing through the earthquake gap. What did people do, he wondered, when they found bones on their property? Antique bones, particularly, and obvious evidence of an old murder. Mrs. Phibbs would find historical bones more interesting than recent bones, no doubt about it.

The police wouldn't give much of a damn about historical bones, except that they'd have to remove them to make certain they weren't evidence of a more recent murder. He remembered a story about a psychopathic killer in northern California who had buried bodies under the rooming house where his victims were staying, which must have stunk like the devil. The authorities had yanked out the entire floor, counting the corpses.

It wasn't farfetched to imagine that same thing happening here: him and Jane and Peewee sleeping at the Dew Drop Inn, eating instant oatmeal and reconstituted eggs for the next three months or six months or a year while their house was dismantled.

Jane's idea of the right thing to do sometimes differed from his own, she being much closer to a model citizen. But Jane wasn't available and wouldn't be home until late this afternoon. All questions of right and wrong aside—if right and wrong was an issue in the case of a dried out old skeleton—his first duty was to get the beam leveled, the floor closed up, and the house safe. He had no duty whatsoever to the skeleton, which didn't have an opinion one way or another.

He pushed his way back to where he had left his canvas sack and removed the stuff inside. Then he crawled back to the crypt carrying the empty sack and loaded in the already unearthed bones. He reached into the hole and picked up the partly-buried skull now. When he saw the big coin clamped in its teeth, he rejected the idea of saying something witty to it. It was clearly another of the Chinese charm coins, and he didn't need Lettie Phibbs to tell him which one.

He held the skull in his hand like a grapefruit, the hair standing up along the back of his neck. His hand began to shake convulsively. The skull's jawbone fell away along with the coin, the two landing in the dirt, and he dropped the skull, too.

"Hell", he muttered, staring at the pieces in the light of the headlamp. The empty sockets of the skull looked sinister to him, as if they were looking *at* him, which was senseless.

"Get a grip," he told himself aloud, and carefully shifted the skull, jawbone, and coin to a safe spot instead of putting them into the sack. It came to him that a little bit of glue would restore the skull once he had a spare moment. That idea was followed by the more rational notion that he was thinking like a nutcase. He went to work searching out bones now, finding the rib cage, which he attempted to lift out wholesale. Several of the ribs fell away from the desiccated cartilage, though, the skeleton dismantling itself as he picked at it.

He pulled himself farther out over the open crypt until he could more easily reach the bottom, pushing dirt and rubble aside, working like a paleontologist. For some reason it mattered that he found all the bones, making a thorough job of it now that he was resolved to see it through. The skeletal hands appeared to be entire, and he saw that one of the fingers wore a ring—a polished but unshaped stone on a silver band. He tried to lift out the entire hand, but it fell to pieces, the ring sinking into the loose soil.

His gloves simply made him clumsy now, and so he removed them and plucked out the ring—a man's ring, obviously. The stone was probably an agate, and the inside curve of silver was dented, as if the man had held his hand up to protect himself and caught an axe blow or the blade of a shovel. He slipped the ring into his pocket—another souvenir.

Jerry began picking the small pieces out one at a time and putting them into the bag. As he worked he thought about the mystery. They weren't Ling Jiao's bones, thank God, since according to Phibbs she was buried out at the cemetery in Anaheim, and in any event she wouldn't be wearing a man's ring. He didn't particularly want to know the identity of the skeleton, especially if it were Ling Jiao's. He had developed a particular sympathy for her simply by hearing a little part of her story. But then bones were bones, practically speaking.

What would he do with them? That was the immediate

question. He ditched the idea of the trash bin in the alley. There were spy cameras everywhere these days, and pitching human remains into a dumpster was a sordid idea in any event, no matter how old they were. He imagined his own bones being hauled to the dump for burial. Whoever this was didn't deserve that fate, or the fate of being boxed up and put on the shelf in a museum warehouse, for that matter.

He found a second femur and various arm bones and added them to the sack, which seemed bottomless, like the bag in the *Arabian Nights*. It was a humbling thing—a human being as a bag o'bones. Both of the shoes were there, the leather dry and cracked. One shoe was hacked open, but the other still contained the skeletal foot. He lifted it out as a package and put into the sack. Beneath it he found another treasure—a Barlow knife with a wide blade and a bone handle. He pried the knife open easily despite rust on the blade and a gritty hinge. The dry environment had preserved it.

He realized that he was sweating and that bright sunlight was shining through a screened vent in the foundation. Over the past couple of hours it had heated up outside. The air felt heavy for some reason, almost smoggy, and he was having a hard time keeping his thoughts straight. A car went past on the street, the engine noise weirdly distant and removed, as if there was something odd about the acoustics of the low space. A wave of vertigo and nausea passed through him, and he felt himself falling into the crypt. He scrabbled backward through the dirt, filled with sudden dread and raising a cloud of dust.

He lay there on his back, catching his breath and looking once again through the swirling dust at the light through the earthquake crack in the floor above him. The light winked on and off—shrubbery moving across the bedroom window in the breeze or maybe the shadows of passing clouds. He was still dizzy despite lying on the ground, and it came to him that he should get out into the open air, but at the moment he was too worn out to move. His mind played with the notion that some sort of invisible vapor had risen from the crypt and poisoned him.

His mouth was parched, and a warm wind blew, unmistakably a dry Santa Ana wind out of the east that smelled of sage and dust. There was an oppressive shift in air pressure that closed his ears, and he fought down sudden nausea and the weird notion that darkness had fallen. He heard the lowing of cattle and a door or shutter slamming shut in the wind, perhaps the barn door, and he had the vague thought that he should latch it and that something had spooked the cattle. At the same time he knew who he was and that he lay beneath the foundation of the house caught in a waking nightmare that was senseless and sensible at the same time.

Abruptly he found himself standing in the open night air, a full moon in the sky. He saw a low mud-brick house with a heavy lintel over the door, the moonlit image wavering as if in a heat haze. The view blinked into darkness, and now he saw two tethered horses beneath a cluster of pepper trees aglow in the moonlight, their willowy limbs swaying in the wind. The shadows sorted themselves into the figure of a woman in a black dress and cape holding the tethers of two horses, waiting for someone. He stood still, listening in the nighttime darkness, knowing that something was pending, and that the woman had betrayed him.

The wind kicked up a dust devil, the loose door slammed, and he turned to look behind him, hearing loud footsteps. A man with a twisted, angry face rushed toward him like death, swinging an upraised shovel back over his shoulder.

Jerry threw his hand up to block the blow, banging his forearm on a floor joist. He shouted, grabbed his arm, and felt a wash of blood, the pain bringing him to full consciousness, the nightmare settling out of his mind like water through sand. He was himself again

The afternoon was as it had been. The skeletal frame of the floor was illuminated by the circular glow of his headlamp, reminding him of the limbs of the pepper trees and the moon in the sky. There was no way he had fallen asleep. This had been a waking dream—his mind playing tricks on him. The old phrase came easily into his mind, as if it explained everything. The dream had been lucid—a hallucination rather than a common dream. He clearly remembered the sudden vertigo and his scuttling away from the crypt. For the time he had been caught up in the dream, he hadn't been himself, and yet he had been conscious of this, which scared the hell out of him.

Phibbs's chatter about adobe houses and farmhouse wells and Cain and Abel stories had probably planted the seeds of the hallucination in his mind, and he wondered if she was a witch. Then he wondered what Jane would say to that, what she would say to any of this.

The inside of his mouth felt like a dry rag, and he was voraciously hungry and sweating like a pig in the coveralls. He had gone without breakfast, which was foolish, and had drunk coffee instead of water, which was outright stupid given the dusty work. Dehydration would explain the dizziness and displacement, and was far more likely than Mrs. Phibbs having bewitched him. Dehydration had been a problem for him in the past, when he had gotten carried away with work, too busy to take a break.

He made a mental inventory of the supplies he would need to finish the work and then dragged himself out from under the low floor, heading straight outside and into the house, leaving the cellar door open behind him.

11.

Lettie Phibbs turned down Water Street after an hour of sweeping the creek with her metal detector. She had the ruined watch to show for it, but very little else, having given the buffalo nickel to Jane Larkin without checking its value first. But it was good to foster feelings of indebtedness in people. The indebtedness that came with a favor was like a bank loan: it paid off over time. She was certain that Jerry Larkin had lied to her about finding it along the creek and had failed to tell Jane about the coin at all—the sin of omission. What exactly was it that he did not want known, even by his own wife?

Peter Carmody had been wrong about the Yansheng charm; she was certain of that. No one had bought it from a junk shop, and it hadn't fallen out of anyone's pocket. It was a clue that pointed toward the past, perhaps part of the story of Ling Jiao, given the coin's origin. Ling Jiao would not have thought of it as a trinket.

She drove slowly past the Larkins house. The blinds were closed, but Jerry's pickup truck was parked in the driveway. There was no sign of him, however—no activity at all. The street was quiet, just a gardener mowing a lawn down the way. She pulled up to the curb and cut the engine, sitting patiently for a time, studying the first four houses on the east side of the street. All of them were reasonably close to where the mouth of the old Flores well was discovered a century ago, choked with rubble and dirt. She had learned its location simply by chatting with Mr. Jenks at the Water Department, which backed up to the Water Street houses.

For a long time she had thought it possible that Juan Flores had buried his gang's treasure hereabouts, perhaps dumping it down the well, before running away to hide himself in the hills. That scenario, however, didn't entirely stand to reason, since getting the treasure back out of a well might be impossible. She wished she had a telescope that would allow her to see into the past.

Nothing stirred at the Larkin house except the bushes moving in the wind. It could be that he was walking the dog. Or perhaps he owned a second car more sensible than the pickup truck and was out gallivanting while Jane made an honest living. Lettie climbed out of the car into the sunlight, opened the trunk, and looked into a boxful of books destined for the Friends of the Library bookstore. After removing a battered old volume, she shut the trunk and walked across the street and up the driveway as noiselessly as she could, hidden from the house next door by a tall privet hedge, heavy with tiny black berries. There was no need to announce her presence: better to surprise Jerry at whatever he was doing.

Blinds covered the windows along the wall of the house, all of them closed. They would hide her movements—a good thing, although it would be interesting to get a look inside the house itself. The top of the garage was visible beyond a cedar gate closed across the driveway. She didn't know what to make of that. Drawn blinds and fenced backyards implied a desire for privacy. She herself enjoyed privacy and believed that people should mind their own business. But Jane and Jerry Larkin had willingly entered her sphere of influence this morning, looking to gain something from that influence. That made their business her business.

She turned her attention to the gate latch, or rather to the big washer on a wire that was looped through a dime-sized hole near the top of the gate. Was it locked? A locked gate was full of implication, and implication was a variety of information. Historians reconstructed entire civilizations out of fragments of information, like a pot healer seeing the ghost of a pot in a heap of broken shards.

She glanced behind her at the empty driveway and sidewalk, and then bent over and peered through a narrow opening between the slats in the gate. The angle was wrong. She scuttled sideways toward the privet hedge, peering between slats as she went, her view changing each time until she saw something that stopped her—the top corner of what appeared to be the cellar hatch standing open. The sneaky son of a bitch was busy in the cellar. No doubt that's where he had found the coin. What else had he found?

She moved back to the gate latch and reached for the washer, giving it a careful tug. The gate began to swing open of its own accord, surprising her, and she grabbed the edge to stop it. She waited for a moment and then edged it farther open for a better view. The cellar door was indeed open, and there were tools lying on the ground alongside—a small sledgehammer and another hammer with a square head on one side and a sort of chisel on the other. A big bucket full of broken brick and mortar sat nearby.

She pulled the gate softly closed again, but the latch fell into place with a surprisingly heavy clank. She turned away and walked down the driveway as quickly as was safe, looking at the house directly across the street, where an old woman was watching her through the window now, the nosy old cow. She had half a mind to give the woman an I-see-you finger wiggle in order to take her down a peg, but she suppressed it and instead looked at the cover of the book she carried, turning it over in her hand so as to call attention to the fact that she had come bearing gifts.

She couldn't simply drive away after having been seen opening the gate, and so she turned up the sidewalk and along the path to the front porch, considering what she would say when Jerry opened the door, wondering if she could sweet-talk him into letting her in.

A dog began to bark when she rang the doorbell—the Peewee creature, no doubt. She hated dogs, filthy things, excreting on sidewalks, slobbering on a person. Jerry's truck in the driveway at least implied that he was at home, although not necessarily in the house. Was he in the cellar at this very moment? Could he hear the doorbell when he was in the cellar?

She rang again and waited, giving him plenty of time, the dog barking furiously for another half-minute and then falling silent, probably waiting for her to make a noise so that it could start up again. There was no further sound from within, just the muffled roar of a leaf-blower at the corner and the traffic along Chapman Avenue.

She stared at the doorknob, scarcely breathing, her hand drawn to the knob and hovering there, a quarter of an inch away. She wondered whether it was locked and whether the dog had gone away. She stopped herself from touching it, however, picturing her embarrassment if she was seen trying the knob. That would be fatal. She thought of the old woman watching from across the street, but she didn't dare to look back. Instead she glanced at the long, curtained window to the left and then stepped back and pretended to be waiting patiently.

Was Jerry hiding behind the curtain? She had a feeling that he was, that there were eyes upon her. She turned away, considered leaving the book on the front porch swing, thought better of it, and headed down the walk again. The woman in the house opposite had disappeared from the window. She climbed heavily into her car, sat for a moment with the motor running, and then drove slowly away, reassessing the mysterious Jerry Larkin. He was hiding something that had to do with the cellar, and he knew that she knew.

Did Jane know? Had she *pretended* not to know about the Yansheng charm?

The jury was still out on Jane, but Jerry had been found guilty. Guilty of what, she didn't know, but she would find out.

12.

THE MEAT AND CHEESE drawer in the fridge had been nearly full, and there were tomatoes and lettuce and a red onion. Jerry had helped himself to all of it, building a Dagwood sandwich that was three inches high, piling on ham and bologna, sliced salami, two kinds of cheese, and lettuce, tomatoes, and dill pickle slices, which he was eating now along with a pile of kettle cooked potato chips. He was ravenous after his adventure in the cellar. A nutritionist would advise chewing each bite forty times, but the nutritionist didn't have a sack of bones waiting in the wings.

"You want a little something?" he asked Peewee, who sat on his haunches watching Jerry eat. He tore off a piece of bologna and handed it to him. Peewee was a dainty eater, which went along with the flat face. He hated to snuffle food out of a bowl, and so he far preferred eating off the floor.

"What's your opinion of skeletons?" Jerry asked, starting to regret the never-ending sandwich. Peewee apparently gave no kind of a damn for skeletons, but he happily ate a piece of white cheddar.

Jerry helped the sandwich along with a second glass of water, feeling restored to sanity, and he gave the last corner of it to Peewee, who made grateful noises while he hoovered it up. There was no reason that the bones couldn't spend another few days under the house while Jerry worked on other projects. That would give him time to figure out a plan before he revealed sensitive information to Jane.

He swept away a rising guilt, and reminded himself that the existence of the bones wasn't actually a *secret* that he was keeping. A secret wasn't a secret if revealing it was merely delayed. Like borrowing money, if it was paid back in a timely manner there was no reason it should generate guilt. The phrase "in a timely manner" echoed in his mind, striking a false note. He bent over to wipe up a piece of tomato from the floor.

Just then, in the silence of the empty house, he heard the distinct sound of the driveway gate-latch closing. The gate had a heavy steel latch, and the sound was unmistakable. Peewee trotted off in that direction, and it came to Jerry that Jane might be home early. But why would she come in through the back yard? He followed after Peewee into the guest bedroom where he twisted the little stick that opened the blinds. The gate was closed and there was no one to be seen. He looked out the back window into the yard, and again there was no sign of Jane or anyone else.

Now the doorbell rang—someone *had* been in the driveway. Peewee ran toward the front door growling and barking. Maybe it was simply a package—UPS ringing the doorbell to alert the homeowner that there were valuables on the porch. Except that a UPS driver wouldn't have meddled with the driveway gate. He crossed the living room into what he and Jane called the reading room, a small den with bookshelves that had a side view of the front porch through a pair of French windows.

He peered out between the curtains just as the bell rang a second time, which set Peewee off again. It was Phibbs herself, by God, dressed for a safari. He stayed still, watching her. There was no way she would see him within the darkened room. And if she did, so what?

She was holding a book—a librarian making a house call. Why had she seen fit to snoop down the driveway before coming to the porch? Why open the gate? It came to him that the book she held was a pretext. She had driven over with the *intention* of looking into the back yard. Her being here meant that the Yansheng coin had wound her up like a tin toy, setting her into motion.

Her hand hovered in front of the doorknob now. She was going to walk in! He wished he had locked the damned door. The thought of his having to confront Phibbs in his own living room was ghastly. Peewee sat on his haunches staring at the door now. Maybe he would rend Phibbs limb from limb so that Jerry could bury her under the house.

But she turned away and descended the couple of steps, walking across the street to her Cadillac, which was parked at the curb just past Mrs. Collins's house. She sat for a moment with the engine idling before driving slowly away, as if she was in no particular hurry.

It came to him that he should put the padlock on the gate. He didn't have to lock it, because Phibbs wasn't tall enough to reach over and slip it out of its hole. In fact there was no necessity for a lock. An old bolt that could be slipped in and out of the latch would do the trick. But why the hell should he have to have a drawbridge to keep out a librarian? Better to set up a trap—a bucket of water to dump on her head. Or a bucket of honey.

He wondered whether he should tell Jane that Phibbs had come snooping. It would inevitably lead to spilling a pot full of beans—his meeting with Phibbs at the Center, the coin, where he'd found the coin, a casual mention of the human skull under the house chewing on a similar coin.

The doorbell rang now, startling him. If it was Phibbs again ...

But it wasn't Phibbs. It was Mrs. Collins, looking squinty-eyed. She was a dapper-looking, blue-haired woman, small and neat and inevitably dressed as if to go out. She was somewhere near ninety years old, the neighborhood watchdog. He opened the door and stepped out onto the porch, greeting her cheerfully.

"There was a woman sneaking around your property," she said, "back toward the gate. I thought you'd want to know—that Phibbs woman from the Antiquity Center."

"I spotted her," Jerry said. "She had a book with her. I took her for a bible salesman."

"I saw her try the gate before walking around to the front door. I noticed you didn't open it."

"Didn't get there quick enough."

"You know that she's been by here before? I've seen her. You can't miss that big black automobile."

"Before today?"

"Yes, in the past couple of weeks. She slows down, looking at things. Two days ago she was on foot, and I got a good look at her."

"Thanks, Mrs. Collins. I'll keep an eye peeled for her. Could be she just has an interest in the neighborhood houses, given that she's from the Antiquity Center."

"That could be, but I'll note the day and time if I see her again."

"Excellent idea," Jerry said, thanking her again and watching as she crossed the street and disappeared into her house. He wished that he had known about Phibbs's spying this morning, before he had walked into her lair and chattered away at her like a squirrel. He would have been more wary.

But what difference would it have made, really? She had talked openly about her interest in the house and the neighborhood. She'd given him a book to read, for God's sake.

But to hell with Phibbs. Knowing that he was working in the cellar would simply drive her nuts. Ideally it would ruin her sleep. Tomorrow he would return the borrowed book. He would make pleasant small-talk, perhaps flatter her on her prodigious beauty. Beyond that he would ignore her, keeping the front door locked for good measure. Right now his hands were tied. Jane had business with Mrs. Phibbs, and the last thing he needed to do was to meddle in that business. It was better to mind his own business, at least for now.

13.

JANE'S OFFICE, the headquarters of the Old Orange Co-op, sat above the Prescott Building on the corner of Almond and Chapman at the edge of the downtown Plaza District. Her and Jerry's house on Water Street was only ten blocks east down Almond, but she had elected not to walk to work, having had the breakfast meeting with Lettie and then the morning at the park and the afternoon in the office.

Jane sat at her big desk, wondering how seriously to take Lettie Phibbs. The woman was certainly decisive—strangely so, given that she had moved from how-do-you-dos to plans for a partnership with the Co-op in forty-five minutes. And then there was her odd reappearance along the creek and what seemed almost like an obsession with Jerry, whom she had only met this morning. And why the need to carry on about the mysterious Chinese charm coin?

The east-facing window, a small one, looked out on the parking lot behind PJ's Abbey restaurant, which occupied a restored Baptist church built in the nineteenth century. Through her south-facing office window she could see the tops of the high trees in Hart Park, half a mile away. The window hinged downward, letting in onshore ocean breezes on warm afternoons.

A big bay with a wide window seat faced west on Glassell Street, looking down through airy curb trees at Satellite Market, the downtown grocery store. The angled windows in the bay gave her a vista of the southeast quadrant of Old Orange and, to the north, a view of the fountain in the Plaza. Peewee's igloo dog-house sat atop the window seat so that he could keep an eye on the sidewalks and sleep in leaf-filtered afternoon sunlight.

Jane found that she was staring, as she often did, at the puzzled-together topographic maps on the east wall. Together they depicted a big section of the Santa Ana Mountains, which would literally be visible if the east wall disappeared. She and Jerry had glued the 80 individual maps up with wallpaper paste and then rolled on several coats of shellac.

She spent a certain amount of time standing in front of it, memorizing the place names and their locations—Holy Jim Canyon, Rose Canyon, Bear Trap Canyon, Bell Canyon, Falls Canyon, Vulture Crags, Grotto Springs . . . It was like trying to memorize a map of the night sky, except that a person could hike back into Holy Jim Canyon and see it firsthand, whereas Orion's Belt was merely an imaginary connection of three almost infinitely distant stars.

She wished she'd brought Peewee to the office today, simply for company, but he would be content helping Jerry repair the damage beneath the bedroom floor. The only earthquake trouble in the office was that a framed photo of her and Jerry had fallen over on the desk, no damage done. Jerry had built the base of the desk out of pine and then topped it with a vast, solid oak top that stretched most of the length of the south wall. It was half desk and half table, which gave her room to work and also to lay out maps, hold Co-op meetings, and dance a tarantella if she had a mind to.

There was a knock at the door now, and a gray-bearded man who looked like a grizzled cowboy actor stepped in, the first customer of the day. He was dressed in an old-school Hawaiian shirt. Adam Honeywell was his name, and he was interested in renting booth space in the Market. He opened a valise and laid out his wares on the tabletop—an array of old flatware pieces, cotton tablecloths, comical cream pitchers, and salt and pepper shakers. The Co-op didn't allow pricey antiques or newly manufactured goods to be sold, but these were used collectibles rather than antiques, and she had always been a sucker for cream pitchers.

Mr. Honeywell had just gone off down the stairs when a woman came in, Anna Fleemer from Tidwell College, carrying good news. The college had agreed to sponsor community classes in practical ceramics. The college would pay for two booths in which to sell locally made craft goods. She wanted to know whether Jane was interested in a quilt-making class too, since there was a woman in the Art Department who was a quilter. Jane was happy to say yes.

And so it had continued into the afternoon, the sun shining through the windows and occasional customers with questions and tidbits of small good news. Then at four o'clock it clouded up and began to rain, just a drizzle at first, and then real rain, and by the time she had locked up at five and was going out the rear door into the parking lot behind PJ's Abbey, the sky was so utterly dark that it seemed as if night was falling. Jane climbed into her Subaru Outback, closed the door quickly behind her, and backed out of the stall.

As she swung around into the lane, she saw Lettie Phibbs's apparently empty Cadillac Escalade with the Antiquities Center logo on the door, parked several spaces away. When she turned out onto Orange Street in the direction of Almond Avenue, however, there was the Cadillac turning to follow her, or at least it was heading in the same direction. The car had appeared to be empty just moments ago. Had Lettie hunkered down inside when she saw the light switch off upstairs in the Co-op office?

Of course not, Jane told herself. It was more likely that Lettie had been inside the Army Navy store and come out through the rear door right after Jane had driven away—a coincidence and nothing more. She watched in the rear-view mirror as the Cadillac crossed under a streetlamp, which illuminated Lettie's unmistakable bubble hairdo.

Jane turned up Almond Street toward home, assuming that the Cadillac would follow, since Lettie might be bound for the Antiquity Center. But when her car came into view at the corner, it crossed Almond and went straight on toward the park. And then, when Jane was crossing Cambridge Street two blocks from home, she saw a black Escalade coming along toward her in the distance. Through the falling rain she couldn't be sure it was Lettie's car, but the sight of it was creepy, as if Lettie had come around the block for no other reason but to spy on her.

Curious now, she watched the rearview mirror as she continued along Almond toward home. The Escalade must have turned off onto a cross-street, however, because the intersection behind her remained empty. The coincidence of her crossing paths with Lettie three times in the same day was a little weird. On the other hand, she and Lettie moved in some of the same circles and their interests overlapped. Probably there was nothing weird about it at all.

14.

JERRY HAD TO FORCE himself to put on the filthy coveralls and crawl back under the house, making two trips back to the crypt: the first towing a plugged-in extension cord and a trouble-light, the second hauling a plastic bin holding a piece of four-by-four post, the paving stone, and other odds and ends. He hung the light on a nail and switched it on, the shadows retreating into the farther reaches, making the low space almost cheerful. But the light didn't drive out the memory of the nightmare he'd had earlier. If he started to feel weird, he was out of there.

He took a gallon-size freezer bag out of the bin, set the two parts of the skull and the Yansheng coin into it and zipped it shut, putting it into the nearly-full bone bag, zipping it up, and tying the canvas handles together in a double knot for security's sake. Still on the lookout for small bones, he set to work scraping leftover dirt out of the crypt with a square plastic storage container that he'd taken from the kitchen.

Toward the bottom he unearthed a silver buckle, apparently hammered into a shallow cup-shape from a silver coin—a third souvenir along with the knife and the ring. Jane would be wowed by the stuff. He added more dirt to the nearby mound until the plastic container rasped oddly across the bottom of the now-empty crypt. As far as he could tell he had found everything there was to find.

What he hadn't expected to find was a solid bottom. It was made up of four wooden planks like those that had covered the top. When he knocked on the planks they emitted a hollow sound, which meant there was a void beneath them—mystery on top of mystery. Maybe they'd reveal a second skeleton and then a third and a fourth—skeletons all the way down.

Leaning his chest on the very edge of the hole, he worked his fingers around the edge of an outside plank and yanked it free. There was a void, all right, but it wasn't empty. He pulled out the other planks and then lay there looking at a cleated wooden box put together with heavy brass screws sitting at the bottom of the chamber. He hefted the corner of the box. It was heavy, not empty. It might as easily be lead fishing weights, or a fruitcake, or the mummified corpse of Estancio Flores's little dog. Or it might be something else. Pandora's box came to mind, but he didn't dwell on it.

It seemed to be a good bet that Maxwell Clemens had discovered the bones almost ninety years ago, given the date on the brick, and given that the brick and the discovery were part of this same mystery. Clemens had removed the skull and put the Yansheng coin in its teeth and then reburied it and built his nutty brick wall around the site. Clemens was a thorough man. Had he discovered this hidden chamber beneath the grave and hidden his own box?

Jerry shifted farther into the hole, bending at the waist and managing to hook his left heel behind a floor joist to offset the problem of gravity. He got a solid, two-handed purchase on the box and straightened up, putting his back into it, the contents shifting inside. He swiveled around, scraping against the floor joists above, and laid the box in the dirt beneath the lamp.

He guessed that it weighed twenty-five pounds, give or take—something like the weight of a big box full of deck screws. The lid of the box was fastened shut with two thick strips of cowhide the width of a belt, the leather secured with square-headed iron nails, which hadn't been in common use since the 19th century. Two shorter strips of leather were nailed to the back of the lid as makeshift hinges.

He took his multi-tool from his belt, forced the end of the tool's narrow pliers under the leather alongside a nail, and attempted to pry the nail out. The old wood was hard, however, and the square nail was stuck tight. He lost all patience and simply yanked the dried old piece of leather to pieces, and very shortly he had the lid open. For the second time that day his mind was unable to make good sense of what he was seeing, which was not a fruitcake.

The box held a heap of coins, dark with age or grime. A number of them were strange-looking octagonal coins, nearly the size of the Yansheng charms but with no hole in the center. They might as easily be bronze as gold. They were like no coins he had ever seen—way too big for one thing. Could be they were fakes or toys.

He fished one out and tilted it under the light, seeing the outline of what appeared to be an eagle's wing and the word "Fifty" at the bottom. He dropped it like a hot thing into the chest and shut the lid, wishing he had a roll of duct tape to fasten it now that he had wrecked the leather straps. He opened it again and took a quick survey. Many of the coins were smaller than the octagons, some very small—several double handfuls of coins altogether. He wondered what that amounted to in dollars and cents. A lot.

Full of nervous energy, he looked at his watch—two-thirty, the day wearing away and one hell of a lot to do before he slept, to misquote the poet. There was no time to sit and look. The stark truth was that someone had buried this box here many years ago. Violence had occurred and a man had been murdered, his body hacked apart and buried along with the box. The problem of the bones was compounded by the problem of the gold, although buried gold was what might be called an uptown problem.

He laughed out loud, giddy with the thought of it, but the giddiness quickly evaporated. *Phibbs had come looking for this very thing when she had tried the gate.* Of course she had. She was an irritating woman, but that didn't mean she was stupid. It was possible, likely even, that she had been waiting and watching for this very thing to happen, chock-full of legend and half-sensible information, certain that the treasure lay hidden somewhere close by the old Flores Adobe. When he had blundered into the Antiquity Center this morning, the Yansheng charm had wound her up like a tin toy.

After scooping a shallow depression in the loose earth that he had removed from the hole, he set the treasure box and the bag of bones in the hole, carefully stacking fallen bricks around and over them, trying to give the impression of a random heap. He set to work scooping clean dirt back into the now-empty crypt, smoothing it out and setting the concrete stepping-stone onto it, checking that the stone was level, and then standing the original pier on top, plumb with the sagging beam under the floor. He measured the length of the post he'd need to take up the half-inch of sag, and scuttled back into the clear, heading out to the garage to cut the post to length, and then back into the cellar to mount it.

At around four o'clock he heard rain falling on the cellar hatch, and it occurred to him that the agitated, nightmarish quality of the cellar had evaporated, as if the rain had damped it down. Maybe it was the gold that had done the magic, or maybe it was a sandwich and three glasses of water. He went into the house one more time to see what the floor looked like in the bedroom.

It looked damned good. The last shim was set perfectly. The floorboards had knitted themselves up just as they had unknitted in the 'quake. Knitting up a crack in the floor was like knitting up the raveled sleeve of care, he thought. He wondered about the "sleeve of care", which had always struck him as odd, as if care wore a sweater. If he was a cartoonist he could sell the illustration for half a million.

He laughed out loud. To satisfy the fates he warned himself once again that the gold might not be gold at all, but brass or bronze or some damned thing. Pewter, maybe. "Hah!" he shouted, which startled Peewee, who was sitting in front of the fireplace like a fat hobgoblin.

"We skunked her, didn't we Peewee?" he said. And it was true. Mrs. Phibbs was undone. There was no way to explain it to Peewee, and no need to explain it to Jane, at least not today. Timing was everything in that regard. Their anniversary suggested itself, since it was coming up on Wednesday—no need to shop for a gift! As for Phibbs, she would have to put the defeat into her hat and wear it, the weight of it pressing on her mind until her head flattened. She had come snooping down the driveway after something that was already beyond her grasp.

15.

BY FIVE-THIRTY Jerry had showered off the long day's dust and made coffee. He sat in the chair in front of the big window in the living room waiting for Jane to get home and looking at her laptop, which he had found lying conveniently nearby. His own laptop was ten years old, give or take, and was slow and only about half useful, like his flip phone, which he referred to as a phlip phone in his mind in order to jazz it up. The mere sight of his phone seemed to irritate and astound people, as if he were carrying an abacus around his neck. Actually people would admire the abacus.

He had struck out on his internet search involving salt-filled bricks. Whatever old man Clemens had been up to with the salt, it had nothing to do with masonry. He sipped his coffee and considered Mr. Clemens, whom he knew nothing about except that he had been a mason and was probably living in sin with Ling Jiao. So what was the man up to with the salt wall and the Yansheng charms?

It seemed reasonable that Clemens had discovered the bones while repairing damage to the fireplace foundation, given the coin between the skull's teeth and the identical coin built into the wall. That meant, probably, that the crypt had been visibly broken open and that Clemens had put it back together again in 1933, if the date brick was an indicator, which it must be.

But Clemens had not found the gold. The bottom cavity of the crypt hadn't been tampered with, obviously, since the gold was still there. No rational human being would dig up a treasure and then bury it again, not in 1933, in the middle of the Depression, and in an era when the government wasn't nearly as interested in looking over people's shoulders as they were today.

He typed "salt and ghosts" into the keyboard now and was swarmed with hits: salting dead bodies, salting the threshold of your home to repel wandering ghosts, pitching salt into the face of an attacking ghost, shooting a corpse with rock salt in order to kill the inhabiting ghost, pouring a line of salt on the floor behind you as you flee a room containing a threatening ghost. Certainly it would be bad manners to offer a salt shaker to a ghost at the dinner table.

The crypt must have been buried and out of sight when Clemens built the house. Later on it had broken open. Clemens had found it and decided to let the bones lie, and had almost certainly put the laid-to-rest charm between the teeth of the skull before putting the lid back on top and covering it with dirt. Then, being a superstitious sort of a guy, he had built the salt wall to contain whatever ghost might be stirred up and stowed the second charm in the wall for good measure.

Maybe it wasn't Clemens who was superstitious. Maybe it was Ling Jiao, his servant or concubine or wife or whoever she was, who was unhappy with the desecration of the grave—a cultural aversion. Maybe *that's* why she was living in the cabin at the back of the property. Or maybe they were both sleeping in the cabin after leaving the house to the ghost of the dead man—to Estancio Flores, if that's whose bones now rested in the canvas sack.

There was a small chance that Clemens had murdered someone and buried the bones himself, like the psychopath in northern California. But that didn't quite fly. It would have been eighty times more sensible to throw the corpse into a ditch and save the Yansheng charms for someone else's grave.

Jerry thought about the gold, about what he would do with it—what *they* would do with it. Clearly he would figure out what it was worth before giving it to Jane as an anniversary surprise. As for the horror story behind the gold and the bones, he would keep that to himself. Jane was fond of horror stories, but only in the pages of a book.

As if the thought of Jane had summoned her, he heard the sound of the Subaru pulling into the driveway. Peewee hauled himself out of his bed and stretched elaborately before trotting to the door. Jerry hastily cleared the computer, closed it, set it aside, and went into the kitchen after a bottle of wine and two glasses.

16.

"IT'S A DATE BRICK," Jerry said, "from the H. Garber brick-yard that was three miles from here up in Orange-Olive a century ago."

"I can see that," Jane told him. "The date is interesting, though. Are you going to open that bottle of wine?"

Rain drummed against the cellar hatch, which would normally be a cheerful, homely sound. Jane couldn't appreciate it, because the cellar wasn't particularly homely. It was a place of shadows and it smelled musty and old to her. Certainly it had potential.

She felt both worry and relief about her last-minute decision to cancel the market. Despite today's temporary sunshine, weather predictions had worsened throughout the afternoon, and now the storm was doing just what was predicted.

She watched as Jerry set the bottle on a plywood table that he had set up on top of sawhorses. He twisted off the cap and poured out two glasses, handing one to her. "Cheers," she said, and they sipped the wine.

"What's so interesting about the date on the brick?" Jerry asked.

"It was the year of the Long Beach earthquake—a big one, killed a lot of people, mainly from falling bricks and debris. This morning's 'quake was along the very same fault line."

"*Was it?*" Jerry said. "That explains a lot about the repairs that Clemens made to the chimney! And today I was down here again making my own repairs. It's like history repeating itself."

"I'd just as soon it quit repeating itself."

"I'll drink to that," Jerry said, and they kissed each other before tasting the wine again, which was something they'd found at MacFrugal's, using an app on Jane's phone to make sure it was a bargain. Jerry regarded the bottle, nodding his head sagely. "A wine expert would say that this has a huge, sulfuric nose, with a hint of burnt bacon."

"There's something pruney about it, too, medicinal, maybe."

"What do you think about a wine cellar?"

"I think it means we'll have to buy better wine. Is this area far enough from the heater, though? The whole point is that the wine stays cool."

"Sure it is," Jerry told her, "and a brick wall would shield the bottles from the heater anyway. Turns out they still sell this kind of brick at a salvage place in Tustin. We could build a double-thick wall sandwiched with insulation."

Jane nodded. Actually it was a good way to dress up the space so that it was less tomb-like. Right now it was like an Edgar Allen Poe story with all this subterranean brick. "How about a couple of chairs and a lamp and a table?" she asked. "Cozy it up a little. Maybe leave the door open to air it out when the weather's good."

"Now you're talking. A bookcase, too, and plaster gargoyles."

"You've thought this through," she said.

"As soon as I saw that we could turn the cracked wall into a door, it pretty much thought itself through. One thing, though. Let's keep this to ourselves, okay?"

"Sure, if you want."

"Once it's done, we can claim the whole thing was here when we bought the place, hidden behind the cracked wall. I looked at the inspection report this afternoon. There was no reference to the condition of the cellar when we bought the house, only the remark that the foundation was solid, which it was until this morning. And here's the thing. Everything we build down here will help to shore up the house, and none of it will be visible to anyone at all, including busybodies from the city—nobody's business but our own."

"I'm for it," Jane said. The idea of a secret wine cellar appealed to her. She held out her wine glass, which Jerry refilled.

"You want to see what else I found?" Jerry asked.

"I do." She assumed that he was talking about the Chinese coin that Lettie Phibbs had mentioned. He took a small, leather drawstring bag out of his pocket with the word "marbles" printed on it, wiggled it open, and shook the contents out onto the plywood bench: a pocketknife, a small buckle, and a ring, but no Chinese coin.

Jerry picked up the ring and showed her the stone. "I was pretty sure it was an agate, and I think I'm right—a Mexican fire agate on a silver band, probably hammered out of a silver dollar. I think that the buckle is the same thing—a hammered coin with a flower etched on it, maybe for a hatband or a strap. It looks homemade, like the ring. The pocketknife is an English Barlow knife, which you can tell by the IXL stamped into the bolster." He pointed at a figure stamped into the band at the top of the knife. "That means it's a Sheffield knife. Sheffield had a company in San Francisco back in the 1800s."

"Wow," Jane said. "You've been busy. These were just lying around down here?"

"Buried in the dirt. I found them when I was putting in a new post under the floor."

"So you think that this stone mason dropped them when he was building the house?"

"They're from earlier than that. They date from the 1850s or '60s. We should buy a metal detector. There's no telling what we'd turn up in the back yard."

"Funny you should say that," Jane said. "Lettie Phibbs told me that you had found an old Chinese coin."

Jerry stared at her for a moment. "This *morning* she told you? At breakfast? How could she know about it?"

"No, later on. She was out with her own metal detector, searching along the creek. She said you'd just been into the Antiquity Center where you'd showed her a coin having to do with dead bodies. According to her, you and Peewee had found it near the weir."

"*Dead bodies!*" Jerry said, "That's *her* theory. She's a meddling old windbag. I'm thinking of setting her adrift in a barrel with six rats and half a pound of moldy cheese." He dug into his pocket and pulled out the Yansheng charm now, holding it on his palm for Jane to see. "I found it right here in the cellar this morning after the earthquake, and I took it into the Center and showed it to Phibbs after I saw you two on the sidewalk. She got nosy about it, so I made up the lie about finding it in the creek. I'm happy to hear that she fell for it."

"She's a difficult woman, for sure."

"Like King Kong is a difficult ape."

"Why didn't you show it to me this morning? It doesn't matter really, but . . ."

"I could have, but I wanted to know what it was first," Jerry said. "I was hoping it was worth something, and that I could surprise you with it. I think this one probably belonged to Clemens—the guy who built the house—or more likely to Ling Jiao. You remember Kat Winkle telling us about them?"

"I do. Did Lettie think the same thing?"

"I'm pretty sure she did, but I didn't want to encourage her. She did an internet search and claimed it was worth six bucks, the same as this bottle of wine. She wanted me to donate it to the Center and take a tax write-off."

Jane nodded, only partly satisfied with the explanation, but not sure why it mattered to her. Was she angry because Lettie Phibbs knew something about Jerry that Jane didn't know? Or that she shared this information about the history of the house with him but saw no reason to chat with her about it? Was this some kind of jealousy on her part? Lettie's comment about married couples keeping secrets from each other had been like a drop of poison.

"I'm worried about you being mixed up with Frau Phibbs," Jerry said, "but I know you can handle her better than I can. She was snooping down the driveway today, probably on her way home from the creek after you saw her. I was eating lunch in the kitchen, and I heard the gate latch clank, like she was checking to see if it was locked."

"Lettie Phibbs? In our *driveway*? It must be get-to-know-the-Larkins day."

"Yeah. After she gave up on the gate, she came back around to the front porch and rang the bell. That's how I knew it was her. I saw her through the window."

"Did you answer the door?"

"No. I didn't want to encourage her. She was carrying a book."

"Is it possible that she wanted to *give* you the book? She told me that she'd lent you one this morning, so the idea isn't far-fetched. You should have answered the door. She probably rang the bell earlier and you didn't hear it, so she went down the driveway to see whether you were in the back. *Were* you in the back?"

"Earlier, yeah. I think the book was a prop."

"A *prop*? Could be your imagination's working overtime."

"Could be, but you know what they say: 'Take a long spoon when you sup with the devil.'"

"She's not a *devil*, Jerry, for God's sake. You should know that she's offered to find funding for the Co-op, starting with the bookmobile project. She's done very well with the Antiquity Center over the years. You can see that when you walk through the door. You *did* see it."

"That's true. But . . . she obviously didn't like me from the first. That's what put me off. Judgmental people are pissants, to use the French term."

"She told me that you were 'baffling'. That's not the same as not liking you. She might think you're making fun of her. Being facetious. I suspect that you exercised your sense of humor on her."

"I told her I ate with my hands, but it made perfect sense under the circumstances—nothing facetious about it."

"Maybe you could humor her just a little bit for my sake. Humor in the sense of going along to get along, not in the sense of cracking jokes that she can't understand. It would make my life *so* much easier right now."

"Sure," Jerry said. "I can do that. Call me the good humor man, just don't call me late for dinner."

Jane smiled at him and said, "We might as well finish the wine. It won't age well. And thanks for the treasures."

"You want the Yansheng charm as a souvenir? To go along with the rest?"

"No. It's too morbid. I think you should give it to Lettie Phibbs and take that six-dollar write-off."

Saturday

17.

BOB HOLLOWAY'S OFFICE was on Tustin Street, northeast of
Old Orange and across from a closed-up bowling alley and a
used car lot. It sat in a building that had once housed a bookstore, a delicatessen, and a café but had come down in the world.
Now it was half-empty. Trash and leaves and cigarette butts lit-
tered the breezeway, and graffiti was faintly visible under green
paint slapped onto the brown, wood-sided building.

Lettie had no idea why Bob had left a message on her
phone, summoning her without revealing why. It had been
three years since she had spoken to him and thirty years since
they'd had a romance. There were more accurate terms for the
affair than "romance", but here they were, still friends by some
definition all these years later.

She was abruptly aware of the swift passing of time and of
the fact that no other man had given two cents for her over the
course of those thirty years. She caught sight of her reflection
in a window and looked away again, feeling that she had seen
another woman's face, one she didn't recognize.

Lettie began to swing open the door to Holloway's office
when she was shouldered aside by a man pushing his way out.

He had the appearance of a petty criminal and reeked of body odor, liquor, and cigarette smoke.

"Fuck you, Holloway!" he shouted over his shoulder, giving Lettie a look of such angry violence that she pressed the door completely open to be well clear of him. She hurried inside and pulled the door shut behind her, twisting the deadbolt in case he came back. She unsnapped her purse as a precaution. Showing one's pistol to a threatening person was often enough to ward off trouble, or so she had been taught in the private training course she'd taken. She left the purse open when she set it on Holloway's desk.

"Don't mind him," Holloway said to her, gesturing her into a swivel chair, "but we'll leave the door locked just in case. His wife took him to the cleaners in a divorce, and he blames me. Complete loser. Is that a pistol?" he asked, tilting her purse toward him. "I like the pearl handle and the gold accents. A .38, I believe."

She drew in a breath and exhaled, still trying to dispel the man's angry emanations, and snapped the purse shut without answering. Bob knew that she was formidable now. The office smelled of burnt coffee and old cigarette butts, and the trashcan overflowed with take-out cartons from Lucky Chinese and greasy bags from Wendy's. She spotted an airline-size Smirnoff bottle in with the trash and wondered whether Bob was pouring it into his morning coffee.

"You're that man's lawyer, Bob? I wonder how you can stand it, fraternizing with his class of people."

"I don't fraternize, Lettie. But I'll take someone's money if they offer it. He paid the retainer in cash. Unfortunately he neglected to tell me about the other woman and the case fell apart. His wife had photographs of them coming out of a room at the Sweet Six Motel down on Harbor Boulevard. He wants his retainer back."

She noted that Bob's hair was mostly gray and that he had a wattle under his chin and baggy eyelids that hadn't been so obvious last time she'd seen him. He was a tall man with broad shoulders, but he was stooped now, and any evidence of youthful vigor had gone out of his face. Youthful vigor was a short-lived commodity.

"It's these modern times, Bob. Self-respect has gone straight out of fashion. The bottom rail is on the top." She shook her head tiredly. "How are the kids?"

"The *kids*? Living out of state. Don't see them much. How about you, Lettie? You still employ that shit-bird Carmody?"

"You don't need to use that kind of language, Bob. It diminishes you. Peter *is* still in my employ. He's a man of many talents, and he's loyal, which makes up for his . . . personality. He makes a good cup of coffee too. I can tell you that from experience. He spent two years as a highly regarded barista." She stood up and crossed to a small Formica table and switched off the office coffee pot. "Shall I open a window to air things out? That burnt coffee smell is mortal."

"The windows are screwed shut. But pour me a cup now that you're on your feet." He leaned toward her, holding out a mug, which she filled halfway before sitting down again. "Here's to cast iron entrails," he said, and took a big sip. "The thing is, Lettie. I was at Benjie's having a drink in that little bar they have in back, and I ran into Fritz Pellman. He's counsel for the city. On retainer, not a city employee. You know Fritz?"

"*Should* I know him?" Lettie asked.

"No. Since I know him, you don't have to. He has no idea that you and I go back to the Stone Age, and he told me that the city was taking a hard look at non-profits. Your Antiquity Center was mentioned in regard to a pending audit. There's apparently a red flag flying."

She stared at him, her heart beating high. "What do you mean *pending*? Who mentioned an audit? This Fritz character? He told you this out of nowhere?"

"Pretty much. Maybe he does know we have a history and it was a tip. I don't know how soon, or whether they'll ask for an independent audit or kick the door in with guns blazing."

"Do you mean with no warning whatsoever? A *surprise* audit? That's not right. Why on earth. . . ?"

"That's the ten-cent question. Someone must have got suspicious of something. Here's the deal. I asked Fritz whether he'd ever run into an accountant named Peter Carmody, and I got a weird response."

"Weird how?"

"Instead of answering my question he said, 'Do you know Carmody?' I didn't get that—his asking me the same thing I asked him. I said that I'd run into Carmody a couple of times and that I thought he worked for you, and that he had the reputation of being a damned good accountant. Fritz nodded and changed the subject, as if he'd already said too much, which he had. He was on his third rum and Coke."

"And that's all you got out of him? What did he know about me?"

"No idea. I offered to buy another round, maybe loosen him up some more, but a woman showed up and they went in to dinner."

"Well . . . That was good—your recommending Peter."

"It wasn't much of a recommendation, but it might be worth something if Fritz was fishing. If Carmody turns out to have a shady history, though, it could put me in a bad light, not to mention you."

"You don't think this Fritz would dig into *our* history?"

"Your history, you mean. You'll recall that I wasn't mentioned in the police report."

She stared at him, trying to figure out what this meant—whether Bob was washing his hands of her, and after what they'd been through.

"Relax, Lettie. Sure, someone might snoop around, out of curiosity. But there's nothing there other than the suicide note, which was completely persuasive, and all of it is ancient history anyway. Water under the bridge." He grinned at her.

"That's *not* funny," she said, fixing him with a hard look. Her husband's body had been found in the San Gabriel River, wedged into the rocks beneath the Pacific Coast Highway overpass near Naples in Long Beach.

"All I'm saying is that you should think about an audit. Are you sure this whole thing didn't start with Carmody? What's the chances he'd sell you out?"

"Are you talking about extortion? That Peter would threaten to provide evidence against me? No, sir. He would not. Peter Carmody is loyal to me, and he has too much to lose."

"If he's been cooking the books he'll have plenty of cell phone photos of you coming out of the Sweet Six Motel with a handful of money, if you catch my meaning. He'd skate and you'd pay the piper."

"Don't be crude. What you're suggesting is unthinkable after what I've done for him. I helped him achieve his full potential. People don't forget that."

"Believe what you want. I just thought you'd like to hear the word on the street. Maybe Carmody is just who you think he is. Maybe he's good enough to stand an audit. You've checked his work?"

"Of *course* I've checked his work. I'm his employer. There's been no hint of a problem with the books."

"There never is until there is. Like I said, though, something put the wind up someone."

She looked at him hard for a time and then said, "If this man Fritz didn't know that you and I were acquainted, how did my name come up at all?"

"Maybe you're living a little high, driving that Escalade." He gestured toward the window. Her car was visible in the lot, parked a good distance from the several other cars in order to keep jealous people from vandalizing it. "What's the sticker price, a hundred K?"

"It's nobody's business. People judge you according to appearances, you know."

"That's what I mean."

She gestured at the office roundabout her. "Perhaps your clientele has lower expectations."

"Calm down, Lettie. I'm being straight with you, for God's sake. Something set someone off."

Lettie shook her head. "I'm at sixes and sevens, Bob. You'll stand by me if I need counsel?"

"Financial troubles are not my bailiwick, but I might find someone who can slow an audit down. In the meantime you might consider your options. You must have a tidy sum put aside."

"Not tidy enough."

"Are you still legally Tilda Lambert?"

"That was in another life, Bob. You know that. I've come a long way in the thirty years since. How about you? Are you still in the business?"

"Nope. The fake identity game is too complicated nowadays. Too high tech and too many hoops to jump through, not to mention serious jail time if you're caught. You might want to take Tilda off the shelf and freshen her up, is all I'm saying."

Lettie smiled at him. "Tilda's fresh enough."

"Do Lettie and Tilda have a concealed carry permit for that pistola in their purse? Because if not, then they should keep it under wraps, especially with this audit pending. No telling what they'll grab if they raid the place. A stolen pistol won't be considered an asset."

She sat looking at him for a moment. "You still employ colorful language, Bob. I have the feeling that you're angling at something here. I was hoping your phone call meant something . . . something *more*."

He shrugged and said, "I've got no angle, Lettie, not with you. Like I said, this is a heads-up for old time's sake."

"Good. That's what I was hoping. I wish we could bring those times back again, Bob." She shook her head.

He shrugged. "Stranger things have happened."

"Do me a favor and ask this man Fritz about the audit, if you can. I need to know what's coming. I've got some irons in the fire."

But now there was a rattling at the door followed by someone knocking. "My ten o'clock," Bob said, getting up out of his chair. "Call me in a few days and I'll tell you what I know."

18.

LETTIE'S MIND WHIRLED as she drove back downtown, considering her options like Bob had suggested. The idea of romancing the current incarnation of Bob Holloway didn't appeal to her, but if it came down to it and she needed his help she might hold her nose and reconsider. *Someone at my back*, she thought, savoring the phrase, *but not someone looking over my shoulder.*

His mention of her husband, Professor Arthur Johnston, that generous and loving man, drew her mind to the past, which seemed to crowd up against the present these days. The police report regarding Art's death had indicated that he had either jumped or been thrown from the Second Avenue Bridge into the San Gabriel River. His car had been found in the parking lot of the old Edgewater Inn with a suicide note on the seat. There was some possibility of foul play—that he had been bludgeoned before his head hit the rocks below the bridge.

The police had questioned her, of course, but it had come to nothing. She had been traveling at the time and so had an alibi, a word that she found ugly. She remembered every detail of the questioning—the doubtful police, the assumption of her potential guilt. But they had no evidence against her. No murder weapon, no witnesses. And to this day she honestly didn't know how the blow had been struck. She didn't *want* to know. The poor man, so scholarly and active, had been declining into dementia, and his death had been a mercy. Art had made no secret of the fact that he didn't want to live when his faculties were gone. His friends had attested to it.

Bob Holloway had stood by her—had lain with her in her own *bed*, for God's sake—telling her only what she had to know, which was as little as possible. His help had cost her a pretty penny, and she had been slow to pay due to the husband's assets being frozen until the case was closed. Bob had been patient in all ways, although he had coarsened in the years since.

Bob's doubts about Peter didn't hold water, of that she was sure. Fairly sure, anyway. She hadn't checked Peter's work beyond glancing at it. Peter had been with her too long for her to conceive of him as a Judas. Just last month they had celebrated her birthday at Orange Hill Restaurant, taking in the nighttime view from the patio. He had given her a beautiful pashmina scarf and a card. *That* was the Peter Carmody that Bob Holloway didn't know.

A horn blasted, and she jerked the car back into its lane and made a hasty right-hand turn down Walnut Avenue to get off the main road, where everyone was in a damned hurry despite the ghastly emptiness of their worthless lives.

She wouldn't half mind becoming Tilda Lambert again, just to get out of the rat race. Giving up the Center would be hard, but losing the Center in an audit would be worse. Everything about her alternate identity was up to date: health insurance, passport, driver's license, and social security number. Keeping Tilda alive had been a small safeguard, and worth the expense. Tilda owned a condo on Molokai that she rented out, the money paying the lease and fees on the condo and the cost of garaging the car. She could walk into it at the end of next week if she chose to.

She *did* have irons in the fire, thank God, and a bolt hole out of the rabbit warren that southern California had become over the years. But she would have to put more coal to the furnace if those irons were going to save her.

19.

FIVE AWNINGS were set up over booths along the stone wall at Hart Park, a miniature farmer's market today, with only a few locals ignoring the threat of rain. Clouds raced across the sky although the sun was glowing through them at the moment, a hopeful sign that probably wouldn't last through the morning. George, the mushroom man, had baskets of white mushrooms the size of baseballs, and the avocado booth was up and running, offering late season Hass fruit, which would last another couple of months, nearly until Fuertes were picked in early November. Bonnie Goodwell's booth, whose Co-op garden plot out-produced everyone else's, had baskets of late-season Valencia oranges and an assortment of produce that hadn't drowned in the rain.

Maryam Saliba's pop-up coffee and pastries booth, hung with festive, multi-colored banners and popular among joggers and bicyclists, was selling homemade cinnamon rolls, one of which Jane was consuming right now along with a cup of Yemeni coffee. She sat with Penelope Potts, a volunteer who operated the Pet Corral under an easy-up canopy. Penny was in her seventies, a retired nurse, and wore a heavy flannel shirt against the cool weather. She was a solid, practical woman and an unpaid member of the Board of Directors.

Peewee sat on his round, oversized pillow, purple velvet with gold piping. Old Grim, Mrs. Potts's Pekingese, sat alongside on an identical pillow, the two dogs ignoring each other. They were friends, but they didn't make a show of it. Jane had recently found the Princely Pet Pillows at MacFrugal's and had bought them with money from the tip jar in order to give the Pet Corral the air of a Middle Eastern bazaar, although it required imagination. Mrs. Potts held onto the leash of a big, snaggle-toothed creature that might have been part pit-bull and part hippopotamus. It stood placidly next to her knee, watching its owner, who was drinking coffee and chatting with Maryam.

The creek had risen in the night, although not quite high enough for the city to barricade the lot. According to Jane's friend Mildred in the Community Services Office, the spillways at Santiago Creek Dam would be flowing heavily today due to rising waters from tributary creeks, and the parking lot would be blocked off at one o'clock, an hour after the market would officially close.

"I wonder if you're a reader, Jane," Mrs. Potts said, changing the course of Jane's thoughts. "We've never talked about books."

"I have to be," Jane told her. "It seems like there's more to know than I have time to learn."

"I meant frivolous books, to take your mind off the learning. We have a book club, you know, that meets once a month. Tomorrow night is the big night. We call ourselves The Circle."

"Not the Plaza?" Jane asked, smiling at her.

"Hah!" Mrs. Potts laughed. "I'm a Plaza girl myself, and I hope you are too, although I'm not fanatical. The book club is a circle as in a *society*. When we started the club that first year we read anything having to do with secret societies—the Rosicrucians, the Illuminati, the Assassins. We called ourselves the

Secret Circle back then. The following year we were the Seafaring Circle. Currently we're the Spirit Circle. We're reading ghost books of all sorts. This month's author is Algernon Blackwood. Have you read Blackwood?"

"I *have*," Jane said. "I just read 'The Willows' yesterday in a ghost anthology that I found at a yard sale. It's currently my favorite ghost story that doesn't have any ghosts in it."

"Then you'll fit right in. We meet at Ruby's in that comfy room in back of the bar, third Sunday of the month. We have nothing against a little something to drink, either. A glass of wine or two can enliven the conversation, at least until it puts us to sleep."

"Sure," Jane said, making a spur of the moment decision, and then surprised at herself for doing so. "I'll be there." She liked Penny Potts, who was virtually always friendly. It was good karma to be friendly in return, and she needed something to take her mind off work, which followed her everywhere. Because of that she had been too busy to cultivate friendships.

She turned up the collar of her jacket against the wind— an ocean wind carrying the cold threat of more rain. The owner of the big dog looked up into the sky and quit chatting with Maryam. He put a dollar bill into the Pet Corral tip jar, thanked Mrs. Potts, and hurried away with his dog at his heels.

"We have only one rule," Mrs. Potts said to Jane. "At our meetings we stick to the topic. No politics, no religion, and no damn talk about illnesses and conditions and that sort of old person's thing. Leave your pain in the neck at home, is what we say."

"Me too. What's the title of the book?"

It's a story collection called *The Empty House*. The title story is first in the book, so read that one if you have a chance. More if you can, of course. It's atmospheric, like 'The Willows'. No blood and guts."

"I don't have a copy, but I can download it, I guess."

"In a pinch. I will say that we're *book* people, Jane, proper ink-and-paper books. We encourage members to buy real books in order to support local bookshops. It's part of our mission statement. Do you know the Bookman, on Katella?"

"Sure," Jane said. "Best bookstore around. I was in there a couple of weeks ago and bought a book on the ecology of ponds. They had half a shelf of them."

"I happen to know that they have a copy of *The Empty House*. If you like, I'll call Dave and ask him to hold it for you."

"Perfect. I'll pick it up later today."

Jane saw Mrs. Phibbs pull into the parking lot in her Cadillac Escalade and drive through the axle-deep creek water into a dry parking place against the opposite wall. Jane had agreed to meet her at the picnic tables.

"There's Leticia Phibbs," Mrs. Potts said flatly.

"Do you know her?"

"Oh, yes. I remember when the Antiquity Center opened many years ago. She was a member of the book club our first year, but she washed out. We're a sociable bunch, and she was a little . . . dictatorial, although I have nothing to say against her beyond that. She thought we lacked seriousness, I guess you might say. She was right, too. Guilty as charged."

"Good," Jane said. "Seriousness is overrated. Lettie and I are meeting this morning at eleven. She has the idea of joining forces with the Co-op."

"Oh!" Mrs. Potts said. "I spoke out of turn. Forgive me. Lettie Phibbs is *very* good at doing what she does. I don't mean to pick on the woman. Ruby's at seven o'clock on Sunday, then."

Jane hurried down to the parking lot, carrying her phone and soaking a shoe leaping across the stream before climbing the stairs. Lettie was just then sitting down at a table out of the rain. She had called an hour ago to set up the meeting, full of a strange urgency and with the news that she'd found a potential donor.

"I'm sorry to interrupt your morning," Lettie said when Jane sat down across from her.

"I was just hanging around the market, what there is of it." Jane set her phone on the table and paused to catch her breath. "We cancelled the real market because of the forecast."

"This terrible rain! They say it's the wettest September in history, over six inches so far, and October is setting up to be even worse. It's the El Niño on the rampage again." Lettie looked at the sky and shook her head. "There's nothing to do about it, though. That's in God's hands. As I said over the phone, I've got some good news, but I wanted to give this to you first." She handed Jane a book and went right on talking. "I stopped by your house yesterday to lend it to Jerry. It has to do with California grizzly bears in the local mountains—right up Jerry's alley, I should think. His truck was in the driveway, and so I thought I could catch him at home, but he must have stepped out. Or at least he didn't answer the bell."

"He might have been working in the back yard and not heard it."

Mrs. Phibbs nodded heavily. "I suppose so. If you'll just give him the book. A gift from the Center."

Jane read the contradictory title, *A Boys' Book of Bear Stories (Not for Boys)*, and wondered whether the apostrophe was misplaced. There was a ninety-dollar price penciled onto the flyleaf. "Wow," Jane said. "This is extravagant. Thanks."

"Not at all," Lettie said.

The book contradicted Jerry's suspicion that Lettie had been "snooping down the driveway" yesterday. Or nearly did. Jerry might see the book as further evidence of a plot. Also, Lettie might have penciled in a faux price. It didn't look like a ninety-dollar book. She stopped herself from this line of thinking.

"Here's the news," Mrs. Phibbs said to her. "I put in a call to the Messerbee Foundation. You've heard of the Messerbee fortune?"

"No," Jane said. "Should I have?"

"Yes, indeed. Sam and Dottie Messerbee are one of the most prominent county families. Sam and his first wife Magdelena acquired their fortune selling orange groves in the 1970s during the land boom when people were flooding into the county. He married Dottie forty years later, after Magdalena's death. Dottie's a bit of a gold-digger, if you want to know the truth. I intend to pitch the Co-op to Sam, and pitch it hard. I'd appreciate *any* information you could let me have in order to come up with an angle, including financials. Sam Messerbee will give us a one-time look. It'll be a *considered* look, but we won't have a second chance to make a first impression."

"That's . . . wonderful," Jane said. "Perhaps I should simply come along to the meeting. I could probably spot an angle if one popped up in conversation. I doubt that he could ask a question about the Co-op that would stump me."

"I wish that would work, Jane, but the Messerbees are a very private family, as you can imagine, swamped with requests for money and time. Sam has agreed to meet with me as a go-between, do you see?"

"Okay. Sure. I'll get you as much information as I can put together. Soon?"

"A-sap. There's no time to waste. And along that same line—and by *line* I mean simple profitability—I've been thinking more about an affiliation between the Center and the Co-op. Not equal partners, mind you, but something like that. I don't for a moment mean to interfere with your independence. But we *are* fellow travelers, after all, and we could better promote our mutual interests by putting up a united front. Does that interest you? Are you willing to consider it?"

A passing cloud cast a dark shadow over the park now, and there was a flurry of drops. The cloud moved on, taking the rain with it, but there were more clouds coming in from the south and southwest. The horizon out toward the ocean was black. Jane had a mistrust of ready-made phrases and clichés, and Lettie Phibbs had a bin full of them in her head. "I'll consider it," Jane said finally, "but I don't quite see how partnering with the Center will work, given the way the Co-op is structured. I'd need to see specifics."

"Of course," Lettie said. "Nothing hidden, that's my motto. Now here's something you can sink your teeth into. It occurred to me that if the Center were to provide a promissory note for a set number of shares—not a controlling interest, of course, but a substantial interest, Sam Messerbee would have no choice but to take me very seriously indeed. He would see that the Center was *committed*, do you see?"

"This is a lot to take in," Jane said. "If your meeting with Mr. Messerbee is coming up quickly, I really don't think I could give all this the necessary attention. I'd have to ascertain that this was in keeping with the Co-op's bylaws, which were established in the original grant."

Lettie looked surprised, as if she hadn't expected resistance. "I take your point, Jane. Well done. I'm perhaps overly excited about the whole thing. I want you to consider an affiliation between the Co-op and the Center for the mutual good of both. Careful consideration. Give some thought to what we can accomplish together. I'll work on Sam Messerbee."

There was another scattering of drops, heavier now, that threatened a downpour. "Here it comes," Jane said, looking again at the sky.

"One quick thing, Jane, before we dash. My friend Bob Hovel, a historian from Santa Ana, would very much like to take a look at your house. He has an interest in the history of the Water Street homes."

"Sure," Jane said. "I don't see a problem with it. Let me talk to Jerry, okay?" Jerry would have a problem with it, of course, but he'd have to lump it. There was no way she could shut Lettie down now, not after she set up this funding meeting.

"Do clear it with Jerry," Lettie said. "I'll be in touch, and soon. You'd better run."

Jane nodded, her mind full of loose ends, and headed back toward the market. Lettie's snowballing enthusiasm was hard to get a grip on, as was the prospect of money from nowhere. The rain picked up, and she dashed down the stairs and across to the market to help Maryam, who was hastily collapsing the coffee booth. Jane went after the banners, pinching off the binder clips that held them to the overhead cable, pausing long enough to pull up the hood of her rain jacket and tighten it down.

The last few customers were jogging away or fleeing to their cars, getting out of the storm and out of the creek bed. Mrs. Potts had the folding chairs stowed in the back seat of her car along with the pillows and was standing under the easy-up out of the rain with Peewee and Old Grim. Jane helped her collapse and stow the easy-up, abruptly aware that she had left her phone on the table with Lettie Phibbs. How had she managed that? The phone had been right in front of her . . ..

She saw that Lettie herself was hurrying toward the parking lot now, her jacket hood over her head, waving the phone. Jane went down into the lot to meet her, happy to retrieve the phone. "You must be more careful!" Lettie said to her, which was true but irritating. A crack of thunder banged out overhead, and by the time Jane climbed into the car with Peewee, both of them were soaked.

20.

JERRY DUCKED into the Antiquity Center carrying the book that Mrs. Phibbs had lent him, *Caminos Viejos*. It was an interesting book to be sure, although he had read only the final chapter, having to do with the Flores gang. It was more than possible that the gold under the house was Flores gold—the right era and location—but he didn't intend to bring up the subject, and he would leave in a hurry if Phibbs brought it up.

Once again there was apparently no one minding the Center. As far as he could see the lights in the kitchen-workroom were out, and the counter area was dimly lit. Maybe Mrs. Phibbs had stepped out to smoke a hubble-bubble. Instead of dinging the bell on the counter, he quietly set the book down and headed straight for the stairs, walking softly on the heavy rugs. There was a velvet rope closing off the bottom landing, which gave him half a moment's pause before he unhooked it and slipped past, re-hooking the rope and climbing straight up and out of sight.

He thought of Phibbs unlatching the driveway gate yesterday, and he found it was hilarious that he was replaying her own caper with the velvet rope. Then he thought of himself standing behind the window curtains in his house watching her on the front porch, and he wondered whether she was doing that same thing now, replaying *his* part in yesterday's caper.

She might easily be lurking upstairs, in which case he would claim to be looking for her. He paused at the landing at the top of the stairs to listen for the sound of activity, but the house was silent, and she was nowhere to be seen. The four rooms opening off the landing and hallway had clearly been bedrooms in the distant past, but two of the doors had been removed, the doorways widened so that the interiors were visible.

He opened one of the closed doors and discovered a bathroom, very up to date and with a shower and tub—black marble with gold veins. A robe hung on a hook and there were toiletries and a basket with makeup on the counter, neatly arranged. It was damp and smelled soapy, as if someone had showered within the last few hours. It wasn't meant for visitors, obviously.

There was a large bedroom behind the next door, also evidently in use and strewn with mission furniture. The bed was neatly made and there was a sweater draped over the back of a chair. A water decanter and glass sat on the bedside table along with a book. He wished he'd brought along a pair of chattering teeth to put into the water glass, just to enliven Phibbs's day when she discovered them. She was evidently living in the Center—not strictly legal, but so what.

He looked into one of the two open doorways, which contained stacks of lawyers' bookcases, books and art objects behind glass, neat, clean, and orderly. The matching mahogany storage cabinets were built in a Mission style, with hammered copper strap hinges and matching drawer and door pulls. The woodwork wasn't original to the house, and must have been expensive as hell. He stood admiring it, considering the joinery and other elements until he reminded himself that he was on a mission of his own.

He stepped through the final open door into a large room lit by wall sconces. Books in several glass-fronted bookcases were perfectly squared up, the glass panes clean to the point of invisibility. The nap in the plush wool rug showed the tracks of a vacuum cleaner, disturbed by a single set of footprints: Phibbs's, certainly.

The footprints led to an oak side-table with a green-shaded reading lamp. A book and a pair of reading glasses sat by the lamp along with a coaster depicting Mission San Juan Capistrano. On the bottom shelf of the side-table stood a stemmed glass and a half-full cut decanter. He picked up the bottle, removed the stopper, and sniffed the contents—sherry and not bourbon, which was disappointing. Alongside the table stood a stuffed leather recliner chair and ottoman. Mrs. Phibbs's Antiquity Center seemed to be her own private domain, not at all a public space.

One wall was lined with waist-high bins similar to those in stores that sold vinyl records. Like the cabinetry, the open bins were built of mahogany, each bin containing several quarter-inch-thick wooden dividers, brass-framed, with brass tabs on top—no expense spared. The paperwork in the bins was organized by decade. Evidently nothing much remained of what had been written down in the distant past. In 1870 the contents were separated into individual years, and farther on down the line there some bins were dedicated to an entire year, the quantity of paper records growing as Orange County got more populated. The items, many of them photographs, were fitted into plastic sleeves so that they could be drawn out without being defaced with greasy thumbprints.

He quickly sorted through the jumble in the 1850s bin, having no idea what he was looking for, only that Phibbs had told him that there was "historical arcana", which was a good word, the more arcane the better. The bandit Juan Flores had been hanged in 1852, so this was the only relevant bin. Most of the contents were manifests written in Spanish, and, as far as Jerry could understand them, they had to do with the sale of cattle and sheep, a couple listing payments to vaqueros working the ranches. There was a list of baptisms and burials at Mission San Juan Capistrano, along with a record of garden yields and the comings and goings of travelers along El Camino Real. There were random letters, some in English, most of them brief and with nothing of interest to say, given that the people who wrote and read them were a century-and-a-half dead. There was nothing arcane about any of it.

He flipped past several old photographs of cross-eyed people, most of the men sporting beards, and then, just when he was fingering the last of the contents, he found a glassine wrapper enclosing a half-sheet of paper that had originally been folded into a small square. It had been unfolded and pressed flat before putting it into the wrapper—six lines hand-written and signed with a scrawled "J", addressed to a woman named Martina. The brief message read, "*Abre la puerta en la casa de Estancio, en la noche del Lunes. Nos vamos a Mexico con el oro.*"

"Bingo," Jerry said under his breath. He had enough Spanish to know that "*Abre la puerta*" meant "open the door", and that the writer intended to run to Mexico with the gold and, obviously, the woman Martina. He refolded it along its original creases, his hands shaking so much that it was nearly impossible to slide it back into its glassine wrapper. He returned it to the bin, turned on his heel, and walked to a bookcase on the opposite wall and stared at the titles on the spines without reading them.

This was surely it—J being Juan Flores and Martina being the shadowy Martina who had been mentioned in *Caminos Viejos*—a mystery woman said to be responsible for the betrayal of a German shopkeeper whom Juan Flores had robbed and murdered. "E", of course was Estancio Flores, whose fate was sealed in the ink used to write the note. Martina would betray Estancio on Monday night. According to legend, she and Juan had never left for Mexico, and in fact Juan Flores had been captured and hanged in Los Angeles, ragged and penniless after being hunted through the chaparral by a sheriff's posse.

Jerry felt a terrible urge to steal the note, to slip it into his pocket, but he knew that there was no reason to do so. He was already aware of what was in it. He didn't need the paper. Except that in some sense the note *belonged* to him, or at least to the house that he and Jane had come to own. He possessed the bones and the treasure, and now he had this third element—the evidence that would complete the picture.

Complete *what* picture? He imagined Jane's response to that sort of empty-headed phrase, which was a simple rationalization for his stealing the note. Temptation was a rabbit hole, and there was no knowing where it would lead except into the darkness.

But in a sense the note *did* complete the picture, if a person knew what the rest of the picture looked like. How much of the picture had Phibbs cobbled together? She had obviously read this note and knew what it meant, but she could have no idea where the old Flores adobe actually stood or what had happened to the gold. Had she connected the Yansheng coin to Estancio Flores's corpse? If so, her guess had probably been right on the money, literally on the money, although she couldn't know that for certain.

Showing the coin to her had been his first mistake. It had sent her straight down to the creek bed with a metal detector, looking to substantiate his story about finding the charm. When she had come up with nothing, she had sneaked down his driveway, homing in on the truth and hoping to see something to confirm it. The bucketful of broken bricks and open cellar door hadn't confirmed anything, but it had raised suspicions.

He returned to the bins, removed the Flores note once again, and slipped it into his jacket pocket. If his borrowing it was theft, so be it. He could smuggle it back into the Center later, after the dust under the house had settled, and put it back into its place. His sin would be absolved, and he would have avoided an eternity in hell.

Time to go, he told himself, and walked out of the room, unavoidably adding more footprints to the recently vacuumed rug. In the hallway he saw Phibbs's head rising up the stairs. He had escaped with seconds to spare. "Hello!" he said cheerily, and she looked up as if in surprise.

"Mr. Jerry Larkin! I thought you might be wandering around the premises. Find anything interesting?"

"Everything is interesting, but nothing in particular. I was looking for you, in fact. I left the book you lent me on the counter."

"And I retrieved it. I'm very glad you took a moment to look around, because I particularly wanted to ask you a favor. Should we descend? Looking up at you is giving me a crick in the neck."

"Of course," Jerry said, following and wondering what sort of favor she could possibly ask for. Yesterday the question would have seemed innocent to him, but nothing about her was innocent now.

She returned to her place behind the counter, taking up a defensive position, it seemed. He realized that the artifact in his pocket had colored his thinking, and he secretly felt it to make sure that the corner of the note wasn't protruding like the corner of his cellar door. She followed the movement of his hand, as if she knew.

She could *not* know, he told himself. Could she? He wondered whether she had actually been coming up the stairs when he came out of the room, or whether she had been standing midway up the stairs waiting for him to come out of the room and *then* started climbing? Had she seen him sorting through the bins?

"Jane tells me that you've volunteered to re-purpose the food truck, to turn it into a book caravan," she said.

"I did. I was thinking of something like an old gypsy cara-van on the outside—filigree work and gaudy paint. Woodwork on the inside—shelves with hold-fasts, that sort of thing."

"Fun and functional!"

"That's it exactly. Why do you ask?"

"Because the Antiquity Center has signed on to finance the project. It would become the first step in what I hope will be a profitable collaboration between the Center and the Co-op. I've already got a line on a truck—a twenty-footer—and what you tell me relieves my mind. I have an old-fashioned sense of things. I abhor plastic and aluminum and gimcrack trash."

"I'm with you entirely."

"I thought you would be. And I can't tell you how happy that makes me. I'm afraid we might have gotten off on the wrong foot yesterday morning."

"Luckily we've got two of them," Jerry said.

21.

LETTIE WATCHED through the kitchen window as Jerry drove away. He was sneaky and unscrupulous, and she wondered how much of his gee-whiz demeanor was an act. All of it, probably, and she'd best be careful not to reveal too much, but to let him do the revealing, which he might be inclined to do now that she had re-established their friendship. When she was satisfied that he wasn't going to return on some pretext, she ascended the stairs and went into the Pamphlets Room to see whether he had fallen for the ruse. There were his footprints all over the rug, leading straight to the bins. It didn't take ten seconds to see that he had stolen the fraudulent note. She should have put the note into a big rattrap.

The theft made it clear that he was guilty as charged, but it didn't answer the salient question: was he still searching or had he already found something that made sense of the Yansheng charm? Something in the cellar? Certainly he had found the charm somewhere on his own property. And his failing to tell Jane about it must mean that there was something more to the discovery. The grave of Estancio Flores?

She headed back downstairs to phone Bob Holloway, considering what to tell him. Not the truth, certainly. Not entirely.

She didn't trust Bob that far, although she had at one time. And he would have no desire to hear the truth for reasons of plausible deniability. He would do a favor for a friend if he was well enough paid, but he would want to avoid complicity.

When she and Bob had been lovers, she'd had someone to confide in. Peter Carmody wasn't a confidential friend. When Lettie had taken Peter's arm walking into the Orange Hill Restaurant for her birthday dinner, he had managed to shrug it off—not angrily, but like a boy who was too old to hold his mother's hand, and needed to make that clear once and for all. Bob hadn't shrugged her off when their affair ended. He had simply gone back to his wife. She'd been hurt by it, but it was the honorable thing. When she had heard that his wife had passed away, she should have called him, but she had been too proud. And now look where the pride had taken her.

Bob picked up the phone on the third ring and said, "Hello again, Lettie," clearly having looked at the caller ID. Secrets were hard to keep in this modern age.

"I've got a two-hundred-dollar favor to ask," Lettie said, and then, after bracing herself, she said, "and something else that's . . . that's priceless."

"Everything has its price," Bob said flatly. "What's on your mind?"

"Can I speak candidly?"

"We've always been candid with each other. No reason to stop now."

"I was hoping you'd say so, Bob." She realized that she was nervously winding a lock of her hair around her fingers. She felt like a schoolgirl, an emotion that she thought she had put behind her decades ago. "What I've got in mind is nothing professional in nature—no legal advice, just a small piece of theater. What do you know about eminent domain laws?"

"Enough," Bob said.

Lettie hesitated for a moment, gathering courage, and

then asked, "Would you be willing to talk about it over a drink?"

"Over a drink? Are we at the candid part of the discussion?"

"If you'd *like*." She held her breath. Would he react to the word?

"Candidly, I could use a drink. Just about any time."

"Tomorrow night?"

"Sure. Let's say Benjie's, in the bar, seven p.m."

"I'll be the one with the rose in her teeth," Lettie said, and hung up the phone. "God help me!" she said aloud, sitting down hard in a chair. Where had she come up with that last line? She'd probably scared the living hell out of him.

She recalled the vodka bottle in his office trashcan this morning and wondered whether Bob had become a mere drunk—whether it was her offer of a drink that attracted him. She had no idea of throwing herself at him, but if she could light a small fire in him, she might end up with a friend by her side once again.

22.

JERRY SAT in the public library, two blocks west of the Antiquity Center, working on one of the desktop computers. The brightly lit library was particularly busy, maybe because of the cloudy day and the pending rain. Most of the easy chairs were occupied by people reading books or working on laptops, none of them seeming to be in a particular hurry. Jane had called to tell him that the market had shut down early, and that she was holed up in the potting shed with Peewee, trying to get it organized for the move up the hill.

He had found a feature article in the *Orange County Register* from 1969, largely having to do with Donald Hyink, Numismatist. Hyink had attended Santa Ana College back in the 1950s and then studied mineralogy at the University of Iowa. The article had to do with the man's being a featured speaker at the first California State Numismatic Society symposium in Long Beach. He had been thirty years old at the time and owned one of the largest collections of numismatic books in the southland, much of it inherited from his father, who had shared the same passions.

There were other articles about Hyink, one about his coin library in Tustin, which was a semi-commercial consultancy, bookstore, and metallurgical laboratory hidden away in a suburban neighborhood that had grown up around the Hyink homestead in recent decades. Zoning laws would nix the venture today, but because of its long history it had been grandfathered in as a commercial enterprise, which apparently had little or nothing to do with the buying and selling of coins. Like Mrs. Phibbs, Donald Hyink dealt in information.

Another article titled "Founding Fathers of Tustin", revealed that Donald Hyink's great grandfather, Pieter Hyink, an arborist, was an associate of Columbus Tustin himself, and had married a woman named Leucadia Carmody in 1878, the two of them building the house on Prospect Street on twenty acres of land, all but two acres of which had been sold off over the years. There were eighty-two exotic trees surrounding the old colonial-style farmhouse on the remaining two acres.

Jerry wondered whether the name Carmody was simply a coincidence, or whether Peter Carmody of the Antiquity Center was a shirttail relative of Donald Hyink. It would explain why a hoser like Carmody was employed by a man of Hyink's standing, although it would not explain why Lettie Phibbs employed Peter Carmody, who had the shit-flinging personality of an unhappy zoo ape. There must be something else to recommend Carmody and to explain his nickel-and-dime part-time jobs.

He closed down the computer, left the library, and walked to the pickup, considering what he would say to Hyink when he called him. Nothing at all about the actual treasure, of course. He would have to keep the conversation hypothetical—a question on behalf of a non-existent uncle, maybe. Later, after he'd met the man, he could decide what was next. He punched the number of Hyink Numismatic Services into his phone, which rang half a dozen times before someone picked it up and said, "Hyink coins," in a flat voice.

"I'd like to speak to Mr. Hyink," Jerry said.

"He's out today on business."

Jerry knew that he was talking to Peter Carmody, a man who didn't waste words. "When is he in?" Jerry asked. He had no idea of involving Carmody in his business, and for a moment he considered hanging up.

"Monday and Wednesday. No walk-ins. Appointment only."

"Monday then, in the morning."

"Name?"

"James Laslow. I'm driving out from Long Beach, so ten o'clock if that'll work, after traffic."

"Ten o'clock. Ring the buzzer. The address is 13340 Prospect Street, but the place is hard to find, so you might want to use your phone to map it out."

There was a click and a dial tone. Carmody had hung up— exactly his style. Jerry sat for a while, staring at the little screen on his flip phone that he was supposed to use to "map it out". For a time he watched the people that were coming and going in the library parking lot, searching through the ten-cent books in the outdoor bookcases or dumping books into the returns bin. Clouds raced across the sky, filling in the distant corners, really packing in.

There was no indication that Carmody had recognized his voice. And why would he? Carmody had been indifferent to him at the Antiquity Center yesterday. He had probably forgotten Jerry's existence. But he hoped that the little creeper wouldn't be working at Hyink's shop on Monday morning.

23.

THE SHED AT THE CO-OP Community Garden sat just above the Santiago Creek high-water mark. The line of debris from the nighttime release of water from the dams was uncomfortably near the mark, although the level was down slightly again this morning. Jane had moved her car up onto Grand Street now that the creek parking was shut down, and had walked to the garden along the park's perimeter walkway. The area that Lettie Phibbs had been sweeping for treasures yesterday had vanished under water. Jane wondered whether the toad had found a dry spot to wait out the weather.

She could hear children hollering on the distant playground along Glassell Street—a boy and a girl, being pushed on the swings by a man who must have been their father, given his enthusiasm. She had liked nothing better than playing outside on a rainy day when she was a girl, stealing time, threatened with a soaking at any moment. She wasn't as wild about the idea now that she was older. That was one of the tradeoffs people made, giving up childhood pleasures for . . . what? Information? Work?

She waved at Peewee now, who was looking out at her through the shed window. He had no desire to be outside in the wet and cold, and so she had put his bed on top of the potting bench. He was happiest when he could look people in the face instead of looking up at their knees.

What to do about the garden shed; that was the problem. It had been built in 1938, when the park's band shell and pool building had gone up as projects of the Works Progress Administration. The shed, with its concrete floor and river rock foundation, had been used as a utility building. It had been restored fifty years back, after the '69 flood had swept part of it away, re-sided with heavy, rough-cut cedar planks and a split-shingle roof with deep eaves supported by wooden outriggers. It looked like a tiny craftsman bungalow. Bags of potting soil and organic fertilizer, seed trays, plastic irrigation pipe, garden tools and garden carts, a sub-compact tractor, and other odds and ends filled most of the space, all very neatly arranged, and all waiting to be moved uphill when there was someplace to move it.

When the Co-op plotted out the community garden, Jane had assumed responsibility for the shed, which was a listed historic building. There was no tearing it down. But the fifty years since its last restoration had taken their toll, and the shed was pockmarked with holes drilled into the boards by acorn woodpeckers. Termites and dry rot had played their part.

The stone foundation was crumbling at both corners along the creek side of the wall, and the building had slumped slightly in that direction. The entire shed, foundation included, wanted to be dismantled and moved up the hill to the edge of the garden, where it would be safe from further floods. There was already a concrete slab poured, and the restoration should have been done this month. But if the weather grew any more apocalyptic, the shed would have to fend for itself.

Jane walked around the corner of the building, taking photos for the sake of posterity, trying to imagine how long it would take to dismantle it, and how easily she could find volunteers to do the work. She meant to use every scrap of the existing building, including the woodpecker-holed cedar planks, which would make good shutters for the high windows along the top and for tool cabinetry inside. According to Jerry, the split-shingles would pry up fairly easily, although she would have to supplement them with new shingles, which she intended to split out of chainsawed sections of old cedar telephone poles from the city yard. All of the lumber, siding, beams, and shingles, would have to be soaked in fire retardant.

Someone shouted the word, "Ahoy!" from a distance, and Jane turned to see Jerry himself coming toward her along the path, taking long strides and carrying a grocery bag, ideally full of food. She had only eaten a pear for breakfast, and it was well past lunchtime. Jerry wasn't wearing a jacket, which was typical of him, and might have been either optimism or foolishness. Foolish optimism, probably, which was one of his lovable attributes except when it got him into trouble.

"What's in the bag?" she asked when he arrived.

"Sandwiches, coconut cookies, and a thermos of coffee," he said. Jerry had a passion for sandwiches and was psychologically incapable of turning down a cookie unless it had white chocolate in it, which he said was made of library paste and corn syrup and was high on his list of garbage foodstuffs. "Worried about the creek?" he asked her.

"I am. It's up and down, up last night, obviously. If the rain decides to really get going, the shed will be floating off Newport Beach."

"The foundation won't float."

"It won't withstand a flood, either. The rocks will be part of the creek again."

As if her statement had called up the Fates, there were three bolts of lightning in the east and a peal of thunder that rolled across the sky. Rain began to fall, pattering through the branches of the sycamore tree overhead, and the two of them went in through the open door of the shed. Peewee greeted Jerry by barking and turning circles, clearly happy to have the family together. Then he lay down on his bed and went to sleep.

Jerry cleaned off a section of the potting bench with a brush while Jane dug a big towel out of the hanging flour sack that they used as a rag-bag. She spread it out as a tablecloth, laying out paper plates and coffee mugs wrapped in paper towels, which she flattened out and folded into napkins.

"I made muffalettas on Italian bread with that olive spread Mindi brought back from New Orleans. Cookie?" He held out the bag of coconut thins.

"With my coffee, I think," Jane said. "Thanks for the grub."

They sat quietly for a time, eating their sandwiches, drinking coffee, and listening to the rain and the thunder, looking out in the direction of the unseen ocean, where the sky was a mass of black clouds.

"So Phibbs is donating the bookmobile outright?" Jerry asked, pouring out more coffee and offering Jane a cookie.

Jane could see the doubt in his eyes and hear his dislike for Lettie Phibbs in his voice. He was making an effort, but he had never been able to hide what he felt. He assumed incorrectly that he had a poker face, which made him a lousy card player in any game but Go Fish.

"The Antiquity Center is donating it," Jane told him. "It's apparently a bargain at $18,000. But it's too rich for the Co-op's blood. Lettie's working with the Friends of the Library to fill it with books. Why do you refer to her as *Phibbs* all the time? It sounds contemptuous."

He shrugged. "Bad habit."

"Developed since *yesterday?*"

"She and I got off on the wrong foot, I guess."

"She seems to feel that same way. Why don't you call a truce?"

"I'm willing. But does this mean that I'll be fixing the bookmobile up for *her?* I'm okay providing free labor to Jane

Larkin's Old Orange Co-op. But the idea of working for Lettie Phibbs is a kind of nightmare."

"She wants nothing to do with the dirty work. That's up to me. Or us."

"But will the Antiquity Center in some sense still *own* the thing? Can she take it back on a whim?"

"No, she can't. It would belong to the Co-op."

"I could afford to donate . . ."

She shook her head. "This would create a useful bond between the Center and the Co-op, mutual gain at the Center's expense. I can farm out the renovations if you'd rather. And I mean that. I use you shamelessly, and I know you've got a lot on your plate with the wine cellar plans. And if the weather gods cut us some slack, we still need to take this place apart and move it up the hill. The bookmobile can wait. But if you just don't *want* to . . ."

"I *do* want to. I like that kind of project, both of them, actually. I'm just . . . Here's the thing that's bugging me, I guess—this business of Phibbs, of *Mrs.* Phibbs, bringing a man out to the house to search the premises. Who is this character? Have you met him?"

"What are you talking about? *What* man?"

"From a historical society in Santa Ana. His name is Hovel. Lettie said she talked to you about it. I'm not crazy about people barging in and nosing into cupboards, especially people like her. You'll admit that she's haywire."

"I'll admit that she's wired differently. But we're all wired differently when it comes down to it. I did tell her it would be all right. We can keep an eye on the historian just in case he tries to steal my jewelry. And who said anything about them *barging* in? She wouldn't haul him out to the house without our okaying it first."

There was another boom of thunder, and they sat listening to its echo, the rain pelting down. Jerry poured them both another cup of coffee. When the noise quieted he said, "If either of them asks to see the cellar I'm getting out the shotgun."

"What shotgun?"

"The one I don't own. It's a humdinger."

"Okay, no cellar. There's nothing in the cellar he needs to see."

"And they stay out of our bedroom."

"*Why?* He'd be interested in the back-to-back fireplaces and the alcove bookcases. It's the nicest room in the house. Also, he'll want to see the tile-work. The fireplace is a sort of showcase, so why not show it off? It wouldn't be a bad thing for the Co-op to have a connection to the Santa Ana Historical Society."

"It seems intrusive to me."

Jane stared at him over the top of her coffee mug. "I sense that this is another anti-Phibbs reaction. We've had neighbors drop in for a glass of wine now and then. Not much difference."

For a moment she thought he would go on arguing with her, but he abruptly gave in. "Okay," he said, breaking into a smile. "A glass of wine, a quick tour, and we show them the road. Meanwhile let's get a rental shed set up at the top of the hill to shift all this stuff into. We won't waste time that way. We can take the roof off this shed the minute the rain lets up."

"Okay. A big enough temporary shed would cost what? Three thousand or so?"

"Hah! I'm way ahead of you. Check this out. On a whim I went down to Rent-a-Shed on Tustin Street. They can drop off a pre-assembled shed on the access road next to the garden, put it right on top of the slab up there. And get this. There's a five-hundred-dollar deposit, but the shed's free for the first six months, *and* we get the deposit back. You know why?"

"I don't have the foggiest idea, but I hope we don't need it for six months."

"Because I told my new pal at Rent-a-Shed about you and the Co-op. Guess who he turned out to be. Go ahead."

"God, Jerry. This is turning into twenty questions, and all the time you've got this big grin on your face. Okay, I'll guess. His name is Pinny Needlekin."

Jerry blinked at her. "How did you know?"

"Out with it unless you want a knuckle sandwich." She held her fist under his nose.

"*Benson Peabody.*"

"You're *kidding,*" Jane said. "I knew Peabody in college! He lived in Married Students Housing and bred Madagascar geckos in big terrariums full of plants. He was a little on the wild side. Rode a Harley and had tattoos that made him look like a criminal."

"He still has the tattoos, and he might easily be a criminal. The geckos didn't pay the bills, so he took up renting portable sheds. When I mentioned your name and told him about the Co-op, he was hornswoggled. Did I do good?"

"*Real* good. When can we get it?"

"Who the heck is Pinny Needlekin?"

"It's the name of my favorite hedgehog. How soon do we get the shed?"

There was a loud crack of thunder that made them both jump and woke up Peewee, who walked over and stared at the remains of the sandwiches. "Monday afternoon at the latest, rain or shine," Jerry said. "And by the way, I cleared it with your pal Mildred. I called Community Services right there on the Rent-a-Shed phone before I signed the papers. Sounds like the rain's tapering off," he said, and when Jane looked out the window he gave Peewee a piece of bread and ham.

"Peewee doesn't need to clean the plates," Jane said. "He believes it's his right."

"The Irish leave out scraps for household fairies. It's bad luck to deprive them."

"Peewee isn't a fairy."

"I figured out that he's a Chinese house god masquerading as a dog. It's unlikely, but it's true. It's obvious that he's the god

Sau. We should probably have named him Porky. Get it?" He grinned at her, obviously enjoying himself.

"I hope to God you didn't utter this kind of nonsense to Lettie Phibbs."

"Nope, but I might, just to see if her head explodes."

"You're almost giddy. Have you been drinking?"

"Not a drop, but I bagged you a shed from Peabody, didn't I? He still rides a Harley, by the way."

"Thanks for bagging me the shed. We can make this work, can't we? That's what keeps me up at night—worrying that the Co-op is Humpty Dumpty."

"Of course it's not Humpty Dumpty. If something falls apart we'll put it back together."

They put the trash into a sack and hauled it out the door to the local trashcan. Jane was happy to find that the rain had stopped and the sky was clearing, although there was still lightning over the mountains, too far away to make much noise. Jerry kissed her smackingly and jogged away toward Glassell Street where he had left his pickup. Jane gathered up Peewee, locked the shed, and headed up the stairs beneath the enormous ficus tree at the foot of Grand Street.

She put Peewee into his travel house, which was belted into the back seat of her Outback, deciding to drive over to the Bookman to pick up the copy of Blackwood's *The Empty House*, which was waiting for her under the counter. She turned up River Avenue, heading downtown, when she passed Lettie Phibbs in her Cadillac, suited out in a yellow rain slicker and matching hat, evidently not seeing Jane as she drove past.

Jane pulled over to the curb out of curiosity, watching in the side mirror as the Cadillac turned down Grand, obviously heading for the park. There was no place else for Lettie to be headed, unless she meant to visit one of the houses along the street. The phrase "turning up like a bad penny" came into her mind, and she thought of the buffalo nickel that Lettie had given her, which she'd put into a ceramic bowl of small treasures that she kept on her office desk.

Maybe Lettie was out metal detecting again in her guise as a detective of history, getting in another search now that the storm had passed on. Jane considered following her to see what she was up to. Certainly Jerry would advise it. But that was reason enough not to do any such thing, and she pulled away from the curb and set her sights on the Bookman, wondering again how she'd managed to leave her phone on the table in the park.

Sunday

24.

JERRY KNEW he was dreaming, and he knew that he had dreamt the dream before, but that made it even more real to his sleeping mind. He could feel the bed sheets and his pillow beneath his head, and knew just where he was, and yet he couldn't move—couldn't turn over or turn his head, couldn't wake himself up.

Once again the antique images and sensations came to him: the sagebrush smell of a Santa Ana wind, the smell of cattle, the warm night. He could hear his heart beating loudly in his ears. He heard a door slamming, and it came to him that he should latch it before the wind tore it off its hinges. He had a growing sense of malignant dread—not something he thought about, but something that had settled into his mind and that he felt in his stomach and along the back of his neck. Something was pending, though—something worse than a broken hinge.

His dreaming mind knew that he would see the adobe house a moment before he saw it, moonlight shining on a window, and away to his left the moonlit pepper tree shifting uneasily in the wind, the fear shifting within Jerry's half-sleeping mind. The shadows of a woman and two horses appeared against the moving limbs. There was the sound of scuffling feet, and he turned to see the figure of a man looming up in his vision, rushing toward him, holding a short spade with both hands.

Once again he threw up his right arm to ward off the blow, knowing the murderous face to be that of his own brother. In that instant the nightmare was blotted out, and he found himself sitting up in bed in the living present, his arm upraised to defend himself. He lowered it and looked at his palm, his hand shaking, his mind at loose ends. A moment ago he seemed to have had a brother. But the images were fading along with the dream's lifelike certainty, and soon it was gone.

He stared for a time at the familiar glow of the streetlight through the blinds. It came to him that it wasn't raining and that it was moderately warm in the house. Jane slept soundly beside him, thank God, but Peewee sat wide-awake at the end of the bed. The clock showed five a.m.

He rolled silently off the mattress, picked up his clothes from the back of the chair, and tip-toed out of the bedroom. Peewee followed along, knowing that early morning wandering almost always meant a treat. Jerry poured himself a glass of buttermilk from the refrigerator and sprinkled black pepper over the top before pouring buttermilk into a bowl for Peewee, who fell upon it greedily. "Sorry you can't have any pepper," he whispered. "It gets in your teeth."

He turned on the light in the breakfast nook and sat at the table, looking out into the feathery leaves of tree ferns that bordered the north side of the house. The nightmare had lost its reality, and yet he had no sense that it had simply been a dream. Instead he had *been* at the adobe, outside on a windy night, standing in the very place of the murder, very near the cistern where the dismembered body would be hidden—the place where their house would be built some seventy-five years later.

It was far-fetched to think that the nightmare was in some sense *real*, but it was impossible not to believe it. It had felt real. It was a damn good thing that he hadn't shouted out and awakened Jane or whacked her with his elbow when he'd thrown his arm in the air. She didn't need to hear about his nightmares, especially this one.

He thought about the note that he had taken from the files at the Antiquity Center and felt a little bit shameful. He would take it back on Monday morning, no harm done. He walked out into the living room and fetched his wallet from the bowl near the door. The folded-up note was slipped in behind the credit cards, and he removed it now and brought it back to the kitchen table, unfolding it carefully.

The note *looked* old: the age-browned paper and the way the ink had seeped into it, leaving a ghostly outline shadow at the edges of the letters. The paper had a ragged edge—heavy paper like a piece torn from an old book. He smelled it. There was an odor that he recognized—black tea?

"What an idiot," he muttered. He had learned that trick in the Boy Scouts, and now he had fallen for it like a tenderfoot. Phibbs had set him up, baited the hook with a rubber worm, and he had swallowed it. He should have seen that it was a fraud. But he hadn't *wanted* to see it, which of course she was betting on. He read the message again. It seemed evidently contrived now—way too particular. All the relevant names were included, if only as initials, the details in keeping with Phibbs's yammering about the murder of Estancio Flores.

Phibbs probably *was* a witch, and had hocus-pocused him. Her story had affected him deeply enough to trigger the repeated nightmare. He recalled the way she had been hovering on the stairs yesterday when he was searching in the room above, probably levitating above the stair runner, casting a spell and laughing through her teeth.

Had this started when he had first shown her the Yansheng coin? She had been discreet as heck with the computer search—secretive even. He sorted through what he had told her, what he had revealed. Not a lot, for sure, but enough to wind her up. She had begun shaking the tree to see what fruit would fall out of the high branches.

And her main suspicion was dead right: he *had* gotten onto the trail of the Flores gold. She could have no idea how far along that trail he had come, and so she had continued shaking things up, planting this note to see if he would come looking for it. How the hell could he have known that Phibbs was such a conniving old heffalump?

His mind turned to thoughts of the bones under the house, packed into their canvas bag. Did he have a repressed fear that he was guilty of *desecrating a grave*? Looked at rationally, the question was idiotic: the bones are not the man. The bones were nothing but calcium carbonate, which would very soon be dust.

And yet it was a sketchy thing to have dug them up without a second thought and stowed them in an old sack. Clemens the stonemason had demonstrated more scruples. Clemens had let the bones lie, keeping them restful with salt and charmed coins. Or had it been Ling Jiao who had possessed the scruples? It was likely that she had given Clemens the charms.

Jerry swallowed the rest of his buttermilk, seeing that Peewee had abandoned him, and shoved the worthless note into his pocket. And right then he heard Jane shout something in the bedroom and Peewee began to snarl and bark. Jerry headed across the living room toward the hallway just as Jane appeared, her eyes wild and staring around her as if she didn't quite know where she was. She stood for a moment, swaying on her feet, her hand to her forehead, Jerry's hands on her shoulders to steady her.

"What's wrong?" he asked, putting his arm around her.

"A nightmare. It was so *real*."

Hell, he thought, scrambling to make sense of what he assumed this meant, and for a moment he nearly lost his balance. "Come into the kitchen," he said. "Was it an earthquake dream?" He tried to smile, but his mouth was too stiff.

"I wish it was," she said. "It was . . . I was somewhere outside—a farm—and the wind was blowing, a hot wind, and . . ." It took her less than a minute to get the details out. It was his dream precisely.

Or. *someone's* dream, he thought. Maybe someone's recollection—a living nightmare that had slept under the house until it was awakened. Now it had moved indoors.

"I was paralyzed until I saw the shovel and knew he was going to hurt me," she said. "And I threw my arm in front of me, and when I did I woke up."

"Like waking up before you hit the ground in a dream about falling," he said, shamefully trying to lead her along.

"Worse." She shivered and drew in a deep breath. "Way worse. I knew I was going to die"

"Glass of buttermilk?"

"No, thanks," she said, giving him a look. "You know I don't like buttermilk."

"How about a bowl of cereal? We've got Cap'n Crunch."

"Are you kidding?" she asked.

"Cheerios, then, for the sake of health." He opened the cupboard door and stood staring into it. A wave of guilt passed through him, but he pushed it into a corner along with the Cap'n Crunch and grabbed the Cheerios. *Dehydration*, he thought. *Of all the stupid goddamned . . .*

"What did you do to your arm?" Jane asked.

"What?" he asked, realizing that his voice was husky. He looked at his right forearm, where he had rasped it against the bottom-side of the floor Friday afternoon, trying to block the shovel blow.

For a second it seemed to him that Jane *knew*, that she was asking a pointed question. But she *couldn't* know. Knowing would scare the hell out of her, just like it did him.

"I dinged it when I was working under the house," he said, which was true, but which ignored the obvious, or at least what was obvious to him. He would fix that problem as soon as the sun came up—the problem that he himself had created when he had disinterred the bones and bagged them up.

He went after milk, two bowls and spoons and a banana and knife, set it all out on the table and poured Cheerios into the bowls. Jane didn't eat sugar on her Cheerios, and Jerry followed suit this morning for the sake of solidarity.

"Thanks," she said, watching as he cut rounds of banana over her bowl. "You didn't think of putting a Band-Aid on your arm?"

"Forgot."

"Putting on a Band-Aid is easier than cleaning bloody sheets."

"We can ask Peewee to lick the sheets clean. He loves the taste of human blood, especially mine."

"We *could* do that," she said, spooning up Cheerios. "What woke you up?"

"Couldn't sleep," he said, pitching the essential truth out the window. "And Peewee thought it was time for breakfast, so . . ."

She looked hard at him. "The weird thing," Jane said, "was that I wasn't me in the dream. I didn't know who I was, only that I wasn't *me*. Does that make sense to you?"

"Sure it does. But you're Jane now. You can take my word for it."

"*How* does it make sense?"

"Dreams make their own kind of sense. What are you up to this morning?"

"I've got a book to read," she said. "Ghost stories, if you want to know." She scooped up the last of the cereal before going after the milk that remained in the bowl, one spoonful at a time. She never simply drank cereal milk or soup out of the bowl. "I knew who I was again and where I was when Peewee started barking."

"I heard him."

"I wonder why he barked. You know he doesn't bark for the fun of it, only when something's wrong."

"He's a sensitive dog, like with the earthquake."

"Sensitive to *what*?" Jane asked. "This was no earthquake." She pushed her bowl away, crossed her arms, and stared at him. "What's going on? You woke up because you . . . *woke up*? That's it?"

"That's pretty much why I wake up every morning. Peewee is sensitive to *you*. He knew that you were unhappy and . . ."

He stopped himself and simply looked at her for a moment while she waited. "I woke up because I had a nightmare—the same nightmare that you described. For me it was the second time. It happened when I was under the house working on Friday. I cut my arm when I saw that shovel coming at me." He shrugged. "There you have it."

A long moment passed, and then she said, "And you didn't bother to tell me?"

"I thought it was dehydration. That's the solemn truth. I got dizzy and I hallucinated. It was weird as hell, but when it was over I crawled out and ate a sandwich and chips and drank a quart of water. I felt fine and I went back to work. End of story. It didn't seem to be a story worth telling. And anyway, ghosts aren't the first things to come into my mind when something strange happens. I don't believe in them." He wondered if this was true. It would have been a couple of days ago.

"Who said anything about ghosts?"

"My point exactly," he said senselessly.

"And when it happened again this morning, you still thought you were dehydrated? Could it be that your *brain* is dehydrated?"

"It freaked me out, sure, but I wasn't about to wake you up and freak you out, too. What good would that do? I had no idea you were going to have the same dream."

She nodded, letting out a big whoosh of breath. "So . . . the house is *haunted*?"

"I guess. Maybe. Sounds too simplistic. Neither of us saw a *ghost*. It makes more sense to me that it was an hallucination that affected both of us."

"I've read about that," Jane said, "about shared hallucination. The French call it *folie à deux*—the madness of two—misery wanting company, probably."

"Nothing wrong with company. There's nobody in the world I'd rather be crazy with. Do you think it might have something to do with shared trauma?"

"Don't try to weasel out of this with your evasive talk. *What* trauma?"

"The earthquake? It scared the hell out of both of us."

Without responding to this she poured out another bowl of Cheerios, which was a good sign. There was nothing like cold cereal to realign a person's chakras. He refilled his own bowl, and the two of them ate together. Outside it was pre-dawn, gray instead of black, and a bird was cheeping in the tree ferns.

"We'll figure it out," Jerry said when they were done eating. He picked up the bowls and put them into the sink. "You going back to bed?"

"Fat chance," she said. "I've got homework to do for the book club tonight. You want to keep me company for a while? Cup of coffee?"

"That's just what I want to do," Jerry said. What he actually wanted to do was to head down into the cellar and get the bones the hell out of there. Get *all* of it out, lock, stock, and barrel. "We'll rendezvous in the living room in three-point-six minutes, give or take. I'll make the beverages."

The tea was sitting next to Jane's chair when she arrived from the bathroom, wearing the paisley robe he had bought her for Christmas on the eve of their moving into the house. "You look cozy in that robe," he said to her, conscious of the fact that Jane was still unhappy with his end-run around the nightmare that wasn't a nightmare.

"Thanks for the tea," she said.

"What are you reading?"

She held the book up for him to see the cover. "Ghost stories. I want to get through as many as I can before tonight's book club meeting." She flipped through the first few pages in order to find the first page of "The Empty House".

"Is it scary?" Jerry asked. "Read it to me."

But she read it to herself instead, and then sat staring at the page for a time, during which he kept his mouth shut and she kept hers half-open, as if she couldn't quite believe what she was seeing.

"Some houses," she read, "like certain persons, manage somehow to proclaim at once their character for evil." She looked at him with a what-the-hell expression on her face.

"I advise you to read a different book," he said, forcing a smile.

"Write your advice on a postage stamp," she told him, "and glue it to your forehead."

25.

An hour later Jerry left Jane to her reading and descended into the cellar where he pulled on his coveralls, playing things over in his mind, thinking about Lettie Phibbs and how she was a contradiction in terms. Her Antiquity Center was a showcase. There was no denying it. She was putting up the money for the bookmobile, which she didn't have to do. She was obviously successful—driving the big Cadillac, finding ways to finance her life and turn the Center into a private museum. Her interest in local history wasn't fake.

On the other hand, she was odd as hell, both her appearance and her mannerisms. He would admit those oddities were superficial, but they seemed theatrical. He couldn't figure out who the hell she really was. *And* she had boldly attempted to break into the back yard. She probably would have walked straight into the house if Peewee hadn't been barking behind the door. She was a meddler, and her meddling was over the top.

He took out his flip phone, opened it, and keyed in the number of his friend Paul Buckman, a man of many secretive skills, whom he had met twenty years ago when they had both worked for a cleanup and demolition company out in Placentia.

"Jerry," Paul said to him, "What's up?"

"Not a lot. I'm wondering how easy it is to check whether someone has a university degree or is lying about it."

"Piece of cake. Used to be harder, but now that everything is transparent there's a clearing house for it, a degree validation site. If you need transcripts, that'll take more work, but I can get them. What's this person's name?"

"Leticia Phibbs, and I don't care about transcripts. She claims to have a master's degree in Library Science from the University of Southern California. If she's lying there won't be any transcripts anyway."

"Unless she bought a phony set. Why would a person lie about having a degree in library science, for God's sake? You think she faked her way into a job?"

"Maybe just for self-promotion," Jerry said. "There's something off about her. Maybe there's a *lot* off about her. That's what I'm trying to figure out, whether she's on the up and up. It could be that we'll be doing some business together."

"An F or a P-H in Phibbs?"

"P-H," Jerry told him.

"You have a social security number? Anything useful?"

"No, and I don't think I can find one without being arrested for breaking and entering."

"Okay. I can find the number if you ever need it. It can open some doors. Degree validation is public record, though. Give me a few minutes."

Jerry put his phone in his coveralls pocket and crawled back in under the floor of the house where he took apart the brick igloo. Paul's "give me a few minutes" was typical of the man. How he did what he did was a mystery—one that Jerry knew better than to ask about. He removed the canvas bag of bones now and lay there for a time staring at the treasure box, considering what to do about it now that Jane was . . . involved. He opened the box, selected four coins from the trove, and pushed them down into the pocket with the phone.

He hauled the bone bag out with him and laid it on the plywood bench, and then crawled back under for the treasure box, clearing the decks, so to speak, making sure that there was nothing left—no pieces of bone or leather or rotted cloth. He heard the sound of rain on the cellar hatch now and wondered if Jane heard it—the end of a few hours of hopeful weather. He would have to be a Cheerful Charlie today, because there wasn't much for Jane to be cheerful about.

He stowed the treasure box behind the brick salt wall, out of sight, and then removed the plastic bag containing the skull from among the rest of the bones in the canvas bag. He set the two skull pieces and the Yansheng charm onto the plywood table alongside a tube of epoxy glue and an empty five-pound Chock full o' Nuts coffee can that he'd found in the garage when they'd moved in. Ten minutes ago the can had been full of 16-penny nails. His phone rang now, Paul already calling back. "What's the news?" Jerry asked him.

"Long story short, I made a couple of calls. No one named Leticia Phibbs graduated from USC, not in Library Science or anything else. They never heard of her."

"I'll be damned," Jerry said.

"You sure she said USC?"

"So Jane told me."

After chatting for another minute, he hung up, thinking about what this meant. Nothing useful. He realized that he didn't give two damns in hell whether Phibbs had a degree in library science. She apparently knew her stuff. She didn't need a diploma to pay for the food truck. Exposing the lie to Jane would poison a well that didn't need to be poisoned.

There was something satisfying in knowing his hunch had been right, though—that he didn't simply have a case of bad attitude. She was a small-time fraud, and it was better to know than not to know. Could be she was a big-time fraud.

Working quickly and carefully now, he applied a heavy line of glue to the top and bottom teeth in the skull, which were still attached to the bone. He dabbed more glue onto the four points where the hinges of the upper jaw met the mandible at the base of the skull. He set the Yansheng coin on the jawbone teeth, picked up the top of the skull, and set it on top of the coin, sandwiching the coin between the teeth while squaring the jawbone with the skull, pressing the parts together. Excess glue squeezed out, which was fine and dandy. This wasn't an art project.

He held the pieces steady while counting out two minutes' worth of seconds, listening in the silence for the sound of the back door shutting, of Jane coming out to see what he was doing. Probably he was safe from that, she having grown a little tired of his company. He wondered what she was thinking, whether she knew that he was as weirded-out as she was. She had an uncanny way of seeing through him. When he was done here, he would see if she wanted to walk down to Snack Shop, their local café, for a rainy morning brunch.

When he let up on the pressure and stepped back, the skull sat there solidly, biting the coin, made whole with the help of a tube of glue. Carrying the skull, the empty coffee can, and the plastic food container that he used to scrape dirt out of the crypt, he stepped again through the door in the brick wall and began scooping up salt from the heaps that had poured out onto the ground. He dumped two inches of it into the bottom of the coffee-can, set the skull gingerly on top of it, and then filled the can to the top with more salt, the skull and the Yansheng coin buried like a bug in amber.

It struck him that this entire process was stark staring crazy, but no crazier than his having twice occupied the mind of a dead man. His and Jane's life together had taken a strange turn forty-eight hours ago when the earthquake jolted the house. Constructing a coffee-can sarcophagus for a haunted skull was apparently par for the course, although he would have to avoid that kind of talk when Jane was within earshot.

He wished he had a lid for the can, but it would stand upright if it was wedged in among the rest of the bones. It swelled the sides of the bag when he zipped it up—not much room to spare inside, but then there was nothing more to add. The bag had become a canvas coffin with an illustration of Chiquita Banana on it.

He left it on top of the bench and pushed out of the cellar into the rain. There was no one at all on the street, no sign of Phibbs in the shrubbery or of her pedaling away on a bicycle carrying Peewee in a basket, bound for Oz. He climbed in on the passenger side of the pickup and opened the glove compartment, pulling out the cloudy vinyl envelope that held the truck's owner's manual. After slipping the coins carefully inside the manual, he slid it back into its plastic envelope, and then hid it under the driver's seat behind doughnut bags and flattened paper coffee cups.

Back in the cellar, he picked up the bone-bag and carried it into the garage, stowing it behind a pile of camping equipment, and then made a second trip to fetch out the treasure box and put it in with the bag. He heaped cloth painter's tarps over the lot of it. When he had time he could find a permanent resting place for the bones, maybe a real grave at the back of the property, a permanent home.

He grabbed a big nail that had recently resided in the Chock full o' Nuts can and knocked it into an L-shape with a hammer, and then went back out again, the rain coming down now like it meant business. The nail slid easily into the lock-hole in the gate latch, the bend in the nail holding it in place along with the help of gravity. Unless Phibbs could fly, or had brought a stepladder along when she came to rob the place, the nail would keep her out. It had been a busy morning, but the underside of the house was secure and so were the bones and the treasure. He felt as if he had done a day's work, and it wasn't yet ten o'clock.

26.

LETTIE PHIBBS IGNORED her lox and bagel and watched Peter's face, looking for signs that he was playing her false. Her discussion with Bob Holloway had put the idea into her head, and she couldn't get it out again. The café was full of clatter and conversation, but they had chosen an out-of-the way table in the back so that they could powwow.

Last night she had dreamt that she had come into the Center dressed in her nightgown and discovered that Peter had run off, leaving the accounting books in disarray and covered in filth, the audit pending in half an hour. She looked out the window of the restaurant at the illuminated sign that read Snack Shop, glowing behind a curtain of rain. Even now, in the light of day, the dream gave her the horrors.

"So then the phone rang at Hyink's," Peter said, bringing her back to the present, "and it was him."

"Who?" she asked, having missed the beginning of his story.

"Jerry Larkin, like I said. You might want to listen to this, Lettie. I set him up with an appointment for tomorrow morning."

"An *appointment*? Excellent! You're certain it was him, though? Did he identify himself?"

"No. He said his name was Laslow and that he was driving out from Long Beach, but it was him."

"Do you think he recognized *your* voice?"

"Maybe. Why wouldn't he? It was you who told him that I worked for Hyink. Maybe that wasn't a good idea, Lettie. Too much information."

"That remains to be seen. What I told him led him straight back to you and Dutch, after all. What did he want? Was he specific?"

"He didn't say."

"You asked him?"

"Of course I didn't ask him, not if I want to keep my job."

"A man like Donald Hyink wouldn't fire his own nephew."

"Cousin, actually, about six times removed. And that's exactly what a man like him would do. Everything is confidential in the coin trade, Lettie, for obvious reasons. I'm just a receptionist. I don't meddle in the customer's business."

"I need to know what he wants, Peter."

Peter stared at her for a long moment. She couldn't see his eyes because of the glare on his glasses, but his mouth was set in a rigid line—no hint of friendship on his face or in his voice. He seemed to be a clever cyborg rather than a human being.

"How *badly* do you need to know?" he asked.

"I don't catch your meaning. You seem to be implying something."

"I'm wondering where all this *need* is coming from. Maybe *I* need something."

"We both need to eat our breakfast before it gets cold," she said, smiling at him. "Did you notice that I'm wearing my birthday pashmina? The one you gave me?"

"Sure."

"It's the only birthday gift I received. It means . . . so *much* to me. So if *you* need something you only have to ask. That's our special relationship. I told you that I thought Jerry Larkin had something up his sleeve, and I merely wonder if you might find out what it is, that's all."

She troweled cream cheese onto the bottom half of her bagel, scattered capers onto the cheese and pressed them in, and then laid on the lox, working carefully, waiting for his answer.

"Lots of things are hidden," he told her.

"Then we'll bring them into the light, starting now. I'll ask you a plain question. Can you be at the Dutchman's during Larkin's consultation?"

"I never work on Mondays, so no. Also I'm opening up the Center at nine, right?"

"Secretly, I mean. Never mind opening the Center."

He shrugged. "I guess I can do that."

"Jerry mustn't know you're there."

"Yes, Lettie. I get it. I'll be a fly on the wall."

"*Thank you,*" she said. "You relieve my mind. This might come to nothing, but if it comes to something, I guarantee we will profit *equally.*"

They turned their attention to their breakfasts now and ate in silence. She considered what she actually knew about Peter Carmody after the three years he'd been in her employ—very little, actually. He rented an apartment in the Flats near the Plaza, but he had no real *roots* in Old Orange. He had mentioned having a sister in Chicago, but had said nothing else about her, as if she didn't matter to him, and when she had asked about his parents, he had told her they were dead. After three years he was still a stranger.

"I appreciate what you do for me, Peter. I couldn't *go it alone.* People shouldn't have to."

He nodded at her. "I guess that's what I'm saying, too."

"Here's something that's just come to light. Something troubling. The Center is being audited, and soon, I believe."

He looked up in surprise, a smear of egg yolk at the corner of his mouth. "*When?* How do you know?"

She could see that her statement had addled him. His voice had gone up an octave and his face revealed what to her looked like fear. "I have my sources," she said. "Can we *stand* an audit?"

"Of course we can. No problem." He picked up his water glass and sipped from it, putting it down again and looking around the restaurant as if he was taking a sudden interest in things. Sixty seconds ago he hadn't given a damn and life was a bore. His sudden animation struck her as false. She thought of her dream again, wondering whether it was prescient, and she thought again of Bob Holloway's suggestion that she consider her options.

Was Peter Carmody considering *his* options? What if he *did* destroy the ledgers and leave town? "Why do you ask *when*, Peter? How much time do you need?"

He shook his head. "A couple of days if we have no choice."

"*We*? I'd have to be *coached*. This is your specialty, Peter—your work. I depend upon you utterly."

"We're *safe* Lettie. I asked *when* because I want to look everything over. Obviously. They'll expect me to know what's in the books, not you, so coaching you isn't a problem. You need to know what *not* to say. We're both equally liable, as you know, so if you're keeping anything from me here . . . Who's your source?"

"There's no reason to name names."

"Maybe. I'll tell you what the problem is, Lettie. I'm starting to feel like a pawn to your queen."

"You're not a pawn. I've come to rely on you *completely*, and to pay you accordingly, I might add. I've put my *faith* in you, and I pray that it's reciprocal."

He smiled at her and nodded his head. The smile was so utterly uncharacteristic of him that she was surprised to see it.

"You don't know how much that smile means to me, Peter. Together we can prevail. If we let them divide us . . ." She shook her head, as if it didn't bear thinking about. "You must see that, don't you?"

"You worry too much, Lettie. I see *everything*, including your new friends, who just showed up." He gestured with his fork toward the front of the restaurant, where Jerry and Jane Larkin were coming in through the door, pulling off raincoats and furling umbrellas.

27.

"I'LL BE DAMNED," Jerry said, hanging his wet coat and umbrella on the rack by the Snack Shop door. "There's Lettie Phibbs giving us the glad eye, and there goes Peter Carmody out the back exit. I thought I saw his car in the parking lot." He wondered abruptly whether Carmody was hurrying over to their house, knowing he had a clear hour or so to snoop around while he and Jane were gobbling breakfast.

Jane waved at Phibbs, who waved back cheerfully. "Who's Peter Carmody?" she asked Jerry, the waitress leading them to an oversized booth by the window.

"He works at the Antiquity Center. Phibbsy called him in to identify the Chinese coin I found in the cellar. He told me that it was trash. He's not a cheerful sort of guy. He gives you the impression that *everything* is pretty much trash."

Jerry watched Phibbs's bustling approach. She clearly had something to say to them—a big smile on her face—and he reminded himself to keep his mouth shut; no more "'Phibbsy'". He stood up gallantly when she arrived at the table. "Good to see you Lettie," he said. "Cup of coffee?" He gestured at the half-empty booth and sat down again. "How about a piece of

Harvest Pie? The autumn pie season is on again."

"No pie for me, Jerry, thanks, and I've already had my morning cup." She directed her smile at Jane now, looking as if she might pop with excitement. "I'll just reveal my very good news and then toddle off. It's *business*, but there's no reason both of you shouldn't hear it."

"No reason at all," Jane said.

"Well then, Jane, do you recall my mention of Sam and Dottie Messerbee?"

"I do. You were going to chat with them."

"And that's just what I did. Time and tide won't wait, as they say. But I have to admit that their response surpassed my expectations."

Jerry wondered what tide she was referring to, but Jane clearly took this as good news.

"Surely you can't have gotten a commitment this quickly?" she said.

"Three-quarters of a commitment, yes. I can't put a value to it, but I'll guess it'll be substantial—a boon for the Center and the Co-op both. Sam particularly wants to meet *you*, Jane. I've told him all about you. Isn't that thrilling?"

"Yes, it is. I'm a little stunned. How soon?"

"Tomorrow."

"My God. Tomorrow? I don't know that I'm ready."

"Ready or not, we have to act quickly. In these matters time is of the essence. We cannot let him cool off. As for readiness, I think I can assure you that Sam Messerbee will be persuaded by your womanly charms, Jane. He's very much a . . . *certain* sort of man, despite his advanced age." She winked in order to make her meaning clear.

Jane continued to smile, although Jerry could see in her eyes what she was thinking. She had no interest in being a woman who would be of interest to a "certain sort of man". That sort of talk was merely irritating.

A waiter arrived with the menus, just as a crowd of a dozen people emptied out of a nearby table and pushed past, heading toward the door in a swarm. "Two coffees," Jerry said over Phibbs's shoulder, anticipating the waiter's question.

"I'm in the way," Phibbs said, stepping past the waiter into the midst of the moving throng. "I'll pick you up at nine, Jane!" And with that she moved away toward the door, looking back and holding an imaginary phone to her ear while dialing the air with her other hand, either an imaginary rotary phone or the universal sign for craziness.

"Did you get that bit about your charms?" Jerry asked. "That kind of talk is Lettie Phibbs in a nutshell. If she'd said something like that to me, you'd point out that it was just her way of speaking."

"Probably I would," Jane said, looking over the menu. "But you're a guy. Not the same thing at all. I'm having corned beef hash and eggs. What about a Bloody Mary? Do we dare?" Jane had a smile on her face that implied she *would* dare, a smile that had not been there ten minutes ago. Phibbs's news was obviously good news.

"Excellent idea. It's that kind of morning. I'll have the hash and eggs, too. Phibbs *is* right, you know. You're easy to look at."

"*Easy to look at*! You clodhopper."

"I'm euphemizing for the sake of political correctness. What I really meant to say is that you're . . . beguiling, a babe, a looker, some might say bewitching."

He waggled his eyebrows at her and she gave him a hard look, although her smile returned immediately. "You know that I hate the idea of selling myself rather than selling the Co-op."

"Of course I know that. The idea of having a photo taken for the Co-op website just about sank the whole ship. You remember that I had to talk you into it, like it was some sort of weird notion? There's nothing wrong with looking good, and besides, you can't help it."

"It was the word 'headshot' I didn't like. I hate the idea that a person has to strike poses like a celebrity."

"Whether it's right or wrong, appearances make a hell of a difference. You'd be a fool to take *me* along to your meeting with Mr. Moneybags. Lettie Phibbs would kill the idea due to my suspicious face and the fact that I'm a clodhopper. She'd be right, too. It's not my game."

"His name is Sam Messerbee, and his wife's name is Dottie. I remember Lettie saying that he was ninety-two."

"Then you're safe. You can outrun him. I say you should get gussied up and blind him with your charms before reeling him in with the facts."

"So you're saying that I'm going along as *bait*?"

"I'd *never* say that kind of cheap thing. The word 'lure' comes to mind, though, as in alluring."

Jerry pushed the salt and pepper and ketchup aside to make way for their drinks, which were just arriving from the bar. The hash and eggs were heading toward them too, from the direction of the kitchen. "I'm happy that you're going to join the book club tonight. It'll give you a break from me and the Co-op."

"God knows I need that, at least part of it. I'll let you worry about which part."

He raised the Bloody Mary glass in a toast, looking at her over a leafy piece of celery and a giant toothpick speared through a line of olives.

"Here's to a change in the weather," he said, and they clinked the heavy glass mugs together and settled down to breakfast.

28.

WHEN JANE LOOKED into the Atchison Room behind the bar at Ruby's Diner, she saw that Penny Potts and another woman had already arrived and had stopped at the bar for glasses of wine on the way in. The two sat in easy chairs at a coffee table. The walls were hung with photos of passenger and freight trains, and there was a mural of the Pacific Surfliner running south along the coast, the sun setting over the ocean. Through the west-facing window lay the lamp-lit railroad tracks of the Old Orange Metrolink station and the parking lot beyond.

"Jane!" Mrs. Potts said to her, "Come meet my dear good friend Mrs. Hazelton."

Jane shook hands with Mrs. Hazelton, a stout woman, probably in her early seventies but with very little gray in her short hair. She had deep laugh lines on her face, and she wore an autumn-colored, leafy, cable-stitched sweater that was almost certainly handmade.

"Get yourself a drink before you sit," Mrs. Hazelton said to Jane. "Talking is dry work."

Jane headed back into the bar, which was nicely empty on a Sunday night. There was no music playing, thank God, only the sound of a model Santa Fe passenger train running around a track that circumnavigated the ceiling.

"Are you a book club member?" the bartender asked. He was particularly good-looking and was probably ten years younger than she was. The term "chiseled features" came into her mind, and he had the build of a dancer. The nametag on his shirt read "Jason". "Just say yes," he said to her. "There's a thirty percent discount on drinks and happy-hour food for club members."

"Then yes," Jane said. "I'm a new member." She waved her copy of *The Empty House* at him.

"That's what I thought. I haven't seen you before. Book any good?"

"It's a collection of stories. Lots of atmosphere. I admit I didn't read them all. Don't rat me out to the others."

"They told you there's a test afterward, right?" He glanced down at her hand when he said this, pretty obviously looking for a wedding ring—some kind of helpless biological response. He poured her a glass of chardonnay, said he'd keep the tab open if she intended to order something else, and then told her to enjoy herself, all very cheerfully.

She carried her wine back into the Atchison Room and took a seat on the couch. "Jason is pleasant," she said.

"Mr. Scrumptious, I call him," Penny said. "He looks like that good-looking fellow on the television."

"*What* fellow, Penny?" Mrs. Hazelton asked. "You can't just say '*that* fellow'. It's not sensible."

"Maybe not, but it's true, and that makes up for something. I can never remember the names of celebrities," she said to Jane. "Do you know that Mrs. Hazelton is Curator of Cultural Heritage at the Little Tidwell Museum on Main Street in Santa Ana? It's high time that the two of you met. She also has a deep understanding of mysticism. She's our resident scholar on the paranormal."

"I deny it," Mrs. Hazelton said. "I have no time for people who claim an *understanding* of that which has never been understood. They always turn out to be charlatans, which is worse than non-believers. I have no sympathy for non-believers, either. They think of themselves as rationalists, but there's nothing more irrational than to disbelieve what one sees with one's own eyes. And to deny that others have seen these things is to accuse well-meaning people of lying."

"I stand corrected," Mrs. Potts said, "but I'm not sure of what. Where do *you* stand in regard to the mysteries, Jane, given that you're a scientist?"

Jane took a sip of wine while she thought about an answer. "Well, I studied zoology, but I don't claim to be a scientist. When it comes to ghosts, I think I stand with Mrs. Hazelton for reasons that I'd actually like to talk to someone about tonight. I love to read ghost stories, though. Jerry warns me against reading them before bed, since they give me nightmares."

They were interrupted when two more women entered, arm in arm, carrying a carafe of red wine and two glasses and copies of tonight's book. One, named Roberta, wore a flamboyant scarf with rainbow colors and calf-length black boots and a beaded belt with a silver buckle the size of a coffee cup saucer. The other, Cecelia, was dowdy, like a bookish professor, with salt-and-pepper gray hair cut short, a cotton blouse illustrated with images of herbs in clay pots, and a tweed jacket with leather patches on the sleeves. Penny introduced them as Mrs. and Mrs. Carson. "They're one of the First Four Thousand couples married in San Francisco in 2004," she said.

"It must have been thrilling to be a part of history like that," Jane said, moving over to make room on the couch.

"You have no idea," Roberta told her. "We drove in from Iowa, got married, and never looked back. We stayed on in San Francisco until Cecelia was hired to teach anthropology at Tidwell. Now here we are." The two of them settled in and poured wine into their glasses.

"It's none of my business, but which one of you was a Carson?" Jane asked. "I hope it's okay for me to ask. My last name is Larkin, which is my husband's name. People ask me why I decided to take his name, and I'm inclined to tell them it's none of their business, so feel free to tell me the same."

"Neither of us was named Carson," Cecelia said. "It was a brand-new day and so we chose a brand-new name, just like you chose your husband's name. Don't put up with busybodies, Jane. Just *claim* it."

"Are you familiar with Rachel Carson's books?" Roberta asked Jane. "We named ourselves after her."

"I *am* familiar with them. I read *The Sea Around Us* when I was eight years old. It made all the difference in the world to what I'm doing now. I didn't figure that out for years, but I see it's true looking back."

"What you're doing now would be the Co-op?" Mrs. Hazelton asked. "Penny has told me about it. And of course I've been to the market on Saturday mornings . . ."

Jane talked for a couple of minutes, hitting the high points and then said, "That's the short version. I'd far rather talk about ghosts."

Penny tapped on her glass with a spoon and said, "We'll call the five of us a quorum, then, given that Cindy and Darla won't be here. Cindy and Randall have gone off to Solvang despite the weather, and Darla is on a date. She wouldn't tell me with whom. I've prepared the usual list of questions, which—I'll say for Jane's benefit—are merely talking points. We're all free to ignore them. And now in keeping with protocol, we'll freshen our drinks before we start the conversation. Visit the necessary room if it's necessary."

"It is for me," Mrs. Hazelton said. "Buy me another glass of the Chablis, Penny. Next round is on me."

Jane swallowed what was left in her glass and went out to order another. In two minutes' time they were settled around the coffee table again, waiting for Mrs. Hazelton's return. In a low voice, Penny said to her, "For your information, Jane, we all call Mrs. Hazelton by her last name out of long tradition. She doesn't mean to be standoffish. Her family couldn't abide her husband, you see, who was much older than she, and when the poor man passed away they tried to convince her to take her family name again. She declined and has been Mrs. Hazelton since."

"And good for her, I say," Roberta put in, just as Mrs. Hazelton reappeared.

"What do we have to say about the first story?" Penny asked. "I'll start by saying that it doesn't seem to have a plot to me. It's all just movement. They go up the stairs and they come down again, getting bullied by ghosts."

"It doesn't want a plot," Mrs. Hazelton said. "It's intended to be atmospheric—a sense-of-dread story, like 'The Willows'."

"I want a character to *do* something," Roberta put in. "Aunt Julia starts out well and then turns into a wimp, and it's the nephew who plays the hero."

"The main character is the house, it seems to me," Cecilia said, taking a healthy drink from her glass.

"Yes, that's right," said Jane. "It takes on the characteristics of the things that haunt it."

"The idea is not entirely fantastic," Mrs. Hazelton said. "Houses can develop a persona. Aunt Julia and her nephew are expelled as interlopers."

For the next hour the conversation shifted back and forth from one story to another, sidelining into irrelevancies now and then. Jane did her best to chime in with comments, although her mind was often on her own house. She wondered if it had "developed a persona".

A chime on Cecilia's phone went off at eight-thirty, and she said, "I've got choir practice in the morning. Early to rise for me."

"By which she means twelve hours from now," Roberta said. "A church choir?" Jane asked.

"Yes, the Church of the Messiah, in Santa Ana. We sing on Sunday and practice on Monday."

"Episcopaisleyans, I call them," Roberta said, winking at Jane.

"That's because your conscience is too uneasy for you to sing a hymn," Cecelia told her.

"A person's conscience *should* be uneasy, I say. I just can't carry a tune."

After the two had said their goodbyes and gone off, Jane said, "I believe our own house is haunted. Or something like it."

"You're serious," Penny said. "I can see it in your face."

"I am. It's silly, probably, but the strangest thing happened this morning." She told her two companions about her and Jerry's identical nightmares. "The thing is, we could feel and smell the wind and hear a gate banging shut, or a door maybe, and everything was . . . *consistent*, like a story. Not like in an actual dream where things don't make sense but you believe they do. I didn't see a ghost. I felt a . . . *presence*, if you know what I mean."

"I do know what you mean," Mrs. Hazelton said. "Manifestations are quite common in these old downtown neighborhoods. You describe this as a dream? You were asleep?"

"I think so. I had *been* asleep. I guess it woke me up"

"Are you familiar with hypnogogic hallucinations? Waking dreams?"

Jane nodded. "I am now. I looked into all sorts of strange things today online, trying to figure it out. I don't think it was that sort of hallucination, though. It wasn't an . . . observation. I was *participating*."

"You mean that you weren't you?" Mrs. Hazelton asked.

"No. I was in a man's mind."

"Or a man's mind entered your own mind?"

"Yes, that was it. And Jerry's had the same dream. Twice."

"Did you feel as if you were displaced in time?"

"In time but not in place. I hadn't *traveled*, if you see what I mean."

"Very interesting," Mrs. Hazelton said. "It sounds as if a spirit is lingering in the house when it should have gone on. It's a common problem. Such emanations and manifestations aren't necessarily malevolent, or not dangerously so."

"It's not the ghost that was malevolent, it's what happened in the nightmare that was malevolent. I'm not sure I'm making sense."

"To me you are," Mrs. Potts said. "You're not going to get a good night's sleep until the ghost is gone."

"But it's not a ghost, not like I think of a ghost."

"My first thought is that the manifestation is a traumatic memory," Mrs. Hazelton said.

"A memory?" Jane asked. "Whose memory?"

Mrs. Hazelton shrugged. "Who's to say? A lingering memory is a variety of haunting. The problem is to rid the house of it."

"Hold that thought," Penny said, gathering up their three empty glasses and heading back out toward the bar. She returned with full glasses and set them around. "It's only once a month," she said, "and none of us are driving more than a few blocks."

Jane opened her purse and took out the drawstring bag. "Jerry found these under the house when he was working on the foundation." She shook out the three objects onto the table.

Mrs. Hazelton peered intently at them but didn't pick them up. "You brought these inside the house?"

"Into the bedroom, yes. I guess that was a mistake."

"Have you heard of the notion of *chindi*?" Mrs. Hazelton asked.

"No," Jane said.

"It's a Navajo term having to do with a hurtful spirit left behind in a dwelling when someone dies. The spirit can be embodied in their possessions—attracted to the earthly things and not wanting to give them up. It's usual for the family to get rid of the person's possessions and remove the body to some distant place for burial."

"So you're telling Jane that the ghost is with us right now?" Penny asked. "Living in this bag?"

Mrs. Hazelton sipped her wine and said, "I'm not *telling* you any such thing. Variations of this notion of *chindi* are common to cultures around the world, dating back thousands of years, each with its own lore. To put it in simple language, a lingering ghost, often malevolent, is attracted to the things of the material world, and those very things can sometimes be used to exorcise the ghost—to help it to move on, or to compel it."

Jane sat staring at the three objects, which in the last five minutes had changed their character utterly, and seemed to her to be made from some sort of dark matter, which was ridiculous. Except that it didn't feel ridiculous. "What do I do with them?" she asked Mrs. Hazelton.

"It doesn't matter much. They're inert. Because they might be an attractant, however, I suggest leaving them in your car tonight rather than taking them back into the house. We can make use of them, however, if you want our help sending the spirit on its way."

"Yes," Jane said. "That's exactly what I want. Like Penny said, I'm not going to get a good night's sleep until it's gone."

"I find all this very exciting," Penny said to Jane. "The two of us tackled a troubled spirit in a house on Van Bibber Street a year or so ago. There's been no trouble with it since, so I'd call it moderately successful. Don't you think so, Mrs. Hazelton?"

"Oh, yes. But I've had my share of failures over the years. My work at the museum has put me in the way of many people troubled by ghosts—to use the easy term. There are tens of thousands of buried bodies in the county. People dig them up regularly, right in their own backyards, and then are troubled by wayward spirits or a wayward imagination."

"I'd like to think it was a wayward imagination, but not two imaginations that are wayward in exactly the same way."

"Then Penny and I will have a go at yours, if you'd like, won't we Penny? It happens we're both free on Tuesday afternoon. We were going to waste the day thrift storing."

"I'd like that very much," Jane said. "Thank you. Tuesday is perfect. We'll have the house to ourselves."

"I warn you that it might look a little silly, me and my bag of tricks," Mrs. Hazelton said.

"It won't look silly to me," Jane told her. "Will noon work? I'll pick up something for lunch."

"Noon it is," Penny said, swallowing the last of her wine.

"I'll tell you something that might sound strange to you," Mrs. Hazelton said to Jane. "Look out for the manifestation in dry weather, if we have any. It's commonly thought that rain dampens the energy of a spirit because of the increase in negative ions that accompany the rain. A dry, breezy atmosphere, with an increase in positive ions, is more likely to animate a spirit."

"I've been praying for dry weather, actually," Jane said.

"Good," Mrs. Hazelton said. "You might try specifying Tuesday in your prayers. We want an active ghost."

Monday

29.

JERRY DECIDED against taking the truck to visit the Dutch-man, the truck being a conspicuous vehicle. It was possible that he had managed to mislead Carmody over the phone, and so to be safe he had borrowed Jane's Subaru. Jane wouldn't need the Subaru for a few hours anyway, having gone off with Let-tie Phibbs to bag Sam Messerbee. And if Carmody happened to be watching their house, the pickup in the driveway would imply that Jerry was at home.

Jerry had looked into the Messerbee Foundation—an internet search that had taken about ten minutes this morn-ing. The man was a good deed doer who had come up from nothing, buying undeveloped land in the 1950s and '60s and selling it at immense profits years later. He had shed tens of millions of dollars in donations to schools and hospitals as well as handing over thousands of acres of foothill land to the Nature Conservancy. The information made Jerry reconsider Lettie Phibbs, at least in a small way. She wasn't leading Jane on any sort of wild goose chase this morning.

He decided to detour past the Antiquity Center. The Prius sat in the lot, and there was a light on inside the Center, so Carmody was occupied. He patted his coat pocket to make sure the four coins were safely stowed, and five minutes later he turned right off Chapman Avenue down Prospect Street, which had a rural air about it that he liked. The street was shaded by immense eucalyptus trees and had no sidewalks, just a verge of shrubs and bedding plants and a shallow irrigation ditch for a gutter.

Where Hyink's shop should have sat at 13340 there was a ranch-style house with heavy shake shingles, probably built in the 1950s. The address on the mailbox read 13376. He u-turned at the corner and came back down, looking for what he had missed. There it was, an alley that he had mistaken for a driveway. There were half a dozen mailboxes mostly hidden by the trunk of an oak tree. Above one of them was a wooden sign painted with block letters that read, "Donald Hyink, Numismatist."

He turned up the drive past several houses along the narrow alley, finally passing beneath a wrought-iron gateway that was standing open, the name Hyink in brass letters fixed to it. He could see the old house now, away through enormous trees, and through the open window of the car he heard the weird chatter of a raven in a nearby tree. It might as easily be a realtor perched in the branches, waiting for Dutchman to drop dead so that the place could be sub-divided and sold off.

The driveway forked, the left fork ending in a closed-up carriage house that must function as a garage. To the right was an empty gravel lot big enough to hold several cars. The lot was fenced off from adjacent back yards with a high stone wall covered in vines, the leaves turning orange.

He drove through a puddle, parked, and got out, listening for the raven talking in the trees again. After a moment it came again, from high up in a sycamore. He spotted its stick nest in a four-limb crotch, the raven perched nearby. A red-tailed hawk stood some eight feet from it, tearing at something that it held in its claw. It glanced back warily at the raven, which was perhaps protecting its eggs or fledglings.

The hawk dropped what appeared to be a half-eaten squirrel onto the sparse grass below and flew off through the trees. The raven plummeted to the ground, picked up the bloody remains, and returned to its perch. It came to Jerry that if his treasure were worth a fortune he would offer it to Hyink in exchange for his house and property, where Mother Nature was still residing in the midst of suburban sprawl.

He checked his jacket pocket for the plastic envelope containing the owner's manual and coins and headed up the path toward the eccentric two-story house, dark pink with white trim. It had a steep, gambrel roof, so that there appeared to be a second roof at a more moderate angle sitting on top of the first like a hat. The shingles were slate, actual slate, which must have cost a fortune, a nightmare to install. The four gables along the front of the house had pointy little roofs of their own. The place was maybe 3,500 square feet, with what appeared to be a full basement, light shining through the ground-level windows. Jerry guessed that the house was late 19th century—an actual Dutch colonial and not a 20th century Dutch revival.

He pressed the buzzer, which sat next to a sign saying that there were no coins or valuables kept on the property—sensible given the lonesome location. The door swung open and Donald Hyink the Dutchman stood before him, a small man dressed in a black suit, solemn as a plump mole. He wore spectacles and was bent with age. Jerry noticed that his hands were strangely long, with slender fingers, and he wore three rings and had a stickpin in his tie, as if he had a passion for jewelry, or at least for precious stones.

"Mr. Laslow," he said, bowing slightly and swinging the door open to let Jerry in. He bolted the door behind them and said, "I prefer to be undisturbed, if you don't mind. My consultations are necessarily confidential."

"I'm happy to hear that," Jerry said. "I was admiring the raven in the sycamore tree. Is he a resident?"

"Oh, yes. The pair have been here for several years now."

"I'm not surprised," Jerry said. "I'd be here too if I lived in a tree." He followed the old man into a room that reminded him of the big room downstairs in the Antiquity Center—wood paneling with shelves of books everywhere, but sensibly cluttered, with books stacked on top of each other on shelves and on the floor—the working library of a numismatist rather than a mere collection of books. He was a rock hound, too, the books separated here and there to accommodate clumps of rock crystal, open geodes, and fossils.

He sat down opposite Hyink at a big desk built of mahogany. The desktop was partly hidden by books and papers, but it appeared to be a single, vast plank some four feet wide and eight feet long, with shiny, flaky patterns in the wildly figured grain. The tree it was cut from must have been a giant. "Nice desk top," Jerry said, running his hand over the polished wood.

"My grandfather purchased the desk in 1889 shortly after the house was built," Hyink said. "Cuban mahogany of a quality that has disappeared from the world this last half-century. I see you're an aficionado of birds and wood, which means you have an interest in the natural world. Are you a collector, by any chance?"

"No, not at all. Baseball cards when I was a kid. I'm an amateur birder, but nothing farther than keeping a log of what I see and where. And I worked as a carpenter for years. I've built some furniture."

"And you live in Long Beach. What part?"

"Belmont Shores," Jerry lied, not missing a beat, but not liking it. He had no idea what he had expected to find here, but the man sitting across from him didn't deserve lies. Necessity was the mother of lies, though, to warp the old phrase, and he could come clean with Mr. Hyink when he knew it was safe. "I want your opinion on some coins that my uncle left me. I don't know a thing about coins."

"You've brought them along?"

"I did." He took the owner's manual out of his jacket and removed it from its dirty plastic envelope, which looked silly to him now. "Not much of a hiding place, but I wanted to be careful." He tipped the four coins out onto the desktop and then pocketed the envelope and manual again.

"Wise," Hyink said, looking down at the coins and raising his eyebrows. "I make it a policy to tell my customers that all undertakings at this desk are recorded—in the mutual interests of both parties. Is that acceptable to you?"

"Sure. Just out of curiosity, though, is our discussion confidential, in a *legal* sense?"

"In a word, no. I'm neither a lawyer nor a priest. The law does not protect a numismatist if he finds himself in a precarious position. Is that a possibility here? Was your . . . *uncle* likely to possess illegally obtained coins?"

"No," Jerry said. "Not at all. Nothing precarious about it."

"Well then, let's see what you've got." Mr. Hyink took a small digital recorder out of his coat pocket, pushed a switch to turn it on, and set it nearby.

Here goes, Jerry thought, realizing that he was agitated now that the moment had come. He was struck by the fear that he was making a mistake, showing his hand like this. But it was too late, because there it lay.

The old man sat for a time simply looking at the coins, as if making up his mind about something. Then he leaned back in his chair, made a tent of his hands, and asked, "Do you have a letter of provenance, Mr. Laslow, revealing the coins' history? Anything at all?"

"No. Like I said, they were a gift from my uncle before he died. He had cancer and was clearing the decks, if you see what I mean."

"Indeed I do. Gold has no value in the afterlife, or so the philosophers tell us. But perhaps your uncle told you how he came to possess the coins."

"Not really," Jerry said stupidly, realizing that he hadn't thought through this. "I didn't know him all that well. The whole thing was a surprise."

"Were you named in his will?"

"No. He dropped these off at my house a couple of months before he passed away, just showed up out of the blue. He said he didn't want anything in the will to be contested, so he was . . . tying up loose ends." The lies and half-lies were coming easily enough to him now that he was rolling, which wasn't anything to be proud of. Undoing the lies, if he had to, wouldn't be as easy.

"Your uncle didn't reveal anything *about* the coins?"

"Not a thing. They were in a box with some other items. A jewelry box, I guess you'd say, with cufflinks and rings and the like. A couple of old watches." This was another half-lie. His uncle *had* given him a box of family jewelry some time back, very much like this, although the only coins inside were a couple of dimes flattened on railroad tracks. Mr. Hyink picked up an ivory chopstick now and shifted the coins away from each other, the two small coins together in front of Jerry and the larger octagonal coins off to the side.

"Here's what I can tell you," he said, pointing at one of the smaller coins with his chopstick. "This is a Liberty Head Double Eagle, minted, as you can see, in 1850. An Eagle was valued at ten dollars, a Half Eagle at five dollars. The Double Eagle, then, at twenty dollars. Its melt value—the value of the gold, not the collectible value—is something on the order of $1,400, although this varies, of course, with the current market for gold. Something of the same is true for its companion, which is a five-pound English Gold Sovereign. It's slightly smaller than the Double Eagle, as you can see, with a melt value of perhaps $1,200."

"Why would a person *melt* them?" Jerry asked. "Aren't they worth more as collectors' items?"

"Not always. Both of these are common coins, with little collectible value, comparatively speaking. They're sought after by collectors of bulk gold—bullion collectors and hoarders. The Sovereign is particularly common. Its melt value is near the collectible value. The Double Eagle, however, especially in the condition of this coin, which is very fine, is worth perhaps twice its melt value, something over $4,000. If a fellow had a bread-box full, he would be quite well off. Remember, however, that if you sell a coin, either as bullion or for its collectible value, you would scarcely be paid the full value. Purchasers would want something for their trouble. A dealer might offer you half its value in order to resell it at a profit."

"Which means that the melt value is all the more relevant," Jerry said.

"Yes, unless you have the patience to sell the coins directly to collectors, on e-Bay, for example, or at coin shows. That could take months, of course, maybe years if your price is too steep, during which time the value of gold will rise and fall."

"I'm not patient enough for that."

"Most people are not." He opened the desk drawer and removed a felt rag and a small squirt bottle with a blue solution in it, spraying the solution onto the rag and polishing the two smaller coins until they glowed. Then he held them out to Jerry, who put them into his shirt pocket.

Hyink shifted the big octagonal coins into a line with the chopstick now, pushing them in front of Jerry and squaring them up to each other. "Your uncle perhaps undervalued these two octagonal coins, commonly referred to as gold slugs. They weigh two-and-a-half troy ounces, so with gold hovering around $1,300 per ounce, the current melt value would be just about exactly $3,250."

"Well, that's good to know," Jerry said. He did a quick calculation of his hoard; call it twenty-five pounds or so. He wasn't sure about troy ounces, but figuring sixteen ounces to the pound at thirteen hundred dollars per ounce . . .

The sum staggered him. Melted down they'd make a half-million-dollar golden cow pie, even if he had to eat half of it in order to unload it. He composed himself, keeping the grin off his face. The old man might not be amused by cow pie jokes.

"But no one in their right mind," Hyink said, lowering his voice and watching Jerry carefully, "would melt a fifty-dollar gold slug in the crucible."

30.

JANE WAS SURPRISED when Lettie pulled up in front of Mimi's Café on 17th Street, where they were meeting the Messerbees for breakfast. There was nothing wrong with Mimi's Café, but it scarcely seemed like the sort of place where a billionaire would eat breakfast. She wondered what constituted breakfast for a billionaire as she followed Lettie into the café. Hummingbird's tongues? Flower petals? Inside the café, Lettie waved at a couple who must be Sam and Dottie Messerbee, sitting in a corner booth.

Sam stood up, smiling, when they approached, and he shook hands with both Lettie and Jane. He didn't look a lot like a billionaire, dressed as he was in an aloha shirt with hula dancers and palm trees printed on it along with the logo "Old Guys Rule". He was several inches shorter than Jane, with a prominent nose, chin and ears, as if his facial features had continued to grow while the rest of him had shrunk.

His eyes were bright, however, and he had a surprisingly hearty voice. The waitress brought two glasses of iced tea and set them in front of Sam and Dottie. Sam emptied six packets of sugar into his and Dottie gave him a squinty-eyed look.

"It's been *so* long since we've had a chance to talk," Lettie said to Sam after she and Jane were settled into the booth. "I mean really *talk*. The Center has done some *wonderful* things—acquisitions, mainly. Our library has grown substantially, and we're planning on sponsoring a spring mini-conference on the California mission days. Tidwell College is *fully* committed."

Sam nodded sagely at Lettie and concentrated on stirring his iced tea, trying to dissolve the inch-deep layer of sugar in the bottom of the glass.

"It's good to meet you, Jane," Dottie said to her. "I particularly wanted to chat with you personally."

Dottie reminded Jane of her own grandmother. She was a tall, youthfully slim woman with silver hair piled on her head and held in place with a jeweled celluloid comb that looked like a traveling jellyfish. "I think I covet your comb," Jane said.

"I found it at the big rummage sale at Leisure World in Seal Beach, at the Community Church," Dottie told her. "I never miss the sale. Do you like a good rummage sale?"

"Immensely," Jane said.

"The Leisure World sale is coming up," Dottie told her. "You'll want to get in early, first thing in the morning on the first day to beat the collectors to the punch. I very much like what you're doing with the Co-op. It must be a ton of work."

"It is, but I take it one day at a time, just like growing a garden."

"These storms must have you stymied," Sam said.

"They get in the way of productivity, that's for sure. But I won't admit to being stymied."

"We're all worried about the storms," Lettie said, shaking her head woefully. "Will they *never* let up?"

"Why don't we let Jane have a word?" Dottie said.

"Oh, of course I didn't mean to . . ."

"Of course not," Sam put in. "Jane?"

"Like Lettie said, the storms have been a pain in the neck, but with this new storm system there's a real danger of a hundred-year flood, or so I'm hearing. That would be a real crisis, and not just for the Co-op."

"What's up with this garden shed that Lettie mentioned? It must be something grand if you're so worried about it."

"It's a small historic structure out at Hart Park," Jane said, "built in the late 1930s near the baseball diamond as a concessions stand. It's on the historic register, believe it or not."

"I think I know the one," Sam said, "although I haven't been to the park in years. I swam in the plunge the day it opened, and I played some baseball there when I was a boy. It was the Orange City Park in those days."

The food arrived then, and Lettie frowned at her toast and scrambled eggs. Afraid that she was going to threaten the waitress with a penny tip in a water glass, Jane went right on with the conversation again between bites of her omelet. "Both the pool house and the shed were WPA projects. The shed is built of river rock and rough-cut cedar, with overhanging eaves and a shingle roof. The Co-op is using it as a potting shed, but it's too close to the creek for comfort. The Co-op has agreed to dismantle it and rebuild it farther up the hill, but suddenly we're in a race for time."

Sam nodded. "There's a lot of history in that park. Sometimes I don't think people give a damn about that sort of thing these days."

"*I certainly do*," Lettie put in. "The Center's mission statement is ..."

"I was in the CCC back in the late '30s," Sam put in, apparently not caring much about mission statements. "We dug firebreaks across the Santa Ana Mountains. A lot of pick and shovel work. A big section of it became part of the Truck Trail, out there near Lost Woman Canyon. Most of the money they paid us went to our folks, you know, being the Depression and all. I was too young so I lied about my age. They knew I was lying, too, but if a kid could grub out a stump, who the hell cared how old he was?"

Lettie nodded, squinting her eyes. "No one, I'd warrant. One thing about that kind of work . . ."

"So what's wrong with the shed?" Dottie asked Jane. "Only the elevation? It sounds like you've got the will to restore it."

"Oh, Jane's got the *will*," Lettie put in, "and where there's a will there's a way." She nodded heavily.

"So I've heard," Dottie said.

"I'm not sure we'll find a way unless Mother Nature cooperates," Jane replied, worried about Dottie's evident dislike of Lettie. "My husband Jerry thinks there is. He took it on as a project. His mantra is 'fix it yourself'."

"I like Jerry and I don't even know him," Sam told her. "But let's talk about the long haul. You think you can pull off this sustainable neighborhood idea of yours? That's a lot on your plate. I looked into it. It'll take some work."

"Right now I'm thinking in terms of the downtown square mile."

"Just Old Orange?"

"Yes. It's a real neighborhood, and the residents are proud of it. We've got a community garden already going, as well as plans for practical craft and building workshops, tool sharing, restoration projects, an animal care center, and a number of other things. Some of it is already in the works."

"These sorts of things were batted around in the '70s," Dottie said. "I batted some around myself. Most of it fell apart because no one could stay still long enough to make it work. What's changed since then?"

"*Need*, for one thing" Jane said. "And the means to make it happen. Sustainable neighborhoods are springing up all over the country. There's one on Bainbridge Island that's a zero-energy community. In one way or another they're going to be the future. What we've got now won't work for much longer."

Sam nodded, although it was a non-committal nod, and it came into Jane's mind that she had said too much—shifted into the political realm without meaning to. Maybe everything was political and there was no avoiding it. "I'm getting way ahead of myself," she said. "I tend to think long term."

"By God, someone has to," Sam said, swallowing the last of his tea.

"I'm happy that we got to know you, Jane," Dottie said, "but we should give up the table now that we're through eating, and Sam's got an appointment with the acupuncturist. If you have any interest in going along to that rummage sale at Leisure World, let me have your phone number."

She handed Jane a little pad of paper with a pen clipped to it, and Jane happily did as she was told.

"When can I call you, Sam?" Lettie asked. "The Co-op is on thin ice, and time is of the essence."

"This very afternoon," Dottie told her. "But we'll call you. It's been nice speaking to you again, Lettie, and thanks for introducing Jane to us."

Lettie smiled and nodded, but the smile didn't last.

Two minutes later Jane and Lettie stood together in the parking lot, an east wind blowing leaves and scraps of a runaway newspaper around their feet. "I think that went well," Lettie said as they watched Sam and Dottie drive away, Dottie at the wheel. "You've got to beware of saying too much, though. You might have put Sam off there at the last with your talk about energy. Energy is a hot topic. Watch out for getting burned."

"Better to be honest about it now than to surprise him with it later. Dottie seemed okay with it."

"That Dottie," Lettie said, shaking her head. "A gold-digger, like I said earlier. Did you see how she spoke out of turn, putting words into Sam's mouth?"

"I think Dottie could eat us both for dinner and spit out the bones," Jane said, as they climbed into the Cadillac.

Lettie smiled and said, "Not if I get my fork into her first."

31.

"So these big ones are *slugs?*" Jerry asked, keeping to the same conspiratorial tone that Mr. Hyink had fallen into. He sat back in his chair now and looked out the east-facing window, which was draped with wisteria vine, the leaves yellow and orange, but hanging on. Golden sunlight angled down through them, stippling the carpet. The *crucible*, he thought. The word had a ring to it.

"Slugs is the popular term, yes. Technically they're known as Humbert Ingots, originally produced in 1851 by a private mint prior to the opening of the San Francisco Mint. In this part of the world they were commonly called Adobe Slugs, because most of them were in the hands of families that held Spanish land grants—wealthy families, I mean to say. In Spanish they were called *esquinados*. The common man had little use for a fifty-dollar coin at a time when a dime would buy him breakfast. They were fairly common in California at the mid-century, although nothing near as common, say, as a ten- or twenty-dollar gold piece. They're exceedingly rare today."

"Are they?" Jerry asked. "That's good news. I was getting depressed thinking of melting my uncle's coins."

"Then I'll anticipate your next question, Mr. Laslow." He lowered his voice another notch and said, "If one of these ingots were offered on the open market, bidding would rise quickly. How high it would rise I can't say, but a decade ago a single Humbert Ingot sold for $460,000. At that time there were only eight such coins changing hands. Anywhere. Hence my asking about proof of provenance. The public appearance of *two* of the ingots would raise eyebrows to say the least, if their provenance was confirmed and not hypothetical."

"So we might round the value up to a half-million dollars apiece? That's . . . hard to grasp."

"But not out of the question. There would have to be various proofs and assurances."

The idea of faking up a letter of provenance flitted through Jerry's mind—a letter that might be worth millions of dollars. His uncle Henry was real enough, as was the jewelry box full of cufflinks and tie clips and old watches that the old man had given Jerry. It was sitting in a dresser drawer at this very moment.

But he quickly saw that it wouldn't do, even if he had the talent for it or could hire the talent to create such a document. He could picture the handcuffs as easily as the cufflinks, and he could imagine the sound of the prison door clanging shut. With California's finders-keepers law, it might not be necessary to have a letter of any sort. The provenance was inherent in the legend of the Flores gold. There was no question that the gold *existed*.

He crossed his fingers for luck and said, "Like I told you, there's no provenance to be had. I wish there was, but my uncle is dead and gone."

Hyink nodded, pursing his lips and looking carefully at Jerry for a long moment. "False letters of provenance abound," he said, "but I advise you against considering such a thing."

"Not me. I was happy with the melt value."

"As I said, no one would melt a Humbert Ingot. These two alone are worth a small fortune, given that they in fact are what they *appear* to be."

"You mean they might be fake?"

"Counterfeit antique coins are common these days. They're professionally produced in China and probably elsewhere. The counterfeits are made up of a tungsten core plated with gold. It's part of my business to authenticate coins."

"Would you do this for me—authenticate them?"

"I'd be happy to. They're of particular interest."

"How long would it take?"

"I would keep the coins for three days, only the two ingots, of course. A certificate of authentication with metallurgical results and identification photos would go some distance toward ensuring the authenticity of the coins. Not all collectors require provenance, but metallurgical authentication is an absolute necessity for coins as rare as these."

As if the appointment had run its course, Mr. Hyink sat back in his chair and crossed his arms. Jerry was surprised to hear a clock begin to toll somewhere in the house. He had been there for an hour. "What's the charge for the process?" he asked.

"Five hundred dollars. You might find someone who would do the work for less. I like to keep my hand in, but . . ." He shrugged. "Obviously the decision is yours."

32.

PETER CARMODY LAY on his stomach in a storage room in the second story of Donald Hyink's house, viewing part of the room below through an old brass floor register. He could see the desk below and the two men who sat at it. Jerry Larkin, unfortunately, was big enough to block part of the view, and the men's voices were often low. Carmody had missed some of the conversation, but he had caught enough of it to know that it had nothing to do with a Yansheng charm and everything to do with gold. He had seen only two gold coins laid out, but apparently there were two others out of sight. This was why Lettie was on edge yesterday at breakfast. She knew more than she let on about Larkin and what he was up to, and she had always known it.

His wrist was cramped from his awkward position, but he didn't dare move. There was too much at stake. If Hyink or Larkin discovered that he was in the house, his plan would go straight to hell, and so would his job. Larkin pushed his chair back now and stood up. The coins had already vanished from the desktop. Hyink picked up his digital recorder, switched it off, and put it into his coat pocket.

The meeting was evidently over, and the two men began to talk about the weather. Carmody rolled sideways into the middle of the heavy rug that he lay on, got his bearings, and stood up. He tip-toed to the door, picked up his shoes from where he had left them on the chair, and went out onto the landing and down the stairs toward the mud room and the back door, assuming that Hyink would show Larkin out through the front door. Peter slipped outside, easing the door shut, and hunched along below the windows to the east corner of the house, where he hid his bicycle.

He pulled on his shoes over now-muddy socks, as he watched Larkin walk to the parking lot. For some reason he stopped short of his car and stared into the trees. Even from that distance he seemed to have a satisfied grin on his face. The morning had gone just right for him, the asshole. There was the clicking sound of a raven, and Larkin waved upward as if the bird was an old friend. The man was certifiable.

After Larkin had climbed into his car and driven out of sight, Carmody sneaked around the corner of the house to the half-stairs that led down to the outside door of the cellar—Hyink's laboratory. He slowly raised his head until he could see through the corner of the window. The room was full of workbenches and metallurgical apparatus. Hyink's white lab coat hung on its hook along with goggles and a heavy apron.

Hyink himself was at this moment hauling back the rug to expose the floor safe. He held what appeared to be a vinyl envelope, and when he had opened the out-of-date clunker of a safe, he put the envelope into it and closed it up again. He replaced the rug, stood up, and went to the desk, taking the recorder out of his coat pocket and putting it into the middle drawer. He walked away up the stairs now, switching off the light when he went out into the kitchen.

Carmody stood for a moment considering things, full of the urge to have a look at the coins now. He possessed the combination to the floor safe as well as a full set of house keys. The old man was oblivious to this fact. Hyink was too trusting—far more so than Lettie Phibbs, who was a suspicious old hag. Making up his mind, he yanked off his muddy shoes and socks, took out his keychain, unlocked the door, and slipped inside barefoot, leaving the key in the lock and closing the door behind him.

He had long ago set up his own secret access to Hyink's computer, which he had mined for passwords and other secret information, including the combination to the floor safe. He'd had plenty of time over his three years of employment to look into the safe and to search out the hidey-holes in the old house, making copies of useful keys. What he had discovered was of little of immediate value, just penny-ante odds and ends—no squirreled away cash or valuable jewelry.

Hyink scrupulously kept real valuables in a bank vault, including his own collection of coins. In that way he was more sensible than Lettie. It had always seemed to Peter that if he bided his time, however, an opportunity would arise. Here was an opportunity, writ large, as the saying went.

Was it *enough* of an opportunity, however? Not without knowing the value of what he intended to steal. There was no point in risking arrest over a nickel and dime theft . . . He stepped across to the desk and removed the digital recorder. He would have a listen to it and then return it tomorrow. Hyink had no more appointments today, and would leave the shop to Peter tomorrow in order to drive out to Riverside to visit his sister. He might not look at the recorder again for weeks.

Peter went out now, locked the door back up, and pushed in behind the shrubbery along the property line, stepping gingerly on the gravel and leaf debris as he made his way along. He put his shoes on when he was hidden by the carriage house, cramming the muddy socks into his jacket pockets. He could see that the kitchen light was on and that Hyink was moving around inside, probably scrambling eggs for a late breakfast.

Peter rolled his bike out when the old man disappeared from the window, and within a handful of seconds he was out of the alley, heading back toward Old Orange and the Antiquity Center, thinking about what he would tell Lettie. And what he wouldn't tell her.

33.

LETTIE PHIBBS DROPPED Jane off at her house and drove toward the Antiquity Center, weighed down by the depressing feeling that there had been a tidal shift in her life this morning. A cool sun shone in the sky, and the wind whirled leaves out of the curbside trees. It felt like fall, not only in the wind, but also in her bones, and she thought about her condo on Molokai, wondering why she hadn't sailed away a year ago.

Dottie Messerbee was a parasite, an impediment. It was easy to see that she envied Lettie, who had made her own way in the world, and that the envy had led to jealousy. Lettie would have to count on Sam to see things clearly. Surely he would understand that without Lettie Phibbs, he would know nothing about Jane Larkin's Co-op. "I am the *impresario*," Lettie muttered, and wished that she had used that very word at breakfast when she'd had the chance. She *would* use the word when she spoke to Sam again.

When she neared the Center, she saw that city workers were tearing up the street. Half the block was coned off. She turned into the neighborhood and found a curbside spot, where she sat for a moment letting her mind work, once again considering her options. Bob Holloway had put that phrase into her mind. It had sounded sensible, but it had taken on an ominous tone over the past couple of days.

Peter, surely, would have good news, she told herself, locking the car and walking up the sidewalk. Jane needed to be taken down a peg. She was too damned full of herself. She wondered if the tumbledown garden shed was too wet to burn. A half-gallon of kerosene would help it along. She recalled the graffiti on the wall of Bob's building, and she imagined scrawling obscenities on the shed walls with red spray paint. That would take some of the starch out of Jane's smile.

She saw now that Peter's car was parked in the lot and that his bicycle was hanging from the trunk rack. Either he had gone out to the Dutchman's and discovered something interesting or he had not. Either he had looked at the Center's ledgers and was confident that they would weather the audit, or he had not. The world was closing in, losing its in-betweens.

She realized that she had a bad case of the dwindles as she opened the door and stepped into the vestibule of the Antiquity Center—her life's work, for God's sake. The wind tried to slam the door shut behind her, but she held on, easing it home, in control of those things she could control. She smelled the lemon oil from the wood polish on the air, and the smell of books and . . . *antiquity*. It was her home, and they wanted to take it away from her. And they might well do that if Peter Carmody turned out to be a weak link.

She heard a voice intoning something in the kitchen workroom, and she stopped dead still and listened. She *knew* the voice, and it took only a moment for her to recognize Donald Hyink's even tone, almost no inflection. But what was Dutch doing in the kitchen? The voice stopped in mid-sentence and then after a moment began again, repeating itself. *It was a recording*, not the man himself. She moved quietly closer, cupping her hand over her ear in order so as not to miss anything.

"Your uncle perhaps undervalued these two octagonal coins," Dutch said. "They weigh two-and-a-half troy ounces, so with gold hovering around $1,300 per ounce, the melt value would be just about exactly $3,250."

"Well, that's good to know." It was Jerry Larkin's voice. She *was* hearing a recording, which was brilliant. And they weren't talking about Yansheng charms, either. She nearly started forward to join Peter, but she stopped herself. Had Peter made the recording to *share* it with her? Or had he gone rogue?

"But no one in their right mind," Hyink was saying now, "would drop a fifty-dollar gold slug into the crucible."

The recording fell silent, as if Peter had switched it off. "God *damn!*" Peter said, and then hooted.

Lettie stayed right where she was, scarcely breathing. *A fifty-dollar gold slug?* She wasn't certain what the term referred to, although Hyink's reference to its value was clear enough.

What it meant—what it *had* to mean—was dead obvious. Jerry Larkin had found the Flores gold and had taken some coins to Hyink to get them appraised. How Peter had gotten hold of a recording of the conversation was a mystery. But it didn't matter. What mattered was whether he meant to share it or to keep the knowledge to himself.

She returned quietly to the front door, opened it, and then shut it hard. "Peter!" she called out cheerily.

He answered "What?" in an irritated voice—not the voice of a guilty man, but with his usual indifference. She found him applying glue to the unattached spine of an old book. There was no sign of a recording device. He had pocketed the thing when he heard the door slam.

"Well," she said, "Did you manage to get out to the Dutch-man's this morning?"

"I surely did, just like you asked."

"And what did we discover?" She set her purse on the counter and then leaned back as if she was taking it easy, holding the smile steady on her face.

"Not a hell of a lot," he said, not looking up from his work. "A complete waste of time."

"What was Jerry Larkin interested in, then?"

"The Yansheng charm. He still thinks it's worth something. It could be you put him off too fast the other day, coming up with that six-dollar valuation. Like you were more interested in it than you were letting on."

"I seem to recall that your assessment was more off-putting than mine, Peter. You told him that the coin was *crap*. That was your very word."

"And I was right. That should have been the end of it. You couldn't leave it alone, and he went off thinking he might have something. I've been wondering what *you* thought he had, given that this whole thing was a wild goose chase."

"*Me?* I had no idea. I was hoping that you would discover his motives this morning. Simple as that. What did Dutch tell him?"

"Same thing I told him, that it wasn't a coin."

"You have nothing useful to report, then?"

"I've already *reported* it—an utter and complete waste of time, and I risked my job for it, sneaking in through the back door to spy on them. I knew better than to do it, but I did it out of loyalty to you."

"Well I'm sorry that it worked out that way. I'm through with Jerry Larkin and his damned coin. What's the news on the audit? Did you look over the books?"

"Yeah, I spent half the night looking them over. We're solid."

"*Solid?*" she asked, peering at him over the top of her glasses. "The word conveys almost nothing to my mind."

"I mean they're spotless. I find your doubts a little bit insulting."

"I don't mean to insult you, Peter. You know I value your skills. It's just that . . ." She shook her head, looking him in the eye. "Sometimes life is a perpetual disappointment. You work hard for half a lifetime, and just when you think you're on an easy slope at last, they put you on trial."

"Just to be clear, Lettie. There won't be any *trial*. Keep on track, and don't talk about how things are unfair. No anger at all in front of anyone. Take a positive view. Remember that you'll defer to me during the audit. Can you do that?"

"Oh my yes," Lettie said. "If anyone defers to me we've all got problems. On the other hand, you'll remember that I have a long memory. I know the Center like I know the back of my hand. I'm the *historian*, in other words, and you're the accountant. I can be useful if it comes to justifying an expense."

"*That's* what I want to hear," he said, and he went back to his pot of glue, carrying out the whole charade like Satan himself.

In the silence she heard the clock ticking, and she didn't like the sound of it—time running out. Her mind was in a boiling rage, and had been since that damned meeting this morning—the way she'd been treated. She imagined jamming sharpened pencils into Peter's ears while his back was turned. She held the image in her mind while she digested her anger.

She had forgotten that everyone lied if there was something they wanted. Was Peter's entire *life* a pretense? She herself had manipulated the truth a time or two, but always for the best. There was no shame in a semi-truth if the result was justifiable. She had always valued justice.

"I'm thinking of closing down for the day," she said. "I've got a touch of something. You've already earned a day's pay with your trip out to the Dutchman's. You'll be out there tomorrow all day, I believe?"

"Just like every Tuesday. Boss's day off."

"He overnights at his sister's in Riverside, doesn't he? He must look forward to that, having family close at hand."

"That's what he tells me," Peter said, clamping the book he'd been working on between two polished-stone bookends. He slid his computer into his backpack. "I can use the day off today," he said. "Don't worry about the audit, Lettie. I've got it under control."

34.

THE FLATS, where Peter Carmody rented an apartment, looked down onto Glassell Street, just north of the Plaza. Lettie Phibbs sat across the street at Café Lucca, drinking a cappuccino and eating chocolate frosted biscotti that she dunked into the coffee, soaking them until they were just at the edge of falling apart. The outdoor tables were in deep shade, the sun hidden behind the building.

The light was on in Peter's apartment, third from the corner, and she could see his shadow moving around beyond the window. She suspected that he was packing his bags, going to ground until the time was right for him to move on to the next stage of his miserable existence. The so-called gold slugs were no longer a mystery to Lettie. She'd looked into them, and she knew their value, which was prodigious. And Peter knew their value. Certainly he meant to steal them.

She straightened her blonde wig, took a last sip of coffee, and spooned up the biscotti sludge in the bottom in order to get every morsel. After dabbing her mouth with her napkin she set out toward the corner, crossing the street to the bank, entering at the side door, and exiting into the parking lot. She climbed into the front seat of her Honda Accord—her burner car—and prepared to wait.

She kept the Honda garaged at her house in Garden Grove, having "owned" the car for years, as non-descript and generic as a car could be. It was clean of dents and other attention-getters, and the red paint was faded, a car that no one would pay a nickel's worth of attention to. Bob Holloway had set up the purchase, complete with fake registration and VIN number. She had never parked the Honda at the Antiquity Center.

She liked to think of the Garden Grove house as her second house—a mailing address rather than a home, which was necessary to her since it wasn't legal, strictly speaking, for her to live in the Antiquity Center, even though she *did* live there most of the time. The house was as unmemorable as the old Honda, and the mortgage payment came directly out of one of the Center's accounts—something that might be discovered in an audit. There was nothing in Garden Grove that she couldn't walk away from, and although she slept there on occasion, it was essentially a hideout—a burner house, she thought, laughing at her own joke. Then she wondered whether it was a joke at all, or was a subliminal suggestion, food for thought.

She started the Honda up routinely, just to keep the engine alive. Invariably she drove it down Beach Boulevard to the ocean, circling around through Sunset Beach and Seal Beach and across the San Gabriel River at the Second Avenue Bridge where poor Art's body had been discovered. She always murmured a word or two of remembrance when she crossed the bridge. On the drive home she stopped into the Parasol Restaurant for breakfast, making the trip a sort of pilgrimage. Now they were shutting the old Parasol down, erasing another part of the world she had known, and so much for pilgrimages.

From where she sat now, she could see the rear entrance to The Flats near the rear façade of Wells Fargo Bank. The door stood open, revealing the staircase inside. Peter's car was parked nearby in one of the spaces relegated to the bank—half-hour parking, which argued that he would be leaving soon. But she was prepared to stay all day in order to keep tabs on him. He had become her destiny. She could remember when she had realized the same thing about Art, which had led to her taking that destiny into her own hands in order to relieve him of his suffering. Leaving decisive things to the fates was a mistake. The fates were a fickle crowd.

She opened a romance novel that she'd taken from the outdoor bookstall at the library—a bodice ripper with a promising cover illustration. She liked a good romance, one with plenty of sex in it, but before she had read three pages her mind strayed to this morning's meeting with Sam and Dottie. It had gone better than she had thought. Her earlier anger came from allowing hypocrites like Dottie to get to her. Sam was obviously smitten with Jane, the old lecher. Dottie was just ants at a picnic.

She saw Peter coming out of his lair now, carrying an armload of boxes, his car keys in his teeth. He set the boxes atop the hood of his Prius so that he could unlock the car. The back seat was already full of clothing on hangers, evidently hauled willy-nilly out of his closet. He stowed three of the smaller boxes on top of the heap and then opened the trunk, where he packed the big box into the space that was left, after which he shut the trunk and hurried away up the stairs again.

He was bolting, and no doubt about it. He had no intention of weathering the audit, and was throwing her under the bus like an old piece of trash.

He reappeared now, rolling his bicycle, pulling the stairwell door shut behind him. She started up the Accord and threw the book into the back seat, watching as Peter hung the bicycle on the rack, fastened it tight, climbed into the Prius, and backed out of the parking space, turning right onto Orange Street toward Chapman Avenue. She followed after him. Her wig and dark glasses were enough to disguise her if Peter was actually paying attention, which he had no reason to do. Even so, she kept two or three cars between them as they circled the Plaza.

Halfway around Peter exited, continuing down Chapman Avenue. Lettie accelerated to keep up with him when they were out of the stodgy downtown traffic. In half a mile he pulled into the Travel Lodge motel adjacent to the Burger King alongside the freeway. She drove on past the motel and turned into the Burger King lot, where she found a parking space, shut off the engine, and prepared to resume her vigil.

Instead of going into the motel office, Peter took the bicycle off the rack, shouldered it, and headed toward the motel stairs, carrying a small suitcase in his free hand. Obviously he had checked into the motel earlier, maybe after leaving the Center. All of this was planned. He went straight upstairs to the second-floor balcony, stopping in front of room 220, where he let himself in.

No doubt he was proud of himself, *making his move*, as people said, after having put one over on Lettie Phibbs, who had treated him like a mother would treat her son, the Judas. "Pride goeth before a fall," she muttered, making herself comfortable and finding her place in the paperback. The sun through the windshield warmed the air nicely, and it felt good to rest.

35.

JANE PUSHED a loaded garden cart out of the old shed and up the gravel path toward the garden, Jerry pulling on the handle at the front end. A squirrel chittered at them from a nearby oak, probably offering advice. It worked better for the two of them to push-pull the loaded carts up the muddy slope. The loaner shed provided by the notorious Peabody was securely in place, perched on skids, and they were almost through filling it with everything that might be threatened if the old shed flooded.

"So you don't mind if Mrs. Hazelton comes over tomorrow afternoon and exorcises the ghost," Jane asked when they reached the top.

Jerry was silent long enough for Jane to know he was looking for the right thing to say. "Do I *mind*? I don't know. It seems weird, I guess—another element of weirdness laid on. You've known her since what—yesterday? We seem to be a magnet for oddball women."

"To be exact, I've known her since last night. So a little less than a day. Penny has known her for years, though. They've worked together on this sort of thing in the past. Several times, apparently."

"Really? Can we get a testimonial from a satisfied customer?"

"Do you require one?"

"Not if you don't, I guess."

"Maybe you can trust me on this. If it turns out to be a waste of time, then it's my time that was wasted, right? She's doing this entirely as a favor. It's not a business venture. She's been the curator of the Little Tidwell Museum in Santa Ana for years."

"Has she? So she's a sort of exorcist plumber who comes out if there's ghosts in the pipes? Does she know there's no *actual* ghost? That we seem to be haunted by a memory?"

"Mrs. Hazelton says it's all the same thing."

"So what does she do, smoke the ghost out with clumps of burning sage? Magical incantations?"

"I don't know. She says she's bringing her bag of tricks."

"Like Felix the Cat's magic bag, but with a newt's eye, an adder's tongue, and a can of ghost-be-gone aerosol."

"This is why you're not going to be there cracking jokes," Jane said. "And she's not a witch, she's a spiritualist. Penny Potts is coming along, too. You'll bring Peewee down here with you, tomorrow, right?"

"Happy to. We should have brought him along today to tow this damned cart."

"So are you okay with this? Because if you're not, I'll call it off."

"If you trust Mrs. Hazelton, then so do I. I've got nothing better to offer. You sure you don't want me and Peewee there as backup? I could pull a gunnysack over its head."

"And I could pull a gunnysack over your head," Jane said. "If you'd like to step out of the doorway, I can push this cart into the shed."

Jerry shifted things out of the way to open up a space, and Jane parked the cart alongside the mini-tractor. The tractor would have saved them some labor if they'd simply stowed things into its bucket and driven it up the hill, but the tractor was loud and smoky and would tear up the muddy hillside, which was already turning into a bog. Jane disliked the tractor's gasoline engine, which was contrary to the Co-op's principles. If they got the grant from the Messerbees she would buy an electric tractor to celebrate.

"I say we're done for today," Jerry said. "What do you think? It's four-thirty. No reason to start on tomorrow's work now. I'll organize things up here for a few minutes and we'll take off."

"If you think so," Jane said. "But if you want to keep working, I'll stay."

"We're both beat. Let's pack it in."

Jane checked the three-day weather on her phone as she descended through the little forest of California junipers. Tomorrow was forecast to be dry, but the Wednesday forecast was worse than she had ever seen. The map put out by the River Forecast Center was red with flood and evacuation messages, and already there were small craft warnings from Santa Barbara to Cabo San Lucas, as well as a dozen beach closures due to heavy runoff.

Wednesday's rainfall was predicted to be a record six inches in the foothills and up to ten inches on Modjeska and Santiago peaks, which made up Old Saddleback, the headwaters of Santiago Creek. People were advised to evacuate Modjeska and Silverado Canyons as well as back-country cabins in Trabuco Canyon. Most of the water would flow through Hart Park toward the Santa Ana River.

The only hopeful thing was that the predictions were changing by the hour. The estimated rainfall totals had gone up and down like carousel horses. It was possible that they'd go down again. There was no knowing what all that rain would mean. There had been eleven inches in Orange County during the month of March in 1983, and although Santiago Creek had risen to the top of the Hart Park wall, the park itself hadn't flooded. On the other hand, in the floods of 1969—allegedly a hundred-year-storm—five people had died in a mudslide in Silverado Canyon and seventeen had been hospitalized. Cattle had been airlifted out of Trabuco Canyon, and people had drowned trying to cross Trabuco Creek. It had been raining at a rate of seven inches a day—the worst flooding since the catastrophic floods in 1938. Now yet another hundred-year-storm was on the way.

She told herself that it was a relief to have the shed cleared out—that was something, at least. But a feeling of doom had settled into her that she couldn't shake. She simply felt puny. She quit her weather app, and her phone rang immediately, the name Messerbee glowing across the top of the screen.

36.

THE FISH BURGER and fries that Lettie had eaten as a late lunch weren't lying easily in her stomach. She'd been sitting in the car in the Burger King lot for two hours, wasting her time. Peter wasn't going anywhere, and sooner or later some officious person would appear at her window and ask her what she was up to. She bunched up her food trash, stuffed it into the bag it had come in, dropped it onto the floor, and turned the key in the ignition.

Her phone rang—a call from the Messerbee Foundation. That had been quick. She switched off the ignition and picked the phone up off the passenger seat, letting it ring again while she composed herself. Her hand was trembling, set off by the name on the screen. "This is Leticia Phibbs," she said.

A voice she didn't recognize said, "I have Dorothy Messerbee on the line if you have a moment, Mrs. Phibbs."

"Yes," she said. "Certainly I have a moment. I always have time to take a call from Dottie." She realized that she was talking to air, and now the phone clicked and Dottie Messerbee came on and said, "I hope I'm not interrupting anything."

"Not at all," Lettie answered. "I was waiting for your call. Jane and I are anxious for news, as you can imagine. Is Sam there also?"

"No. On Monday afternoons he's at his Optimists Club meeting. The Foundation discussed your proposal thoroughly, however, and I'm calling with our decision."

"I can't wait to hear it," Lettie said, suspecting that Sam was not at a club meeting in the afternoon. Did he not want to talk to her? "I'm looking forward to conveying good news to Jane."

"It would be better that I convey the news to Jane," Dottie said in an even voice. "We were quite impressed with Jane and with her plans for the Old Orange Co-op, and we have decided to fund the Co-op specifically. But we—that is to say the Foundation—saw no logical reason to include the Antiquity Center in the funding. I want to be candid about that."

"Of course, but it seems to me that . . ."

"The Antiquity Center is doing quite well," Dottie said, not giving Lettie a chance. "In the interests of clarity, we believe it's doing a bit too well—resting on its laurels, let's say. The Old Orange Co-op is forward-looking, and a grant of money at this juncture would mean a world of difference to it. The Foundation sees no clear benefit in the inclusion of the Antiquity Center."

"I don't for a *moment* believe that this was Sam's decision," Lettie said, overcome with anger. "I'm quite aware that the so-called *Foundation* is you and Sam, and now that you've got your *hooks* into the poor man, he . . ."

Lettie realized that Dottie had hung up the phone, and immediately she pushed the callback button. A recording answered, advising her to contact the Foundation at their website with questions about grants and endowments. She stabbed the disconnect button and pitched her telephone against the passenger door.

She sat for a time staring out through the windshield at the Travel Lodge, her mind agitated. And now Peter pulled the curtain aside and stood looking down at the parking lot.

It seemed as if he were staring at her, but of course he wasn't. Peter's life did not include her any more. He was moving on. Did Jane Larkin's affairs still include her, or had Dottie Messerbee severed that connection too?

37.

"Hello," Jane said into her phone, stepping out of the garden shed into the open air, suddenly dizzy with anticipation.

"Hello, Jane!" Dottie said, sounding cheerful. "I have news that is quite moderately nice. The Messerbee Foundation has agreed to make an unrestricted endowment to the Co-op. 'Unrestricted' in the sense that the Co-op is authorized to spend the money as it sees fit. The sum will total $100,000 per year for three years, with adjustments possible depending on the Co-op's progress. We'll ask to see financial reports as well as a narrative of yearly activities each June, at the end of our fiscal year."

Jane was stunned. "Wow," she said. "That makes me deliriously happy, Dottie. You have no idea."

"I rather assumed it would, Jane, which is a crass thing to say. But I love this part of my work. Will that sum make a substantial difference?"

"It's already made a difference in me. I feel ten years younger. It'll make an *enormous* difference in our dealings with the city, which has been generous to us. But the City Council doesn't like betting on a lame horse, and we're scheduled to be audited next year. We need to be self-sustaining according to the stipulations of our MacArthur grant. This will make all the difference in the world, Dottie."

Jerry walked toward her now, singing the theme song from *Ghost Busters* and making little dance moves. She held her hand up to silence him. He nodded and put his finger to his lips.

"Lettie will be pleased, too," Jane said into the phone.

"I'm afraid she was less than pleased," Dottie said. "I spoke to her before I called you. The Foundation decided to grant the money solely to the Co-op, with the stipulation that it not be shared with any other non-profit entity. Lettie's idea of shared funding is fiscally unwise, especially because the Antiquity Center received funding from the Messerbee Foundation two years ago. When we looked at her June report it was difficult to see that another grant was appropriate."

"Oh, that's too bad. I feel as if she's responsible for me talking to you now."

"Perhaps that's true, although all of the information she provided us was consistent with what we read on the Co-op website and in the literature you gave us this morning. *You* were responsible for convincing us, Jane."

"Thanks," Jane said. Somehow Dottie's confidence made her particularly grateful, although she would have a difficult time with Lettie.

"If you'll allow me to overstep my bounds a little bit," Dottie said, "I'll suggest that you review all regulations about non-profit organizations sharing funds. I see potential disaster. Have you done that?"

"No, but I plan to. Lettie suggested you and Sam as potential donors on Saturday morning and then told me about today's meeting on Sunday. I was taken entirely by surprise."

"I thought as much. Lettie seems to be in a particular hurry. I don't say that she doesn't mean well, just that I don't know quite *what* she means sometimes. I'll be bold and suggest that you impose a one-week stay of execution on any plans that she comes up with. Trust your own instincts."

"I will," Jane said.

"And that rummage sale at Leisure World takes place a week from Friday. Like I said, I never miss it. Would you like to come along?"

"Very much, yes."

"I'll get back to you with the particulars. Sam says that you're the real deal, Jane, and he's nearly always right. Don't sell yourself short."

"I won't," Jane said, and that ended the conversation. Jerry was standing in the doorway with an expectant look on his face, and Jane filled him in, leaving out the part about Lettie being denied a stake in the grant. She would have to find a way to say it without it reflecting badly on Lettie, and she didn't want any I-told-you-so lectures right now.

"I feel wonderful," she said. "Weird how your mood can change in an instant."

"A good weird," Jerry said. "You want me to sing 'Here Comes the Sun'"?

"No, definitely not. But let's go out and celebrate tonight."

"Sure. It's early enough to make it to the beach. How about Crystal Cove?"

"Good idea. Full moon tonight, too. Very romantic." Jane widened her eyes at him, which never failed to make him smile.

"Let's bar the door and get out of here," Jerry said. He grabbed his toolbox off the potting table and the two of them went outside and shut the shed door behind them. It was a frail thing, built of overlaid boards and loose on its hinges. A possum could pull the hasp off, lock and all. Jane held a one-by-four board across the closed door to reinforce it, and Jerry drilled screws into the studs on either side, setting the screws tight. Jerry yanked on the door handle. The door was firm now, not even a rattle.

"I'll put plywood over it tomorrow," Jerry said, "and over the shutters too, like the three little pigs. It's still sticks instead of bricks, but it's better than straw."

They walked along the perimeter trail hand in hand, Jerry carrying his toolbox. Jane found that she couldn't quit smiling.

"Who the hell is that?" Jerry asked suddenly, dropping her hand.

Jane looked where he was pointing and saw a figure darting away up the Grand Street stairs.

"I can't believe it," Jerry said. "I think it was Lettie Phibbs. She was watching us through a pair of binoculars, and she ran for it when she saw that we were headed her way. She was wearing a blonde wig."

"It couldn't have been Lettie, not wearing a wig. Why would she wear a wig?" They arrived at the stairway and hurried to the top, just in time to see a car make a left-hand turn onto River Street. "That's not her car," Jane said.

"That doesn't mean it wasn't her. Who else would be spying on us?"

"Why would *she* be spying on us?" But she recalled Lettie waiting in her car in the parking lot Friday evening after work. And there was no reason for Jerry to be *wrong* about the binoculars and the wig. It wasn't the kind of thing he'd mix up. "This morning at breakfast I told her we were working down here," Jane told him. "She might have wanted to speak to me, but not to both of us. Not to you, I mean. She might have been embarrassed."

They climbed into the pickup, drove around the cul-de-sac, and headed in the direction of downtown. "Embarrassed why?" Jerry asked.

"Because the Messerbee Foundation disallowed the Antiquity Center and the Co-op from sharing the grant in any way."

"So they cut her out? No wonder she's wearing a wig."

"Yes, but it's not all that funny. The Foundation apparently made a considerable grant to the Antiquity Center a couple of years ago and decided not to do it again."

"Of course they decided not to," Jerry said. "She took their money and bought rare books and rugs and lamps to decorate her domicile."

"You don't know that."

"I'm going to tell you something, but don't get mad at me for not telling you sooner. I checked into her alleged degree in library science from USC. She never attended USC."

"Are you *sure*? A fake degree?"

"No degree at all. It's public record. It just took a phone call to find out. I didn't mention it to you because I don't want to wax attitudinal, which is exactly what you mean by saying Phibbs wouldn't want to talk to me."

"Does Lettie know that you know about the degree?"

"No."

"Good. This thing with the grant is hard enough on her. I don't care all that much if she's lying about the degree. I wouldn't make an issue of it. I might even be mistaken about her saying it was USC."

Jane didn't think she'd been mistaken, but she put this piece of information out of her mind. This morning it would have been unsettling, but now, after Dottie's phone call, the Co-op's uncertain future was less uncertain—pennies from heaven. There was no good reason to play Lettie's game unless playing them made perfect sense. They were coming up to the Plaza now, where they would turn east at the first exit, and Jane realized that she was in no hurry for the first time in a week.

"Let's circumnavigate," she said to Jerry, using his own term for going around the Plaza twice. He slowed down and moved into the inside lane, out of the way of the speed demons. The multi-colored fountain lights made an evening rainbow of the sparkling water, and there were people out and about, strolling and sitting on park benches, walking their dogs, taking advantage of the weather. The lights were on in the cafés and shop windows, couples and families looking at menus, people at outdoor tables drinking wine and talking, waiters carrying plates of food.

"Forget the beach," Jane said. "Why waste time driving? Let's throw on some clean clothes and walk back down here."

They turned east toward home and saw that the moon was already up, hanging over the Santa Ana Mountains in a sky swept clean of clouds—an enormous harvest moon like a pale orange face.

38.

At loose ends, Lettie drifted past the Travel Lodge once again. Peter's car was parked in the same slot, and the light was on in his room. He wasn't going anywhere. Two hours ago at the park she had seen Jane talking animatedly on the telephone in front of her preposterous shed, and Lettie had known damned well it was Dottie on the other end of the line. Jane was apparently elated with the news, despite knowing that Lettie had been cut out of the deal. It was easy to see that through her pocket binoculars. Jane, fickle as a child, would glom on to Dottie Messerbee now.

She drove east toward the Plaza in evening traffic, looking into the lighted windows of cafés and shops. There had been changes in Old Orange over the past thirty years, but it still maintained its character. *Like me*, she thought. Having a vision is what did it, and seeing that vision through. The sidewalks were crowded because of the little window of fair weather: couples walking hand in hand, students from the college.

Not a single one of them would miss her when she was gone, but going was inevitable. Now that her options had been defined and she was no longer at the mercy of chance, her mind was easy, and she thought of warm trade winds and the smell of plumeria blossoms and the placid lagoon that stretched forever beyond her window on Molokai. She wondered why she had stayed away so long.

She drove south toward the park, taking her time, thinking to have a closer look at the garden shed now that night had fallen. When she turned down Grand Street she saw that Jerry's pickup truck was gone, and she pulled into the open space along the curb, put her galoshes on over her shoes, and set out.

She walked around the moonlit shed, giving it a good look. The door was barred with a board and screws rather than a padlock. That was convenient. It would be easy enough to open. Reasons to open it crept into her mind, reasons that had to do with teaching Jane a life lesson. She smiled when she realized that she was still considering options—that she was still in the game, that Molokai was waiting beyond the horizon.

She headed downhill toward the creek, almost no distance at all now. Moonlight shone on the rushing water, which must be dredging up God knew what small treasures from the creek bed as it flowed toward the sea. It was like life itself. Over the course of it you lose everything you've gained, all the trinkets you've accumulated, stolen by time.

She looked toward the deserted parking lot, the creek running through it, and the lamps that illuminated the empty park. Once again it was borne in upon her that she was alone, and that everything she had thought she knew last week had been swept away. The future was a blank slate, which was sometimes for the best.

Tuesday

39.

THE SUN SHONE on Tuesday morning as if it had been doing its job all along. There was no hint of the storm that lay off the coast like Godzilla, waiting to wade ashore. A faint offshore wind blew out of the east—a mild Santa Ana wind, which wasn't rare between storms when high-pressure and low-pressure systems swapped places on a whim. It was a perfect day to work.

Jerry had been down to the lumberyard early, and the bed of the pickup was full of plywood that he'd pre-sawn this morning according to dimensions he'd written down yesterday. His tools were stowed, his portable generator braced up against the tail gate, and the bed cover cinched down to keep it from bouncing on top of the load.

A day's work and four hundred dollars-worth of lumber and screws might make all the difference in the fate of the shed. On the other hand, an extra couple of inches of rain could eradicate the day's work and the shed into the bargain. But then a well-placed meteor could do the same thing, so what the hell.

A horn honked out on the street, and he turned around to see Lettie Phibbs's Cadillac pulling into the curb in front of

Mrs. Collins's house. For a moment he considered climbing into the pickup and driving away. He could hide somewhere nearby for ten minutes and then come back home for Peewee and their bag of lunch.

But Phibbs was already climbing out, waving at him by wiggling her fingers. A man appeared from the passenger side, coming around the front of the car. He was dressed in a brown tweed coat and pleated pants, and he wore a pair of spectacles. He was tall and slightly stooped, with salt and pepper hair, heavy on the salt, obviously the history buff from Santa Ana. Jane's idea that Phibbs would call the house instead of barging in had proved wrong.

"Hello, Lettie!" Jerry said, swallowing his anger and walking down toward the sidewalk to meet them.

"This is my good friend Bob Hovel," she said to Jerry. "He hails from the Santa Ana Historical Scholars Club, a *very* erudite group."

"Jerry Larkin," Jerry said, shaking Hovel's hand. The man had apparently slept in his suit, but that wasn't a crime from Jerry's point of view. And he'd had a drink or three. It was just past ten o'clock, so that was understandable, him being a scholar and all.

Hovel gave the house a long, sideways squint and said, "Mid 1920s, I believe. It has elements of an Ole Hanson house, although I don't believe that Hanson strayed this far north of San Clemente."

"I bet you're right," Jerry said, "but our house was actually built by the first owner. Lettie tells me that the man was a stone mason who strayed south from San Francisco."

"Ah!" Hovel said. "But surely one can see a Hanson influence in the turreted entry. Your mason knew his business, I can tell you that. Very interesting indeed." He stroked his chin.

"Jane told you we were stopping by this morning, I believe," Phibbs said.

Jerry shook his head. "She went in to work early. She must have forgotten."

"Oh my. I so wanted to introduce her to Bob. And you're running off, too. Down to the park, I don't doubt. Jane has told me about that pesky shed."

"That's it exactly." He considered telling her to take a hike. Jane hadn't forgotten to tell him anything. On the other hand, here they were. Ten minutes would put this in the past—no glass of wine, no sitting down, no necessity to mind his manners. "I've got a little time to spare," he said, "but I'm meeting a friend at the job site in fifteen minutes. I'll just shut the driveway gate so that I'm ready to go."

He left them where they stood, closing the gate when he went through and hooking the nail back through to jam the latch. He shut the garage door and locked the hasp with a padlock. He didn't trust Phibbs for a cold moment. Turn your back on her and she'd be fetching her burglar tools from the back of her Escalade.

Peewee was barking like a maniac when Jerry entered the house, obviously anxious to tear the interlopers to pieces. He went into the kitchen and fetched a dog treat out of Peewee's special drawer and then lured Peewee into the guest bedroom and shut the door. Allowing Peewee to harass Phibbs and Hovel would be pleasant, but he would forego it for the sake of getting them the hell out of the house. The two of them were on the porch when he opened the front door. Hovel rapped his knuckles against the heavy cement stucco of the entryway. "They made stucco with Portland cement in those days," he said.

"*Portland* cement!" Phibbs put in brightly.

"Hard as a rock, too," Jerry said. "That's first-degree mortar." He grinned at Phibbs, who surprised him by looking horrified.

"*What?*" she said.

"He made a pun," Hovel said. "Very funny."

"Ah! Of course," Phibbs said. "I'll be on my guard now, Jerry Larkin," and she stepped past him into the interior.

"The curved seating in this entry turret is very nice," Hovel said. "What sort of wood is it?"

"Mahogany," Jerry told him, wondering why the man had to ask, since southern California was loaded with historic homes, and mahogany was commonplace.

"Leather cushions, I dare say." Hovel poked at one of the cushions. "Very comfy."

"They are," Jerry said. "Faux leather, actually. I nap on them from time to time, but with the bench curved like this, I wake up bent like a barrel stave. Over there's the kitchen."

He headed across the living room and through the arched doorway. The kitchen had been remodeled before the mason's heirs sold the house—shaker cabinets, white handmade tiles on the countertops, red accent tiles, wall niches and open shelves for decorative items. Jane's collection of cartoony, animal-shaped pitchers from the 1930s stood in the niches. Jerry pointed out his own favorite. "There's nothing better than pouring milk onto your cereal through the mouth of a pig dressed in a sailor suit," he said.

Phibbs looked more baffled than amused, but Hovel nodded seriously. "Quite a collection," he said. "Do you mind if I take photos?"

"Maybe some other time," Jerry told him. "I'd have to clear it with Jane."

They looked into the bathroom next and the guest bedroom. "Peewee is guarding the study," Jerry said, rapping at the closed door. Peewee barked now for good measure, and Phibbs stepped away, clutching her purse in front of her defensively.

Jerry contemplated booting them out, but Jane had wanted them to see the back-to-back fireplaces. The living room side was characteristic of the era, with a mahogany mantel and a face built of clinker brick and small river rocks. Rectangular earth-toned tiles covered the hearthstone.

"Surely those are Batchelder tiles," Hovel said. "You've seen the Batchelder tiles at the Ebell Women's Club in Santa Ana, Mr. Larkin?"

"No, but I hope to someday."

"There are good examples in the old YMCA building, too, on Main Street. It's a derelict building, I'm afraid. The Scholars Club has been making an effort to attract restoration money, but it's pricey, what with earthquake retrofitting and all."

"Sycamore Street, I believe," Phibbs said. "At Civic Center Drive. Your memory is shaky, Bob."

"Sycamore Street, of course. It's age, Lettie. It comes for all of us." He smiled broadly at Jerry.

"And these tiles are much more primitive than Batchelder's," Phibbs said. "They're the work of the mason himself, I believe. Jane mentioned that this fireplace is double-sided."

"Jane told you it was two-sided?" Jerry said. "Three days ago you told me that you knew the old Clemens house well and were a friend of Kat Winkle, our realtor. I bet you would have seen the house when it was being shown. Why all the mystery now?"

He stared at her, waiting for an answer, debating kicking her in the shin. "But sure," he said when she failed to respond. "I'm happy to give you a look." He opened the door of the bedroom and ushered them in. Jane would be thankful that they'd made the bed this morning.

"Is that earthquake damage in the ceiling?" Phibbs asked immediately.

"It is. We were lucky that was the extent of it."

"No structural damage?" Her eyes darted around the room, taking in the floor and the walls, probably searching for telltale signs that the 'quake would have led to foundation trouble. Obviously she knew he had been working under the house.

"None at all," he lied. "Half a dozen books fell onto the floor in the living room and this crack in the ceiling plaster, but that's it."

"You're lucky," she said, nodding heavily. "These old foundations were often weak. No building codes at the time, you know. I've been told that a house on Palmyra Avenue sustained damage to a brick foundation wall."

"Ours is solid concrete," Jerry said. "No damage at all."

"More homemade tiles," Hovel said, "and with these Chinese tiles set in. Very eccentric, but right in keeping with the Arts and Crafts spirit. Surely you'd allow *one* photo. This is unique. The Club would be *vitally* interested."

"Sure. One photo," Jerry said. "Of you and Lettie and the fireplace." He took Hovel's phone, dropped it into his own shirt pocket, took out his flip phone and snapped a photo, catching them with a look of surprise on their faces. "I'll show this to Jane. She'll be happy to know the two of you dropped in and had a look around."

Lettie's face looked as if she'd taken a swig of vinegar. Tough shit, Jerry thought, giving Hovel his phone back and herding them back out into the living room and through the front door.

"Well that was an interesting tour, Jerry," Phibbs said, having collected herself. "Bob is particularly interested in cellars, aren't you Bob?"

"Indeed I am," Bob said. "They're a rare breed in southern California."

"No time for the cellar, I'm afraid," Jerry said to Phibbs, moving them down the path toward the sidewalk. "It's been a real pleasure, Bob." He shook Hovel's hand again for good measure and then folded his arms and looked hard at Phibbs. Her cheerful face was gone again, and she stared at him hard, ugly as a fright mask.

"We're *not* through," she said. "*I know full well what you've found.*"

"I know you do," Jerry said. "I showed it to you Friday morning, a big, fake, Chinese coin with a square hole in it."

"If that's your game, Jerry, then here's something for you to think about. I intend to file papers with the County to place your property under eminent domain based on historical significance. You leave me no choice. I can initiate the process as a citizen, and my reputation with the Antiquity Center will carry *plenty* of weight. Am I right, Bob?"

"Well, yes," Hovel said. "Technically speaking. Historical houses in the county have been placed under eminent domain several times in the last decade. As Lettie said, any citizen can initiate the process. If there's support for the process, the county will simply condemn the house. The owner is compelled to move out, with compensation, of course, and then various entities decide what to do with the property."

"They'll eminent domain our house because I found a six-dollar Chinese charm that you think I dug up in the cellar?"

"I didn't mention your cellar, Jerry, and you know I'm not talking about the Yenshing charm. I *know* what you found. I won't tell you how I know, but I have a witness."

"Let me guess. That would be your man Carmody, witness for hire."

"In a word, yes. He and I are on the same page. So don't be coy with me, Jerry, and I won't be coy with you. Peter was working for Dutch on Monday morning, upstairs doing the books. He couldn't help but overhear your conversation."

"You're lying. Carmody wasn't there."

"Oh, but he was."

"Not working he wasn't. I'll put in a phone call to Hyink to double check."

"No. You certainly won't. We can both put in phone calls until the sky falls in. But there's no profit in it. You already *know* that I'm speaking the truth. I'm aware of the so-called Finders Keepers law applying to found treasures, and Peter and I both witnessed your saying that you found what you found along the creek, on public land."

"Then what's with the eminent domain thing?"

"It's easy. I don't give a damn whether you keep your house or lose it. I'm saying that wherever the hell you found the gold I can tie you up six ways from breakfast. Am I getting through your thick skull?"

"No. You're completely full of crap, Lettie. You're not going to do anything of the sort. I did a little digging of my own and discovered that you have no degree in library science from USC or anyplace else. That much of you is a fraud, and I'll bet a shiny new dime it doesn't stop there. Your only degree is in the science of bullshit. Do you really want to start this up? What'll happen to your plan to partner up with Jane? Are you tossing that into the dumpster now that the Messerbee Foundation told you to go to hell? That's why you're here, right? You're trying to recoup your losses, and so you came out here to threaten me."

"Now see here, sir," Bob Hovel said, shaking his head and looking grim. "Leticia Phibbs has a reputation that precedes her. Her Antiquity Center . . ."

"It's been a long time since I punched an old man," Jerry told him evenly. "Stay out of this unless you want to eat your dentures."

"Settle *down*, Jerry," Phibbs said, changing her tone. She stood for a moment as if considering things, and then in an even voice said, "Jane has nothing to do with this. I'd warrant that she doesn't know what you've discovered under your house. I'm right, aren't I? That's where you found it, and you haven't mentioned it to Jane. Good. This is between you and me. I simply want my fair share."

"What share would that be?"

"I should think that's obvious. I've spent years searching for the Flores gold in every way open to me. My interests, as you know, are purely historical." She shook her head sadly, as if chagrined that anyone would think otherwise. "The Flores gold would put the Antiquity Center on the map. The Center would profit, not me. I have no personal interest, except an interest in doing what's right."

"*And* you have no share, Lettie. I don't give a damn about the Antiquity Center. Anyone with eyes can see that it's not a *center* at all. It's a private collection in a private house posing as a non-profit. That's why you were cut out of the Messerbee deal. It's time for you to leave now."

"Well!" she said, her face screwing itself into a furious passion again. I've warned you!"

"And I'll warn you. If I catch you trespassing on my property, I'll show you what a shotgun looks like. Get the hell out of here. You too, Hovel."

He watched them walk to Phibbs's Cadillac and drive away, Phibbs flipping him off out the window. He waved in response and walked back to the house. The shotgun comment wasn't good. Maybe the dentures threat wasn't good. He had let Phibbs shake him up, which also wasn't good. He locked the door behind him, thinking that he'd have to padlock the gate as well as the garage.

In the study he did a computer search for the Santa Ana Historical Scholars Club. Nothing came up. Of course it didn't. Bob Hovel was a fraud, too. He moved the photo of Phibbs and Hovel from his phone onto his computer's desktop and then called Paul Buckman.

"Paul," he said, "I'm sending you a photo of the Phibbs woman and a friend of hers, allegedly named Bob Hovel from the Santa Ana Historical Scholars Club. I don't think there's any such club, and if there is, then I bet Hovel's not a member. He's a ringer of some sort, and I'm wondering about his relationship to Phibbs. And there's one more person involved—a guy name Peter Carmody, late thirties probably. I don't have a photo of Carmody, but I'll take anything that pops up about him. Could be he's a forger."

"So this Phibbs woman is a real problem?" Paul asked. "The master's degree sham isn't the issue?"

"It's the least of it. She threatened to file papers to eminent domain my house because of its historical importance. It's not an idle threat. It's a little piece of extortion that I can't tell you about, not over the phone."

"Send me the photo. No one can hide their past these days. We'll track her down. You in any kind of rush?"

"No. I threatened to shoot her, so that should keep her away for a day or two."

"You aren't serious?"

"No! Of course I'm not serious. I got mad is all."

"Good. But don't do that again. And like you said, watch what you say over the phone if this thing escalates."

40.

"CHRIST, LETTIE, you might have told me what was going on before you went nuts on the sidewalk," Bob Holloway said as they drove away up Water Street. "What the hell was that talk about *gold*?"

"It was you who told me to look out for my options, Bob. That's what it was about—an option."

"I nearly got punched."

"Too bad you didn't. We could have tied the bastard up in a lawsuit." She turned right on Almond, heading toward the Center, where Bob's car was parked. Her mind buzzed like a hive of hornets, and she wondered if she was on the verge of a stroke.

"You did notice that he called you out on the USC lie?"

"That's immaterial."

"It's *not* immaterial, Lettie. It means he's looking at your past. We talked about that in regard to the audit. You were the one who was worried about it, for God's sake."

"And you told me *not* to worry about it. You said it was water under the bridge."

"So you think it's a good idea to walk out onto the bridge and start shouting? What's this Larkin character got that you want? Specifically. I want to know what I walked into. That was extortion, you know—threatening him with eminent domain papers. Are you prepared to push that?"

"No. I was just rattling his cage. He's got nothing that would interest you, Bob, just some trinkets he dug up in his yard. And forget the extortion. He's not going to do a damned thing, that I guarantee."

"Tell me about the treasure, then. The word is lodged in my head."

"Like I told Larkin. I'm acting in the interest of the Antiquity Center. There's no profit in it for me."

"Right. Why would I think there was? Jesus, I can't believe we let him take that photo with his own phone."

"The photo was your asinine suggestion. Was that the liquor talking?"

He stared at her as if she were an utter stranger. "I was playing a part, just like you asked me to do at Benjie's the other night when you were gobbling down gin martinis and showing off your boobs in that spandex dress you managed to haul over your head. You're not subtle, Lettie, I'll give you that. Now I discover that you set me up. No one sets me up. I'm going to give you a pass on it, though, because you paid for the drinks." He shook his head, as if in disgust.

Lettie couldn't reply, and she couldn't look at Bob. She would never be able to look him in the face again. She slowed down to pull into the Antiquity Center lot, dangerously close to tears. It didn't pay to be emotional, but she wasn't made of stone, not like Bob. She was surprised for a moment that Peter's car was nowhere to be seen, but then she remembered that he was working at the Dutchman's.

Bob opened the car door and got out, then bent back in and looked at her hard. "I'll make myself clear," he said in a flat tone. "If you've involved me in a criminal conspiracy, then the past is going to rear its ugly head, and your late husband's skeleton is going to step out of the closet. I'm not going along for that ride. Whatever I need to do to clear myself, that's just what I'll do, even if it comes to putting you away. You're dead to me, Lettie, and for your own good, stay that way." With that, he slammed the door and walked off.

She sat in the car weeping, looking at the vine-covered fence in front of her so that Bob wouldn't see her face as he drove out of the lot. He might think she was crying over him. She *was* crying over him, even though he'd insulted her. She had thought that she knew him, that there was something valid in him. There used to be. There was no shame in crying for what used to be.

She slammed her hand against the top of the dashboard. God *damn* him, the two-faced piece of shit. If she had shot him between the eyes when she was in his office on Friday morning, no one on earth would have solved the murder. What he knew about her would have gone to the grave.

"And you're dead to *me*, Bob," she said aloud, but she found little satisfaction in it.

41.

MRS. HAZELTON PLACED her air-ion counter back into its cloth sack and slipped it into the carpetbag she had brought her gear in. Finished with her preparations, she sat now in one of the two chairs in the candlelit bedroom. Penny Potts sat in the other chair, both of them silent and looking down at their hands as if meditating. The mercury level in the barometer had been rising throughout the past hour, and the positive ion count had increased along with it. Jane couldn't remember how many parts per trillion. It was hard for her to picture invisible things and even harder to connect them to this silent vigil in her own bedroom.

A small wooden table hauled in from the living room sat in front of the fireplace hearth. On top of it stood a square, two-gallon, Yorkshire Mason jar, the wide lid sitting alongside. A candle in a silver stand burned inside the jar next to an unwrapped Jolly Rancher candy, the grape-like smell of the candy perfuming the air of the room. The candle and candy were meant to enliven the ghost, which could then be trapped in the jar simply by quickly screwing on the lid, like capturing a winged insect. The pocket-knife, buckle, and ring that Jerry had found beneath the house lay in the jar, too, making the contents of the jar look like a sort of tableau.

Mrs. Hazelton had warned Jane that none of this made good sense. It was better, she said, to let things take their course, as if the talk of ions and barometric pressure was merely part of a ritual chant, and the candlelight and objects in the jar were theater props, meant to create an atmosphere that led to the suspension of disbelief.

Jane sat on the bed, leaning back against the headboard, listening to the warm Santa Ana wind rustling the shrubbery beyond the window. Leafy shadows moved across on the sunlit spaces between the slats of the blinds. It was easy to imagine a human figure in the shadows—the illusion of someone bending and rising, perhaps lowering something into the ground.

She felt a murmuring of anxiety that made her think of low-level electrical current—an agitation that might turn into distress if she allowed herself to be carried away.

Something seemed to be pending in the quiet room, and she wondered whether it was actual or imaginary. Although it was almost certainly another illusion, there seemed to be moving shadows in the mirror set in among the old fireplace tiles, too—a shifting of dark and light in the murky glass. Once she noted the phenomenon it was difficult to look away.

In the mirror or on the mirror, she wondered. If she were closer to the mirror would she see something more than shadows? Something more than her own face? Someone else's face ...?

The candle in the Mason jar guttered and flared despite the dead air in the room. Mrs. Hazelton muttered something, but Jane couldn't make it out. Her friends looked gauzy in the dim light, as if she were seeing them through a haze of rain. The wind gusted, making a moaning noise in the chimney of the fireplace, and a cloud of ash drifted out of the hearth and hovered in the air, the flickering light of the candle glowing through it.

She could smell the wind now, a dusty, sagebrush smell mingled with the smell of livestock and the cloying smell of ripe concord grapes, and the smell of the creek and the wet and rotting vegetation along its banks. A door slammed shut again—a barn door, perhaps. She could hear the lowing of cattle, and she wondered whether a coyote had gotten into the barn.

What barn? The question passed over the surface of her mind and was gone again, as if borne away on the wind. She watched the shifting veil of ash. Shadows moved within it, obscuring the guttering candle flame and assuming the shapes that she recalled from her nightmare. She gave herself up to them, pressing down the fear within her. The features of the room altered, and the notion that she was dreaming was gone.

A willow tree stood in the distance, moonlight filtering through the lacy foliage. What had been the suggestion of a human figure hidden in the moonlit willow took the shape of a black-haired woman in a black dress and shawl, holding the reins of a pair of horses, one of them meant for her. Jane stood in the open air some distance from a low-built adobe house.

Her thoughts were staticky, a confusion of half-formed images flickering through her mind like postcard memories: the dark outline of Old Saddleback in the far distance, glimpses of the adobe house half-built, the empty window frames waiting for glass panes to arrive from Los Angeles, the brickyard piled with wooden forms, the posts for the grapevines strung with twine, the plants mere stumps in the newly spaded ground, the face of the woman standing in the shadow of the willow . . .

She felt a rising horror in the knowledge that she was losing herself, assuming the persona of a stranger, and the cold fear generated by this sliver of awareness made her hold tightly to her own identity. The moonlight over the mountains became the candle flame glowing in the jar, and the air was laden with the smell of grape candy.

And then it was moonlight once again. She stood next to a dry, brick-lined cistern, its wooden lid cast aside. A small box sat on the ground nearby, the box that her brother had come to steal, and her mind was full of the thought that the woman in black had betrayed her, and that she must bury the box in the cistern. She touched the ring on her finger, which had been given to her as a token by the woman who stood now with the horses. But the woman's very presence meant that it was too late, and that the ring was a false gift, the kiss of Judas.

The wind gusted, the unlatched door slammed twice, and there was the sound of rushing footsteps directly behind her. She turned too late, seeing the grimacing face of the man she knew to be her brother, the shovel in his upraised arms reflecting an arc of moonlight as it descended. She threw up her hand and felt a moment of shattering pain as she fell.

The bed banged sideways and Jane latched onto the headboard—another earthquake, her mind told her. Then she remembered the shovel and the searing pain, which were gone along with the nightmare wind, the fear and the shadow of the past, the reality of the memory. She was in her right mind now, however. She recollected dream images, which a moment ago had been moving, sensory reality.

Mrs. Hazelton stood by the wooden table, watching her. The lid of the jar was screwed down now, and although the candle inside the jar had fallen and gone out, there was a hazy glow inside, like chemical phosphorescence. Penny Potts was nowhere to be seen. Jane slipped off the bed and opened the wooden blinds, letting in the sunshine.

"Your ghost has cooperated," Mrs. Hazelton said, breathing heavily and indicating the jar. "I knew it when the candle went out, and I knocked my hip against the headboard when I went for the lid—just quick enough. I should have had the lid in my hand. I've never felt anything of the like before—the pent-up fear and anger . . ."

"It woke me when you knocked against the bed," Jane said. "I thought it was another earthquake. Where's Penny?"

"In the bathroom, sick. She left the room a few minutes ago. A spirit presence is often nauseous, but it'll pass now that he's trapped. That was a good bit of work, if I do say so myself. It was a powerful presence, Jane. You were absent for a good ten minutes. Did it seem like that? Time is often distorted."

"I don't know. I had no sensation of time passing, just . . . just *waiting*. What did you see?"

"Moving shadows. And there was a faint, barnyard smell. I heard footsteps and random noises and felt its desperation, anger, fear. It was all disconnected."

"But could you see the images? The willow tree and the woman holding the horses?"

"I avoided participating. I recited a rhyming poem—my method of blocking the manifestation from affecting my mind. My job was to watch for the candle flame to go out. I just wanted to get a lid onto the jar."

Jane nodded and took a deep breath. The room was simply a room, free of haunts and dread. They moved the small table back out to the living room and took the jar out to the farthest corner of the back yard. Jane was exhausted, but she vacuumed up the ash on the bedroom floor, dusted, and straightened the covers on the bed—leaving the bedroom in perfect order before going into the guest bedroom, hoping to take a long, dreamless nap.

42.

LETTIE SAT UPSTAIRS in the room in which Jerry Larkin had stolen the forged letter—the room in which she sat to renew her spirit. She could almost imagine it was summer, what with the warm breeze moving the curtains in the east-facing casement windows. But the summer feeling wouldn't last. It was midday, but she poured herself a glass of sherry, trying to keep her mind idle. She had no further duties. None at all. She meant to enjoy the tranquility of the Center—of her home—before she lost it forever.

The thought came to her that she might vacuum the rug one last time. She loved the absence of footprints, the pristine colors of the undisturbed wool. She was reminded of Jerry Larkin's invading this space like a sneak-thief, and how she had spent half an hour eradicating his spoor after he had lied to her face and gone away. But she was too tired to fetch out the vacuum cleaner now. Quite likely she would never touch it again, given that she was simply waiting to go. She wiped away tears and gave the room a considered look.

She could see that there was something odd about the rug now, although maybe it was just a trick of the light. She stood up to investigate, walking across to the locked cabinet in the corner. It was no illusion. A swath of rug had apparently been smoothed out in front of the cabinet and along the bookcases. It was about a foot wide, as if someone had tried to efface footprints, maybe by backing out along the bookcases dragging the edge of a book.

It had to have been Peter Carmody. And it had to have been this very morning, because the track in the rug had not been here last night.

She opened the door of one of the bookcases, pulling out a heavy copy of *Wildflowers of Orange County*, letting the book fall open. The key to the locked cabinet—her private cabinet— lay between the pages as ever. She fit the key into the cabinet lock, turned it, and opened the door. In the center sat a common hotel safe bolted to a fixed shelf. The safe was securely locked, as she always left it. She punched in the four-number combination and swung the door open.

The stacks of bills were piled neatly inside as ever: fifties, twenties, and hundreds rubber-banded in bundles of thirty bills—her earthquake fund, as she liked to call it. Her world was shaking right now, and she thanked God for having the wisdom to put the money aside over the years, over $30,000. She breathed a heavy sigh of relief.

But why had Peter covered his tracks on the rug? Had he sneaked in to jimmy the cabinet door on the off-chance that the safe would be unlocked? She had never told him about the safe, but she had opened it on occasion when he was working. Although she wouldn't have believed it three days ago—*hadn't* believed it—she knew now that he had always been a rotten apple. Of course he knew about the safe.

She took out a stack of hundreds and riffled it with her thumb, dropping it onto the rug the moment she saw that the interior bills weren't bills at all, but were carefully cut rectangles of newspaper. She stepped away from the safe with her hands held out in front of her, her breath coming in short gasps. She removed a stack of fifties with a shaking hand. More newspaper. The little turd had cleaned her out.

Methodically she removed the rubber bands and thumbed off the actual bills, one on the top and bottom of each stack. He had left her just over $1,000 all told, not out of a twisted sense of generosity, but simply to hide his crime so as not to set off any alarms until he was long gone. She might not have looked in the safe for another six months.

She left the slips of newspaper and the rubber bands on the floor. The room was spoiled now. The magic had gone out of it. She stuffed the bills into the pocket of her muumuu and returned to her chair, although she didn't sit down. She drained the sherry in her glass, poured herself another and drank it in a single draft, then threw her empty glass against the far wall, where it shattered, leaving a spatter of sherry on the paint.

The sight of her birthday pashmina draped over the back of the chair enraged her, and she plucked it up, smashed it over her mouth, and screamed into it, over and over until she was out of breath and heaving with exertion. She strode out of the room and down the stairs, straight into the kitchen, switching on the garbage disposer and dangling a corner of the pashmina into the grinder.

The cloth was immediately wrenched out of her hand, twisting her wrist, the pashmina flailing in the machine, which jammed to a stop and buzzed like a plague of locusts. She reached for the switch, but the power shut down by itself. The furious ten seconds of chaos had overheated the machine. She stood with her hands gripping the edge of the granite counter slowly counting, trying to settle her mind, which was close to panic.

She clutched the scarf and gave it a pull now, but it was trapped in the blades. The sight of it sickened her, and she turned away, surveying the kitchen and workroom, realizing that she was entirely ready to walk away from all of it. She thought for a moment, and then with a calm deliberation she pulled the battery out of her power screwdriver, shoved the battery into its charger, and plugged it in.

Upstairs in her bedroom she remembered the sherry bottle, but she couldn't afford to become fuddled with drink. She clipped a sleeping pill in half with a pill cutter and swallowed the half down, set the alarm for 5:00 p.m. and lay down in bed, staring at the ceiling, waiting for the pill to work, her thoughts going around in her head.

Considering her options hadn't solved anything at all. The irons she had been heating in the fire had gone cold due to the machinations of underhanded men. Bob Holloway was the most hateful of them all. He had pretended to be her friend and companion—*had* been her lover—prattling about old time's sake in his office and then insulting her and throwing her over in her hour of need, leaving her to fend for herself.

But by God she had fended for herself pretty up-and-walking good, hadn't she?—and she wasn't through yet. She was *not* defeated. She would not *be* defeated, not by the likes of Peter Carmody and Jerry Larkin. She recalled her conversation with Peter at Snack Shop on that rainy Sunday morning—just the day before yesterday, for God's sake, when the world had been a different place. It was her mention of the audit that had turned the tide, putting the fear into the craven little rat.

Peter had gone off to the Dutchman's at her request and seen an opportunity to cash in. He had considered his options for about thirty seconds and then seized on them, literally, by breaking into her safe and stealing her nest egg. There was an irony in it worthy of . . . of Shakespeare. What had the Bard said about being more sinned against than sinning? She had seen *that* notion play out in newspaper and rubber bands.

Peter's stealing from the Dutchman was one thing. Hyink was insured, and his reputation would scarcely suffer. But

Peter's stealing her money in her hour of need was personal. Unforgiveable. She would be a fool, though, to think that Peter had any interest in forgiveness.

Her angry thoughts drifted away, and her mind grew placid, turning to the future, to her "Molokai Getaway", as the travel agent had referred to it so many years ago when she and Art had made their first visit to the island. The word *getaway* brought up practical thoughts of the route she would take when she took to the open road, one that would fox anyone who thought of following her. She made a mental list of what she would take with her when she abandoned the Center: a few old books, jewelry, her collection of Zuni fetishes, her toolbox. She wondered if her old bathing suits would fit her, and whether she should make a quick trip tomorrow to Hilo Hattie's for a sarong or two and an evening dress and a floppy sun hat.

After a time one thing drifted into another, and in her dream she found herself on the patio of the Hotel Molokai on a warm night, the fronds of the coconut palms stirred by the soft trade winds and the hula moon rising over the ocean.

43.

Jerry wrapped up the shed work late in the evening, and walked down to Santiago Creek, standing at the edge of the wall and watching the creek flow past high and wild. The water was some two feet from the top, a foot higher than it had been a couple of hours ago. Dry weather earlier in the day had brought out joggers and walkers and kids on bicycles, moving along the walkways on either side of the creek, but storm clouds were moving in now, evening was coming on, and the park was quiet.

He trudged back up toward the shed, surveying it from a distance. He had set pre-cut plywood sheets onto the heavy sill that topped the rock foundation and fixed them to the studs beneath the old siding. The windows had disappeared beneath the plywood. For good measure he had tacked vertical strips of zinc-plated L-flashing over the corners to seal them. Except for the shake roof and the wide eaves with their corbels and outriggers, the place had temporarily lost its character. Or at least he hoped it was temporary.

Time to give it up, he thought, and he took one more circuit around the shed, pushing on the edges of the plywood, checking to see that everything was tight. He looked at his watch—nearly seven-thirty—and sent a text to Jane telling her that he and Peewee would be home in half an hour. Peewee had gotten tired of watching Jerry work some time ago and had retired to the shed, where his bed was set up atop the potting bench. He lay on his back snoring now, with his paws in the air, not offering to help Jerry load tools into the cart.

After everything was stowed in the pickup, he rolled the cart back down the hill, picked up Peewee and his bed like a giant taco, and put him into the cart while he screwed the last plywood panel over the plank door and fixed it with the cross bars. He had done everything he could to help the shed along, but the knowledge didn't cheer him up. There were good odds that it had played out its useful life, and that he had spent his day at the park building it a coffin.

While Jane started dinner, Jerry went out to the back yard with a battery-operated work-lamp and hung a big tarp over the area where he meant to bury the ghost jar, as Jane referred to it, tomorrow morning. It was easy enough to attach the tarp to limbs on the avocado tree with bungee cords, and then toss the other side of the tarp over the block wall in order to run rainwater into the Water Department parking lot behind them. It had been Mrs. Hazelton's idea that the ghost should be banished to the farthest corner of the property while it awaited "a proper burial". The name "Mrs. Hazelnut" passed through his mind, but he banished it as too dangerous to utter.

Jane had hidden the jar beneath an overturned flowerpot on the garden table to keep it safe, and Jerry had promised to wait for her before messing with it. The pot was big enough to plant a small tree in. Jane appeared behind him now, stepping in under the tarp just as the first raindrops of the evening pattered down. A small gust of wind shifted the tarp overhead.

"You want to take a look at it?" she asked.

"I'm full of anticipation," Jerry said, picking up the heavy flowerpot with both hands and setting it on the ground. The square jar with its metal, Mason-jar cap looked like something out of an anatomical lab rather than a kitchen. There was a gray, gelatinous substance pooled up around the ring, buckle, and knife, and a small pool of yellowish wax spilled from the fallen candle and candleholder.

"What's that gray mung in the bottom?" he asked.

"Mrs. Hazelton says that it's most likely ectoplasm. It looked like a cloud of gray smoke at first, right after the ghost went into the jar. It settled into that shape."

"Did it? It looks dusty."

"The dust is from ashes that blew out of the fireplace," Jane said.

A wet-smelling wind rippled the canvas, and there was another moment of rain. Scattered stars still shined in the sky, however, appearing and disappearing behind fast-moving clouds. There was something slightly horrifying about the small collection of ashy trinkets enshrined in the jar. Jerry would be happy enough to put it into the ground tomorrow morning, although it was a pity to bury the Barlow knife.

He wondered whether the knife alone would be safe to keep, but he didn't dare ask Jane. Retrieving it would mean opening the jar, of course, which might let the ghost out, and they'd have a haunted avocado tree for God knew how many years—ectoplasm in the guacamole. He suppressed a laugh, which Jane seemed to see in his face.

"I find it difficult to say the word *ectoplasm*, seriously," he said, "without ..."

"Without sounding like a fool? Of course you do, but I don't," Jane said. "Not anymore. If Mrs. Hazelton says that's ectoplasm, then so do I. If you had been there today, you'd take it seriously."

"I already am. Mrs. Hazelton must be an interesting woman. I wonder whether the ghost would escape if the jar broke. Why not just unscrew the lid and let it fly away?—not that I mean to be doubtful."

"Don't you? She didn't use the word 'ghost,' actually. She described it as a left-over fragment of the dead man's traumatic memory."

Jane zipped up her sweatshirt and put the hood up. The temperature was dropping and rain pelted down hard for a moment. They both stood waiting to see whether the storm was serious or undecided.

"I've never thought of a ghost as a memory, but I guess it makes sense," Jerry said. "Or as much sense as any of this. So that's a Jolly Rancher stuck in the wax?"

"Grape flavored. I think the heat of the candle started to melt it, although I don't know. It might have melted when the ghost got to it."

"Ghosts like the taste of grape?"

She stared at him, and he realized that she wasn't going to answer.

"Fire Stix, maybe? That was my Rancher of choice, but it might have a gates-of-hell vibe that would scare the ghost away." He smiled at her, but she didn't smile back, and he realized, too late, that he was taking the wrong tone.

"I guess I decided to buy into this, Jerry. I'm kind of surprised that you still have an attitude toward it after having the same nightmare twice. That's why I didn't want you around the house today, making a joke of everything. I mentioned that at the park yesterday."

That was troubling—her calling him by his first name. "I'm sorry," he said. "I guess I try to lighten things up sometimes."

"Why do difficult things *need* to be lightened up? You think that makes them float away?"

He shrugged. "I guess I don't know. Maybe I haven't been paying attention."

Jane was on edge. Of course she would be, with the storm threatening to wash away a year's worth of her work. He wondered if this was a good time to bring up the problem of the bones, which were still in the garage, zipped into the canvas bag, and which, he realized now, he should have mentioned days ago—Sunday morning, say, when he had hidden them in the garage in the first place. But the last thing he had wanted to do was to make things even more worrisome for Jane, especially when she was shaken up by the nightmare. More honestly maybe, he hadn't wanted to set her off. Honesty was starting to look like a slippery fish, though. He had found easy routes around it, even with himself. And Jane had always had a way of digesting her anger fairly quickly.

"We've been too busy to talk these last few days," she said. "That has to change. It's getting cold out here, though. I'm going in to check on dinner." She turned around and walked away without another word.

He decided that he would save the full disclosure until after a glass of champagne. The bones could go into the bottom of a grave along with the Mason jar and the treasure, at least for the time being. As far as he was concerned, they could stay there. He covered the jar with the flowerpot for safe-keeping now and followed after her through the back door and into the kitchen.

"What did you do to the salmon?" he asked, trying to shift the conversation to cheerful small talk. The smell of steamy coconut milk rose from the rice cooker.

"I painted it with wine, garlic, and Dijon mustard and wrapped it in parchment. You want to mix up some dressing for the salad?"

"Sure. I've got this great idea, though. Why don't we chill some anniversary champagne? I bought a couple of bottles and put them in the wine rack. It'll be quick if we put them in ice water."

"It's not our anniversary until tomorrow," she told him. "I'll have a glass of fizzy water with a slice of lime. You knock yourself out, though."

Jerry couldn't think of anything to say to this, but it was obvious that Jane wasn't going to relent. "I *am* sorry. Sometimes I just don't think, and . . ."

"Stop *apologizing*, for God's sake. Do you think I didn't know who you were when I married you? I didn't make a *mistake*, you know."

"Me neither," he said. "I didn't mean . . ."

"I *know* what you *didn't* mean. Right now I want to hear what you *do* mean." She stared at him without smiling, letting this sink in. "Sometimes just say what you mean. I think there's a *lot* you haven't said in the last few days—this problem you have with Lettie Phibbs, for instance. There's more to it. Like why she was looking around in our driveway and what she thought she could find down along the creek. You fixed the problem of the floor on Friday afternoon, right? So what's with all this messing around under the house that you've been doing? Lettie's obviously obsessed by it, and so are you. What's going on?"

"Heaps," he said. "I'll fill you in over dinner. Nothing left out."

"Good," she said, and turned her attention to the food again.

He took a lime out of the fruit bowl and then went to the refrigerator for a bottle of sparkling water. He *did* have a lot to tell her—more than she wanted to hear. He had been living a secret life this past week. Right now he couldn't remember why he'd kept everything from her. What had he been protecting her from?

He pulled open the refrigerator and saw that both bottles of champagne reclined on the top shelf. "Hey! I found the champagne," he said. "Peewee must have put them into the fridge. I say we open one. We need . . . bubbles."

Jane pulled the baking dish out of the oven and scooped the salmon filets onto the plates with the spatula. "Why don't we open one now and save the other one for tomorrow?" she said, holding the spatula like a weapon. "I'm declaring this anniversary a two-day celebration."

∞

"You hid the bones from Lettie Phibbs after digging them out of this crypt?" Jane asked after they had made inroads into their dinner. "You want more rice?"

"No to the rice, thanks. Yes to hiding the bones from Lettie Phibbs. But I didn't do that until Sunday morning, after we both had the nightmare. That was when I wondered whether there was a ghost, or whatever it's called, living in the bones. I thought that Lettie might come back looking for them when we were out of the house, so I hid them in the back of the garage and locked the door. I figured the trinkets were safe in the bedroom. My mistake, but an honest mistake."

He poured them each another glass of champagne, emptying the bottle.

"And that's when you checked to see whether Lettie lied about her education."

"Yeah. She was looking like a fraud to me."

"Uh huh."

"I should have told you, obviously, but I didn't see it as that big a deal. You two had plans together. I didn't want to mess things up. You already knew I didn't trust her because of her snooping around the house, looking into our business. When she showed up this morning with the phony historical man, I had to tell her to go to hell. She actually wanted me to let her search the cellar."

"*Search* it? Did you get out the imaginary shotgun?"

"She was lucky I didn't." He shrugged and took a sip of the champagne, which was very damned good. "I might chase this champagne with a glass of cognac," he said. "It's been that kind of day."

"For both of us. And thanks again for boxing in the shed."

There was the sound of thunder now, and then of rain pounding against the skylight—a determined rain. "It's started," Jane said, a flat, final-sounding statement.

After a long silence she said, "After thinking about yesterday's phone call with Dottie, I decided to break off the Co-op's association with the Antiquities Center. Then Lettie called me and apologized for being out of line when she came out here with her friend this morning. She was afraid she'd interrupted something important and that you were miffed."

"Miffed? The woman is a walking miffler. That's her purpose in life."

"Anyway, she wants to talk things through. She's stopping into the office tomorrow morning."

"Not *early*? Tomorrow is day two of our anniversary. There's no need to set the alarm, I hope."

"No need at all," she said, smiling at him. "So what are we going to do about the bones? They can't live in the garage or anywhere else around here."

"No, but I didn't like the idea of them being buried under the house, and not just because I figured they were the source of the damned ghost. Imagine the turmoil if the authorities knew there were human bones under there."

"You might be right about that. But they're evidence of a murder. There's no statute of limitations on murder, you know. We're inviting all kinds of legal trouble if we don't talk to the right people."

"Yeah, but I'm not persuaded by the crime aspect of the argument. No one's interested in a backwoods murder that took place 150 years ago. The whole thing is a matter of legend any-way as far as anyone knows. It's not some kind of cold case. Why would the authorities give a damn?"

"*Lettie* knows they exist, right? You said you hid them from her."

"She *thinks* she knows, but she's got no evidence of any-thing. My idea was to bury them with the jar out back. Like Mrs. Hazelton said, in a real grave. It'll literally put this thing to rest. And we're not burying *evidence*, we're simply shifting the bones to a more appropriate place. We can sleep on it for a month and if we change our mind, I'll discover them again and we can call the Old Bone Bureau and tell them to send a hearse."

Jane looked at him doubtfully. "*Sleep on it?*" she said.

"Not literally, now that they're moved out from under the bed."

The rain was coming down so hard now that it sounded as if someone was beating on the kitchen skylight with rolled up newspapers, and in the glow of the neighbor's side-porch lamp they could see a haze of shattered rain rising from the driveway. "Why do you have to go into the office tomorrow?" Jerry asked. "Not just to talk to Lettie Phibbs?"

She shrugged. "No. Who knows what tomorrow will bring? I need to be on the job. I know that doesn't make any sense, but it's the way I feel. Why don't you come down there and join me when you're done in the back yard?"

"I'll bring Peewee," he said.

He stared at her for a moment, thinking things out, and then said, "I've got one more surprise up my sleeve. Full disclo-sure, like I promised. My days of keeping secrets are over."

"Really?" Jane said. "Another surprise? Should we drink that cognac first? Maybe kill the bottle?"

"Nope," he said. "It's a *good* surprise. I meant to give it to you tomorrow on our actual anniversary, but like you said, who knows what tomorrow will bring? Give me a half a second."

He headed into the bedroom now and fetched the two pieces of gold that the Dutchman had shined up for him. They were hidden in a dresser drawer, waiting to be wrapped in the morning. He slipped them into a colorful argyle sock and tied the top, then went back into the kitchen. Jane had a frankly skeptical look on her face.

"You're giving me an old sock?"

"If you want the sock, you can have it, but the surprise is in the toe."

She shook it next to her ear. "It clinks," she said.

"Just open it."

"You must mean untie it. A person doesn't open a sock."

She untied it and shook the two coins out into her hand, stared at them for a moment, and then squinted her eyes at him. "Is this gold?"

"Yeah, an English Gold Sovereign and an American Double Eagle. Gold as gold can be."

"Where'd they come from?"

"From the treasure under the house."

She gaped at him. "What treasure is that?" she asked. "The one you neglected to tell me about?"

"The one that the skeleton was sitting on top of."

∞

Jane closed the book she'd found at The Bookman, having to do with ponds. The distinction between water boatmen and lesser water boatmen wasn't holding her interest. It was past midnight, and her eyes were too tired to read. She was also too tired to sleep, or too unsettled. Of course that was the trouble.

She sat listening to the storm for a time, an orchestra of rain playing against the windows, water running in the gutters and splashing into the flowerbeds, and the occasional moaning of the wind. She could hear the wind chimes on Mrs. Collins's front porch, and there was an off-and-on rattling noise like a loose screen that reminded her of the door slamming in the nightmare.

Jerry had drifted off to sleep as soon as his head had hit the pillow at ten o'clock, as had Peewee—the two men in her life, both of them sleeping the sleep of the just. The two gold coins lay on her bedside table like talismans, and she opened the drawer now and pushed them inside, hiding them from sight.

Come what may, she thought, she and Jerry would weather the storm. The sun would shine and the world would dry out. But Jerry's idea of burying bones and gold in a hole in the back yard was almost literally a skeleton in the closet, and there was no way she could "sleep on it" a minute longer. She tapped Jerry on the shoulder, and he awakened as quickly as he had fallen asleep.

"What's wrong?" he asked.

"I can't sleep. I'm worried about the damned bones and I'm worried about this treasure that's come out of nowhere. Tell me again why the treasure belongs to us. I know there's a Finders Keepers law, because you told me, but that can't be the end of things."

"It's not," he said, sitting up. "The problem is going to be figuring out how to get at its real value. I talked to Hyink about that. The quick way would be to melt it down and sell it as bullion ..."

"I don't mean that. I mean why is it *ours*?"

"Because the law clearly states that a treasure trove belongs to whoever finds it unless it's on public property or belongs to someone else—someone who lost it or misplaced it. Then there are complications. We found it on our own property, so it's ours unless someone else has a prior right to it."

"Someone related to this Flores man, this criminal? How do we know that he didn't leave any heirs? It's a common last name."

"The money was buried a hundred and seventy years ago. It's hard to believe that . . ."

"But we don't know for sure, right? I can't imagine offering that argument in a court of law, that it stands to reason it's ours. We can't lay claim to the treasure unless someone recognizes our claim. We can't just hide it in the pantry. What if someone pops up and disputes our claim and it's discovered that we never reported having found it in the first place?"

"But it's in our possession. Of course we found it. Hyink would verify that much."

"So you *asked* Mr. Hyink about that?—told him where you'd found the gold?"

"No, I gave him a hypothetical case."

"What was it?"

"An anonymous uncle."

She stared at him. "You mean you made up a story."

"You could put it that way."

"What other way is there to put it? We might call it a lie, I guess."

"A white lie."

He winked at her, which was irritating, but she let it slide. "I'll bet hypothetical uncles won't stand up in court, either," she said, "which is where we might find ourselves one of these days. You said you were worried that Lettie Phibbs might know something about all of this. Do you think she'll remain silent?"

"If she knows what's good for her."

"And you're happy with that?"

He shrugged. "Hypothetically."

"I guess I'm not happy with any of it, which is why I can't sleep. Don't get mad when I say this, but all of this subterfuge and the white lies and hidden secrets reminds me a lot of the way Lettie does business. That's why I'm breaking things off with her."

"You're saying that I'm turning into Lettie Phibbs?"

"I'm saying that everything has consequences. You know what they say about gaining the world and losing your soul."

"This is completely different. The gold is ours, it's not hers. There's no subterfuge about it."

"That's not what I mean. I mean that unless we come clean with all of this, it's going to turn into another nightmare. I don't want any more nightmares. And the Co-op can't afford any nightmares either, if you see what I mean."

Jerry sat for a moment thinking and then said, "I do see what you mean. Of course I do. How about this?: I'll be picking up those ingots from Hyink on Thursday. I'll come clean with him, ask him who to talk to, by which I mean a lawyer, and what to do with the gold in the meantime."

"Good. And we'll do the same with the bones, right? Find someone who actually knows about these things."

"Sure. Can I bury the ghost? Mrs. Hazelton recommends it, and I'm pretty sure that there aren't any legal ramifications involved. I have to have *some* fun with all this."

"Good night," Jane said, and switched off her lamp.

44.

LETTIE PHIBBS SAT in the parked Honda opposite the Burger King in the half-empty lot of a 7-Eleven store and a Star Doughnut shop. It was just past eight p.m. There was a five-dollar barbershop, too, but it had closed at six. People came and went, mostly into the 7-Eleven, paying her no mind at all in the forty-five minutes she'd been sitting there. She'd had no dinner, and she was thinking about doughnuts and the risk involved in stepping into the shop and buying an apple fritter—minimal risk, surely, in this part of town.

But the thought was extinguished when the light in room 220 across the street switched off, the door swung open, and Peter wheeled his bicycle out onto the walkway. He leaned in through the open door to grab his suitcase and then shut the door forever.

Forever, Lettie thought, realizing that the time had come. She was on the brink of a change from which there would be no turning back. Her life in Old Orange was finished, or nearly so, and it was time to move on. She thought about what she was leaving behind, including the contents of the Center—the rare books, the jewelry, the Navajo rugs, the historical documents, many with collectible signatures.

There were the plein-air paintings, too, many of them originals. If she had the opportunity she would return and remove the three Edgar Payne paintings from their frames. They were worth far too much to abandon. She could lay them out flat on the bottom of her suitcase . . . .

Her mind was full of second thoughts and re-considerations, but she exerted her will and very carefully shut them out. There would be no more opportunity for her, not here in southern California. Her very life in Old Orange was too much to abandon, but here she sat in her car with the motor running, getting ready to leave ruination behind. She was more thrilled than frightened by the thought.

When Peter drove the Prius out of the lot and headed east toward the Dutchman's, she checked the time on her wristwatch. She would give him six minutes. She knew just where he was going, and it made no sense to arrive at the same time. It would be equally fatal to arrive late. He certainly knew just what he wanted out of the Dutchman's house, and he wouldn't spend more than a few minutes fetching it.

If she was wrong—if he wasn't returning to the Dutchman's, but had already stolen the gold—then so be it. It meant he was running, and she didn't have the leisure to chase him. In that case, good riddance to bad rubbish.

When the long minutes had passed, she drove out onto Chapman Avenue and headed east in light traffic, careful, as always when she drove the Honda not to attract the attention of anyone at all. A traffic ticket associating her with the car could be a disaster. A few minutes later she turned up Prospect Street and drove along slowly in the shadows of the overhanging eucalyptus trees, not seeing Peter's Prius. That was no surprise, since he had no excuse for being here at this time of night and had probably parked down the Dutchman's alley. No one was out and about in the neighborhood—everyone snug in their beds or glued to the television screen, living their small lives. She found a place at the curb far from a streetlight and parked, shutting the door as soundlessly as she could when she got out.

There were no sidewalks, so she walked in the street atop a litter of damp, crescent-shaped eucalyptus leaves and smashed berries. The smell of them perfumed the night air, and the shadows of the trees hid her from the bright moonlight that appeared and disappeared through tearing clouds. She wore a black coat and dark clothing and moved soundlessly in her sneakers. If someone saw her, she was merely out on an evening walk, wearing a pair of gloves against the chill. Being seen would put a crimp in her plans, but time and chance, as the bible said, happen to everyone.

She turned up the alley, keeping to the far wall, the moon hidden now. A motion-sensor lamp blinked on over a garage, and the sudden light brought her heart into her throat. But the house remained dark, and there was no clamor. Hyink's wrought-iron entry gate loomed ahead in the darkness—open wide. She strode through it, relieved to be out of the alley and in among the dark trees and the privacy of the Dutchman's acreage.

Strangely, Peter's car wasn't in the lot, and for a moment she doubted herself. But there it was in the old carriage house, visible beyond the open doors. She saw at once that his license plates were wrong—not Peter's egotistical personalized plates, which read "CARMODY", but standard California plates, almost certainly bought on the internet, since Peter wouldn't have the courage to steal them himself. Her $30,000 was almost certainly in the car. She would take that back tonight.

She stood for a moment making up her mind, and then walked into the darkness of the garage. Using the flashlight function on her phone, she peered in through the windows at the junk on the seats of the Prius, wondering where he would have stowed the money. The car doors were locked, and there was no time to rummage through the litter inside anyway. She switched off her light and slipped deeper into the darkness to wait.

∞

Peter returned the audio recorder to Hyink's desk before opening the floor safe and taking out the nicely heavy coins, which lay inside a soft leather coin pouch. He wore gloves, even though he was leaving town, and it wouldn't take a genius to figure out who had stolen the coins.

There was little chance that the police would try to chase him down—two coins, after all, with a hypothetical value . . .. Insurance investigators were more likely to take an interest in the theft if the value of the coins could be proven. But without fingerprints there was nothing that would tie him to the theft—nothing that wasn't merely circumstantial. His DNA was everywhere on the property, after all. His leaving town wasn't evidence of anything.

He had no idea of fencing the coins or offering them for sale on legitimate websites. Crypto-markets on the dark net were easy enough to access. Maybe he would trade them for Bitcoins. Maybe he would sit on the coins for a couple of years first. He closed the safe and turned the dial, closed the hatch over it, and pulled the rug back into place. The yard was bathed in moonlight now, but he walked boldly through it, full of the urge to whistle "Zippity Doo Dah".

But he bottled up his exhilaration, which was probably half due to nervousness, and continued steadily around the side of the garage and into the interior darkness, clicking open the car doors with his key fob. The interior lights came on, weirdly bright in the almost total darkness. In the sudden illumination, Lettie Phibbs stepped out from behind a cabinet wearing a blonde wig and holding a pistol in her hand.

∞

"Stop right there," Lettie said, cocking the pistol with an audible click. "I'll shoot you, Peter, after what you've done to me."

"What?" he asked stupidly, staring at the pistol. "I haven't done anything."

"Liar!" she said. "You robbed my safe, and now you've robbed Dutch, your own kin. I listened when you played the recording of his conversation with Larkin. I know that you have no intention of seeing out the audit when it comes. You've betrayed me."

He stared at her, his mouth half-open, his hand still outstretched, holding the key fob. "Okay," he said, lowering his arm now and turning toward her. "Let's bargain. I'll return your money and keep what I've taken from Hyink. We'll go our own ways."

"And I'll serve time for embezzlement while you lounge by a swimming pool somewhere."

"We're both complicit, Lettie. You know that."

"Will the *auditors* know that? Did you sign your work? I've paid you under the table for years. You're a ghost, and you haven't even *looked* at the books. They'll put it all on me. I'll be under the microscope once you're gone."

"God couldn't put the books in order, Lettie. And you'll be under more than the microscope if you don't put the gun away. Shooting me won't help your case. For God's sake, take the money and run."

She smiled at him and cocked the pistol. "That's good advice, Peter. Surely it is. Stop talking now and turn around."

"Lettie, don't . . ."

His voice had risen a couple of octaves—a little boy's voice now, enhanced by fear. And he looked like a frightened boy, one who badly needed to be shamed and humiliated.

"Don't what?" She stepped forward and pressed the gun between his shoulder blades. "Remember that this weapon has a *hair* trigger." He began to shake now—his entire body, as if he'd gotten a chill. "Is my money inside the car or in the trunk?" she asked. "There's no point in lying to me, Peter. We're past that."

"Back seat," he said. "In my suitcase."

"Is there a weapon in the suitcase? If you lie to me, I'll shoot you in the back."

"No. The money's on top, in a travel bag."

"Open the door slowly and take the bag out of the suitcase. Your life hangs in the balance." She ground the pistol into his back, savoring the phrase.

"Give me a chance, Lettie," he said in a quivering voice, and she realized that the skinny little creep was crying, for God's sake, not out of regret, but craven fear. He bent in through the car door and unzipped his suitcase. She saw a black vinyl zipper bag on top of the jumbled clothes.

"Open the bag," she said, taking a step back. "Show me what's inside, but don't reach into it." She heard him inhale sharply as he turned around and faced her, holding the bag and peering out at her from under the hood of his idiotic sweatshirt.

He moved in slow motion, his hands shaking so badly that he had a difficult time grasping the zipper. When he held out the open bag there was a tube of toothpaste on top, a razor, a toothbrush, and a small squeeze bottle. "It's underneath," he said, and he threw the bag into her face with both hands.

She gasped and trod back, sweeping the bag aside. He lunged at her, reaching for her wrist, going after the pistol. She jerked her arm back and hammered his own wrist hard with the pistol grip, pulling away from him. He was making a whimpering noise in his throat, obviously addled, as if he didn't know whether to run or fight. She feinted with the gun, snatching the hood of his sweatshirt when he cringed and yanking it down hard over his face, blinding him, leaning into him now and shoving the pistol against his chest.

He ducked into her and bit her wrist. Her hand jerked with the sudden pain, and the pistol went off with a muffled crack. She was shocked by it, realizing that she had shot him, and she watched in horror and fascination as he staggered backward, clutching his chest, his eyes staring. Blood flowed through his fingers

"You stupid little fool," she croaked, and took a double grip on the pistol, ready to shoot him again. She couldn't leave him alive. Not now. He turned and hunched out of the garage into the night, staggering toward the alley as if would simply walk away. The night was deadly silent—no shouting or alarms.

"No you don't," she said to his back, and she stepped up behind him and clubbed him hard against the side of his head with the butt of the pistol. He took three staggering steps forward and she hit him again twice, hard. He fell beneath a big tree, rolling onto his back, where he lay twitching in the weeds. She stood over him, watching his mouth open and close, as if he was eating something. Blood pumped out of the wound in his chest, soaking his sweatshirt.

Then the life went out of him and he stared sightlessly at the sky, a Halloween dummy in a fright mask. She poked at him with her foot for good measure, but he didn't move. The night remained silent, and after a short time she heard crickets starting up.

She bent over and poked at his pockets, feeling the hard edges of coins in a small bag. She drew out the bag and headed back into the garage, fetching a cloth grocery bag out of her purse, dropping the coins into it. In a hurry now, she yanked a t-shirt out of Peter's open suitcase, wrapped it around the pistol and put it into the bag. She found her money in a pillowcase on the floor of the back seat, and pulled her gloves off, turning them inside out, before stuffing the pillowcase and the gloves into the bag along with the pistol. After retrieving her purse she hurried away toward the alley, not looking down at Peter's corpse. She was done with Peter Carmody. His soul, if he ever had one, had gone to the devil.

There was no sign of activity until she reached the street, where she saw a man on the sidewalk walking his dog. She slipped behind the big oak tree next to the mailboxes and waited until he stepped up onto his porch and disappeared from view. A crack of thunder rattled the sky, and the rain began to fall as she hurried to her car, anxious to get back to the safety of the house in Garden Grove and the bottle of white wine cooling in the fridge. Looking back down the Dutchman's alley as she drove away, she was horrified to see a big coyote slinking beneath the wrought-iron arch.

Wednesday

45.

JANE DROVE SOUTH on Glassell Street, crossing the bridge over the creek at Hart Park. On her right-hand side the creek surged out from under the bridge in a wild torrent. No longer confined by the high, stone walls of the parking lot and the concrete walls of the bridge, the creek bed widened out to twice its width and the rushing water flowed out into the open spaces, swirling around the oaks and sycamores and leaping against the rock walls of the adjacent freeway onramp.

In the park itself, the water washed along the top of the barrier walls, running smooth and deep, gray under the low sky. She caught a glimpse of the garden shed on the rise above the creek, sheathed in plywood now, rainwater pouring off its roof and running downhill. The road beneath the freeway overpass was flooded, and she moved into the middle lane to make her way. The few cars on the road crept along with their wipers at high speed.

She passed the empty parking lot at MacFrugal's, the store's interior lights glowing through the murk of rain. A single car waited at the drive-up window of the taqueria near the road, and she had the wild idea of stopping for a breakfast burrito to take to the office with her. But she drove on past. Jerry was bringing Peewee and lunch to the office later on in the morning, and there was no use giving into her appetite now.

She turned left at Fairhaven Avenue, forced to drive down the centerline between two west-flowing rivers that were curb-deep. She might find herself stranded if she didn't head back downtown soon, but she was determined to see what the creek looked like in the broad expanse of bottomland west of the Cambridge Street Bridge. It was essentially a lake, the tips of the saguaro cactus in the little succulents garden rising out of the flood. It looked as if there was a good ten or twelve feet to go before the water would invade the back yards of the houses that lined the side of the creek—more water than seemed possible.

She made her way back toward the office, creeping along now, hearing distant thunder. The rain sheeted on the windshield, and the overworked wipers gave her only brief moments of clarity. She switched on the radio, and the weather report was dire—nonstop rain throughout the day, thunderstorms, heavy winds, and the peril of falling trees due to wind and saturated ground.

She had an on-and-off view of empty streets, sandbagged storefronts, and flooded intersections as she crept along, finally turning down Orange Street past PJ's Abbey. Diehard breakfasters sat inside in window seats, drinking coffee and eating French toast and omelets and feeling safe and warm.

Jane parked right outside the rear door to the upstairs offices, grabbing her canopy umbrella and her purse. She slid out of the car, slamming the door behind her and hoisting the umbrella. She was thankful for her long raincoat and her waterproof boots as she slogged toward the rear door, her key already in her hand. In her office she flipped on the lights, turned up the thermostat, and breathed a sigh of relief.

The homey feel of the office calmed her nerves, with its woodwork and map-wall and windows overlooking the downtown shops. She could see lightning through the bay window, flickering in the west beyond the roof of Satellite Market, and she watched the wind-tossed branches of the curbside sycamores and the leaden hue of the sky, everything obscured by falling rain. Coming into work early had seemed vital last night, but she couldn't remember why.

She sat staring at the heavy front door with its translucent window of chicken-wire glass. Painted on the outside were the words OLD ORANGE CO-OP, written out backward from her viewpoint. There wouldn't be any customers today. She tried whistling "Pennies from Heaven", and found that the melody came easily into her mind, making her think again of the gold coins that Jerry had found under the house, and their possible value, which sounded absurd to her despite Jerry's talk about ingots and melt value and bullion. Lettie Phibbs had asked her whether she would use Jerry's money to save the Co-op if things got bad, and Jane found that she was still puzzling over the question.

The treasure didn't seem like anybody's money. It had come out of the ground rather than falling out of the sky—pennies from the crypt—but it seemed like everybody's money despite Jerry's talk about the Finders Keepers law. It was stolen money, after all. People had been murdered because of it. But if that was so, then why not use the Co-op to turn bad money into good money? Instant success, financially speaking. Except that it was something like instant coffee, never as good as coffee you made yourself.

The buffalo nickel that Lettie had given her at the park lay on the desktop, and she picked it up and looked at the date—1938. It was a beautiful coin regardless of its value. A quick computer search revealed that she could buy a roll of twenty of them for ten dollars, which made it worth a dollar in some sense. At the ninety-nine-cent store it would only be worth a nickel.

She dug her phone out of her purse and called Mrs. Hazelton, happy that they had exchanged phone numbers yesterday afternoon.

"I've never heard such thunder," Mrs. Hazelton said after the mutual hellos, and for a time they talked about the weather.

Jane was happy simply to have someone to chat with on this stormy morning, but after a few minutes she asked, "Does your job as curator at the museum have anything to do with bones? Bones that might be of historical significance, let's say?"

"Yes indeed, although the bulk of the museum's collection is housed elsewhere. We make it available to scholars, who are usually interested in the bones of indigenous people. Years ago the museum had displays of bones, but that's gone out of fashion, thank God. Why do you ask."

"I was wondering what would happen if, say, bones were discovered in the Co-op Community Garden at the park."

"You'd be surprised at the complication of funerary laws, historical preservation laws, and criminal laws that would come into play," Mrs. Hazelton told her. "It's a complicated business. Until the bones were removed the garden would be closed. If they were found to be of historical significance—the bones of indigenous people, let's say, or a family cemetery for family members in the rancho period—then the investigation would close the garden for a good long time. You might want to speak to Cecilia Carson about it. She's done some field work along these lines. The problem arises on a fairly regular basis. I've interceded with the Sheriff-Coroner on a number of occasions on behalf of private parties. It's nice to have help with this kind of thing."

They chatted for a time, and then Jane said, "Thanks for the information," and rang off, deciding to leave the real question under her hat. Tomorrow morning, after she talked to Jerry about it, she could call Mrs. Hazelton back and make it more particular.

She heard the sound of the parking lot door banging shut, and for a moment she thought it might be Jerry and Peewee, but she had only been in the office for forty-five minutes. There was the sound of someone climbing the stairs, the back door opened, and Lettie Phibbs stepped in.

"Lettie!" Jane said, trying to sound cheerful, although she realized that she dreaded the sight of the woman, who was even more dreadful than usual this morning. She had on a wide-brimmed samurai hat covered in a big plastic shower-cap, the hat broad enough to keep her shoulders dry. Her yellow rain gear dripped water onto the planks of the floor. Weirdly, she wore a long black wig that Jane couldn't help but stare at. There was something nightmarish about what the hat and wig did to her face.

"I'll just be a second of your time, Jane, if you've got a second to spare," she said, closing the door behind her and taking a couple of steps into the room. She looked around, nodding her head as if satisfied with what she saw.

"Of course, Lettie. Lots of seconds to spare. I don't think it'll be a busy day. You want to hang up your coat?"

"No time for that. I'll need to skedaddle if I want to get back down to the Center through the flood. It's already been a long morning. I've been busy as a beaver and twice as wet."

"Quick cup of tea? I can plug the kettle in."

"It's tempting but I don't think so. Like they say, I've got places to go and people to meet."

"I hope not too many people on a morning like this."

"Just *one*, to be truthful, but I think it should be a productive meeting." She winked, but Jane didn't get the joke.

The rain picked up now, pelting the south-facing windows, and there was the sound of the wind shrieking under the eaves. Satellite Market across the road was invisible through the downpour.

"Your garden shed wouldn't survive this kind of assault," Lettie said. "Did Jerry box it up like he said he was going to do?"

"He did. But you're right. If this gets worse the garden shed will be the least of our worries."

Lettie nodded heavily and said, "Like carving a scrimshaw when you've got Moby Dick on the hook." There was a cracking noise outside on the street, and Jane saw a branch from the curb tree fall into the street. Lettie didn't turn around, but was staring at Jane as if waiting for a response to the Moby Dick comment.

Jane had no response to offer, and she was suddenly out of small talk. "What did you want to chat about?" she asked.

An abrupt smile appeared on Lettie's face. "I guess I just dropped in to make amends. I brought you a little gift."

"You shouldn't have, and there's no amends to make."

"In fact there are." She reached into her open purse and removed a small pistol, pointing it at Jane, who rolled her chair back from the desk in response, staring at the pistol now and not at Lettie.

Jane stood up, her heart pounding, and leaned on the desk to keep her balance. "Stop right there," Lettie told her. "You have *nothing* to fear if you cooperate. Listen carefully to me, because I'm going to make a confession. I shot my employee Peter Carmody dead last night and left him on his back in the mud. He attempted to steal two valuable coins that your own Jerry had dug up from under your house. I'd warrant that Jerry failed to mention it to you—that he had found the Flores gold?"

"He told me last night," Jane said evenly.

"Well, Peter got it into his mind that the gold belonged to him. But it did not. To put it simply, it belongs to me—not to Peter, not to Jerry, and not to you, Jane. The Antiquity Center has a historical right to it, and I simply won't allow it to be stolen by opportunists. Peter wanted to argue about this, and so I shot him. It was as simple as that. For your sake, I hope Jerry is not as pig-headed."

Lettie stepped to the desk and picked up Jane's phone, dropping it into her open purse. "I'll just take this back, too," she said, picking up the buffalo nickel. "What you need to learn, Jane, is that what goes around comes around. Today you're in for an education, so get your coat from the coat rack. You'll need it where you're going."

Jane did as she was told, pulling on her coat and fastening every button, zipper, and flap that could be fastened, Lettie holding the pistol on her the entire time. "Why don't you let me talk to Jerry about the gold?" she asked. "I can reason with him."

"*Talk?* I'm through talking, especially with unreasonable men. You're a hostage, Jane. We'll see how much your life is worth to your loving husband. There's only one kind of reasoning that men like him understand." She produced a heavy plastic cable-tie from the pocket of her raincoat and said, "Turn around now and hold your hands together behind your back. Don't make any sudden movements. That was Peter's mistake."

Jane felt the cable-tie zip closed around her wrists. Rain battered the windows, and there was a double crack of thunder that seemed to shake the building.

"Out the back," Lettie said, herding Jane toward the door to the parking lot. "Easy does it. Don't think I won't kick you downstairs."

46.

JERRY STEPPED onto the top of the big flowerpot overturned in the bottom of the grave and climbed out. The rain had made the digging easier than it would have been in a drought year, and the tarp overhead was doing a pretty good job of keeping the area reasonably dry. Even so, the soles of his shoes had collected enough mud to add an inch to his height. He scraped the bulk of it off with his shovel, pulled out his tape measure, and found that he had another two feet to go. Six feet was deeper than necessary, but under the circumstances deeper was better.

He intended to put the jar into the bottom of the grave and fill the hole most of the way to the top. Then he would wrap the treasure chest in a trash bag and leave it and the bones a foot or so under the surface until he and Jane could come up for air long enough to figure out what to do with it. All of it was out of the garage now, sitting on the table beneath the tarp.

He picked up his coffee mug and drained the half-inch of cold coffee left on the bottom, including the chewy grounds that had found their way into it. He had nothing against cold coffee. It had always tasted like work to him, as did water from the garden hose or an early-morning glazed doughnut. Maybe he would pick up a bag of sinkers from Lew's Doughnuts on his way to Jane's office. There was nothing better than a doughnut on a rainy morning.

He wondered where Ling Jiao's cottage had sat. Maybe on this very site, in the shade of this very avocado tree. Could be he was standing in the living room of the cottage right now. He looked at the dug-out dirt heap, recalling what Phibbs had said about people bringing in items that they'd found in backyard dumps. It was too bad she was a nickel-plated troll, because she had an interesting side to her.

He spotted what looked like the mouth of a clear-glass bottle sticking up out of the dirt below the edge of the firewood bench, and he grabbed the shovel and wiggled the blade under the object, giving it plenty of clearance so as not to break it when he pried it up. It came out easily, encased in a big lump of wet dirt. He washed it under a rivulet of water running down off the corner of the tarp so that he could read the raised words on the front: "Citrate of Magnesium. As a laxative, take a wineglass full every hour as long as necessary." The glass was faintly rainbow-colored, but there wasn't a chip in it. He laughed out loud, wishing he could take it to the Antiquity Center to hustle it to Phibbs, who was desperately full of crap. He would keep it, though—the first piece for his collection of backyard artifacts.

Thunder muttered in the distance, and the wind gusted. As if on cue, the rain increased, drops the size of marbles beat down onto the tarp, collecting in the center and forming a small lake. It came into his mind to tent the sagging tarp by slipping the standing umbrella into the hole in the garden table and simply opening it, but before he could act on the thought, the phone rang. *Jane*, he thought, checking in.

47.

JANE WALKED along the muddy concrete walkway that ran from the end of River Street to the bottom edge of the Co-op garden. Lettie followed behind, carrying a small tool-bag instead of her purse. Her free hand was in the pocket, holding the pistol. Although the River Street neighborhood was deserted and the heavy rain made the world a blur, Jane hoped that someone had seen them get out of Lettie's car—had seen that her hands were bound behind her. Surely they would know that something was wrong.

The walkway was raised a couple of inches above the ground for the first fifty yards, but at the edge of the garden a wash of water flowed down the hillside, and the concrete was covered with liquid mud. She saw that an orange tree had fallen in the garden, its roots visible. The hillside itself seemed to be giving way, pulling apart the railroad ties that helped terrace the plots. A torrent of water flowed down the path that bisected the garden, plowing its own channel to Santiago Creek. The creek had become a river, the far side nearly invisible beyond the gray veil of rain. Chaparral shrubs and oak trees stood up out of the water that swirled and eddied around them.

Lettie prodded Jane in the back with the barrel of the pistol and told her to head downhill, and Jane stepped down onto the muddy path that led to the garden shed, walking on her boot heels in order to keep from going down in the sludge. She saw that the shed door wasn't fixed in place—that Jerry's piece of plywood leaned against the wall alongside. The three pieces of lumber that were meant to bar the door lay on the ground.

At first she thought that Jerry had forgotten to seal the place up last night, but of course that wasn't it. She knew why Lettie had been busy as a beaver this morning. Jane felt the barrel of the pistol pushed against her lower back now, inches from her hands, which were useless to her. Lettie tossed the tool bag up against the foundation wall and pulled the shed door open, the bottom scraping away mud that had washed down from above.

"This way!" she hollered, pushing her samurai hat back up onto the top of her head. "Get inside! Safe and dry!"

Once again Jane cooperated, walking in through the open door, out of the rain at last.

"Stop right there!" Lettie shouted. "Don't move! You don't want to die now!"

"Let me have my phone. You don't need it."

"I intend to give it to Jerry. It'll open his eyes. Radio silence for you."

In the darkness of the nearly empty shed, Jane saw that rain was coming in through the roof in a steady flow back in the corner. A pool of water beneath was already climbing the foundation wall under the potting table.

"Hold still!" Lettie shouted behind her, "I'm going to cut your bonds. Sink or swim, it's all the same to me."

Jane felt cold metal sliding along her wrists now, and felt rather than heard the clippers sever the plastic cable-tie, which fell away from her wrists. She turned as the door slammed shut behind her, and in the utter darkness took a two-step run at it, hitting it with her upper body, putting her weight into it. It opened an inch and then slammed shut again. She heard Phibbs grunt on the other side, evidently anticipating her and blocking the door with her weight.

There was a cracking explosion and the simultaneous appearance of a hole in the wall a foot away—a bullet hole. Jane ducked away, tripping in the darkness and going down onto a knee-high pile of bags filled with garden soil.

She squirreled around behind them to shelter herself, but Lettie was busy outside now, screwing Jerry's impregnable ply-wood door into place. Jane stood up and felt around overhead for the hanging pull-chain for the overhead light, wondering if Lettie had been mean enough to remove the bulb. She hadn't been, or hadn't thought to. The low-watt bulb cast only a twi-light glow, but it was better than no glow at all.

A dim light shone through the bullet hole, which had splintered the wood on the inside. Jane listened for further sounds of Lettie at work on the door, but heard nothing, and after another moment Jane pulled the larger splinters away from the hole in order to get a view of the outside world, a view that was suddenly worth a fortune to her.

Through the hole she saw that Lettie had ascended the hill and was just now stepping up onto the concrete walkway. She carried her tool bag in one hand and pressed her samurai hat to the top of her head with the other, holding it against the gale. She stopped momentarily to scrape mud from the soles of her Wellingtons by dragging them across the edge of the con-crete, and then she set out in the direction of her car, quickly disappearing from sight.

48.

JERRY PULLED his phone out of his pocket and looked at the screen—Paul's number and not Jane's.

"You busy?" Paul asked.

"No," Jerry said, "believe it or not I'm out working in the back and found a household dump from the old days. I dug up something fun."

"So did I—something you need to know. I tracked down Lettie Phibbs for one thing. Back in the '80s she was a suspect in the murder of her husband, a professor at Tidwell College named Arthur Johnston. They found him drowned in the San Gabriel River. There was a suicide note, but also a good chance he was hit on the head and then thrown into the river. No water in his lungs."

"Was Phibbs arrested?"

"Nope. Questioned and released. She was out of town at the time. No one was charged, and the cause of death went into the record as undetermined, which was strange—maybe someone pulling strings. And get this: she was represented by a lawyer named Holloway who looks a lot like your historical man. I found an old *Press-Telegram* photo of him and Phibbs walking into the Long Beach police station out in Alamitos. That was thirty years ago and the photo's grainy, but for my money it's the same guy."

"I'll bet Phibbs killed her husband, or had him killed. Plenty of motivation."

"Could be. One more thing you'll want to hear. I called a cop friend on the Tustin PD to find out if Peter Carmody had ever had any legal problems, and he told me that Carmody turned up murdered early this morning on the property of some kind of coin merchant out on Prospect Street. He was shot in the chest and coyotes had made a mess of the corpse. Does that make sense to you?"

"Yeah. Could it have been Phibbs who shot him?"

"No suspects, but I didn't ask about specifically about Phibbs. I didn't want to seem to know more than I should. Neither should you be, by the way. You don't want to be part of an investigation unless there's no way to avoid it. Carmody's car was in the garage on the property, and apparently stuff from his suitcase had been thrown on the ground. Looks like he was robbed."

"Of what?" Jerry's mind was going full tilt now, and he was pretty sure he knew the answer to his own question.

"The coin man reported that Carmody had stolen two antique gold coins out of the floor safe."

"So someone knew Carmody was out there at night and hid in the garage, waiting for him to come out with the coins."

"Maybe an accomplice who got greedy and didn't want to share the merchandise."

"It has to be Phibbs. I gotta run, Paul. I'll tell you how this plays out."

He hung up the phone, the rain pounding down now, running off the precarious tarp in a waterfall and pooling up on the ground. There was a loud, close, clap of thunder, and he heard Peewee barking from inside the house. The grave digging was going to have to wait for better weather.

He dialed Jane's phone number. What if Phibbs didn't want to "talk things over", as Jane supposed? What if there was something else she wanted? She already knew absolutely that the treasure wasn't any kind of legend, and she knew right where to find it.

When Jane didn't answer he flipped his phone shut, opened it again, and pushed redial. It went to voice mail, and when the message beeper went off, he said, "Call me quick. Phibbs murdered Peter Carmody last night, that guy who was sitting with her at breakfast Sunday morning. Don't let Phibbs near you. Get out of the office now and head over to Ruby's when you get this call. I'll meet you there as soon as I can."

Jerry left the bones and the treasure and the ghost jar right where they were, safely out of the rain, at least for the moment, although water was running into the grave now. He would put the treasure back into the garage and worry about the rest later. Peewee was still barking, and he wondered whether there was someone on the front porch.

Heading across the yard, he held onto his rain hood and kept his head down simply to breathe, thinking that he had no weapon and that Phibbs had a gun, which she obviously didn't mind using. Probably she'd be happy to use it. He slowed down along the path next to the garage, wary and moving slowly despite the rain. When he looked past the corner of the garage at the driveway, he was astonished to see that there was a car parked a foot from the garage door—an old Honda Accord. Someone had backed through the gate, knocking the gate off its hinges. The storm had hidden the sound of it.

In that moment a woman with black, stringy hair stood up from behind the fender on the far side of the car, a pistol in her hand. She was dressed in a yellow rain-suit and a pyramid hat. It took Jerry a moment to realize that it was Lettie Phibbs, wearing a different wig, her mouth twisted into something like a smile. She had left her car running. Exhaust rose from the exhaust pipe, the taillights glowing red against the garage door.

"Look what I've got," she shouted at him, and held up a cell phone. He recognized Jane's checkerboard case. "Jane let me borrow it!"

49.

THROUGH HER bullet-sized circle of vision Jane could see that the railroad ties used to terrace the garden had slewed around and were slowly bumping and moving in heavy mud. The uprooted orange tree appeared to have moved downhill. She could see it from sideways-on now, but it seemed to be held in place by branches. If the hillside itself gave way, God knew what would come down with it.

Lettie would be at the house by now, confronting Jerry. Jane sent out a prayer that Jerry could deal with her, whatever that meant, and then she took her raincoat off and set it on top of the bench. She was wet and cold, but she wouldn't freeze, and work might warm her up.

There wasn't much useful left in the shed—no tools at all. She and Jerry had made sure of that. She tossed through a heap of broken seed trays, pieces of clay pots, and empty bags under the bench, spotting a gardening glove crammed in among it. She unearthed the right-hand glove, too. They were both worn through at the fingers but were better than nothing. Water was leaking in under the door, spreading into a pool, which was definitely not good, and she picked up a bag of potting soil and crammed it against the threshold, the water immediately creeping in around it.

There was more water leaching in from under the foundation itself, and so Jane packed bags side by side along the bottom of the wall, cramming them together, thinking that it was as futile as building a wall around a sandcastle to keep the ocean out. Doing nothing wouldn't help, though. She had moved half the bags out of the pile before she exposed a buried piece of two-by-four lumber.

She levered it out and banged it against the floor to knock loose clinging soil from broken bags. The wood was three feet long and heavy enough to use as a battering ram. The idea of battering away at the shed that they had worked hard to preserve was ironic, but if the shed was going down anyway, there was no way she was going down with it if she could help it.

The noise of the rain beating against the wooden roof was deafening, and abruptly it turned into the clatter of what had to be heavy hailstones. And then all sound was shattered by an enormous clap of thunder that echoed down the sky in successive detonations. What sounded like solid water poured from the sky, the shed roof leaking heavily in three different places.

She hefted her battering ram, drew it back, and hammered it against the plank door as hard as she could, shaking the entire shed with the blows but accomplishing nothing at all. She set her feet and put her weight into it, hammering it over and over, beating on it until the old planks on the inside splintered and smashed but held together, fixed in place by the plywood and the cleats screwed across the outside.

She heard a noise that reminded her of last week's earthquake, a muffled rumbling like an avalanche, and she thought of boulders in the creek bed tumbling along the concrete floor of the parking lot. She wondered whether the hillside above would make any noise when it came down, or whether it would be a silent wall of mud and debris.

The ceiling was the only thing that wasn't plated with plywood, and she climbed onto what was left of the pile of bags and punched away at the wood sheathing overhead until the ceiling jumped and shuddered. Splinters flew once again, and now she knocked open a hole. A solid stream of cold water poured through it onto her head, and she ducked away, breathing heavily, her strength gone.

She tossed the two-by-four aside and made her way to the bullet hole in the wall. What she saw in the gray, circular world outside was a muddy chaos of railroad ties and fallen trees in a slow-moving mass, big chunks of the walkway broken and shifting, half of the Co-op garden angling across the little forest of juniper trees on the slope above the shed.

50.

EVERYTHING WAS CLEAR to Jerry now that it was too late. "Where the hell is Jane? If you hurt her . . ."

"Save your breath, you stupid, useless man. You're in no position to make threats. I didn't *hurt* Jane. Jane and I could have been good friends if filth like you hadn't set her against me. Jane is safe, God willing and the creeks don't rise." She laughed out loud, as if she'd made a joke.

Lightning lit the sky now, and she held up her hand, looking at him sharply, and counted with her fingers. A crack of thunder boomed, and in that moment she pointed the pistol at the ground near his foot and pulled the trigger. The sound of the gunshot was lost in the sound of the thunder.

"No need for that," he said as calmly as he could, and he held his hands up. He wondered what she meant by "God willing". What did God have to do with any of this?

She held up one of the adobe slugs in her free hand, one of the two she had taken from Carmody after murdering him. "Will you give me what I want," Phibbs asked, "or will you sacrifice Jane's life for a few gold coins?"

"It's all yours, Lettie." He gestured for her to follow him, moving toward the rear of the yard through the downpour, aware that she was close behind him. Rainwater was pouring over the dip in the side of the tarp now, streaming into the open grave.

"Stop right there!" she shouted. He thought about trying for the shovel in order to hit her with it, but it was too far away. Then he thought of the haunted nightmare and the hacked-apart bones, the cursed treasure still bringing death and ruin.

She ducked under the edge of the tarp and looked at the articles on the bench. She grinned at him and nodded her head in satisfaction. "Jane is quite secure, at least for now. If you're stupid enough to challenge me, I'll shoot you. Then poor Jane will have to go it alone, and if she survives her trial, she'll find you dead in this hole you've dug, pickling in muddy water."

"I fully understand," he said, his words cut off by another crack of thunder.

Phibbs stood stock-still until she could be heard again. "Pick up these things." She pointed with the pistol at the stuff on the bench. "You're going to haul the lot of it to my car and put it into the back seat. All of it! *You keep nothing.*"

"I hear you!" The goal now was to get Phibbs the hell out of their lives and to find Jane. He set the canvas bag and the big Mason jar on top of the treasure box and set out toward the driveway again, tilting the pile against his chest, bowing his head, letting the water run off his rain hood. He thought of Peter Carmody, eaten by coyotes, and he sensed the presence of the pistol aimed at his back.

"Stop!" she ordered, when they got to the car. She swung the back door open with her left hand and motioned with the pistol. "Careful with it," she said, "but don't waste time. I've got a long drive ahead of me, and wouldn't you like to know where? Wedge that jar in between the other two pieces, nice and tight."

He did exactly what she wanted, and when he backed out, momentarily blocking her view, he unscrewed the lid of the jar, leaving it loose on top—fresh air to the ectoplasm. Senseless, probably, but a nod to Mrs. Hazelton.

Phibbs shut the door and adjusted her hat over her idiot wig, which had slid sideways, hanging on because it was trapped by the pyramid hat. "Listen to me," she said. "I'm going to call you in half an hour, so keep your phone handy. I'll tell you where Jane is located. She's scared, but she believes that the great Jerry Larkin is coming for her, the man who thinks everything is funny. If I suspect you've gone to the police, I won't call you. Simple as that. Jane's life is in your pitiful hands."

Keeping the pistol trained on him, she walked around to the far side of the car and climbed in, put the car into gear, and drove away down the driveway, turning left onto the street and disappearing, her license plate number hidden by black tape.

51.

WATER SWIRLED around Jane's feet now, flowing in through the roof and bubbling up from under the foundation. It was easy to imagine the mudslide collapsing the walls and the roof caving in, trapping her in the debris and pushing her into the flooded creek. She battered away at the ceiling again, fueled by fear, but merely wore herself out. Lettie would have found Jerry by now and made a devil's bargain. She hoped to God that he had humored her. Then she wondered whether Lettie had meant to kill Jerry all along.

She was swept with futility but kept banging away, widening the hole. How she would get through it was a good question. She tossed the two-by-four down and went to the potting bench in order to drag it nearer to the hole. She yanked and pulled on it, trying to lever it away from the wall where it was fixed with nails—too many nails.

She picked up her battering ram to use it as a prybar, but right then the shed began to groan like a living thing, shuddering and turning on its axis, the rock foundation coming apart, water flooding in. The light fixture sparked overhead, the lights went out, and for a moment Jane was in twilight darkness. There was a cracking and tearing sound and the shed skewed around again, tilting crazily. The uphill corner tore open, splitting open the roof and pulling apart the corners of the wall below it. A limb from the fallen orange tree thrust through, driving its way in, and the corner of the shed opened from floor to ceiling, heavy mud oozing through like lava.

The big limb was wedging the shed apart, the entire tree pushing the west-facing wall toward the creek, filling the gaping corner with leafy branches. It was time to go, or at least try. She grabbed the limb and began to climb, the tree itself shifting under her, rain beating down through the open roof. The tree itself filled the hole it had made, and she had to slither and pull herself between the limbs. Broken off branches gouged her side as she hauled herself upward, her boot braced against the crotch of two limbs. She levered herself into the open, pushing on slippery shingles through green leaves and small limbs until she was free of her prison, the muddy ground some ten feet below her.

The rain pelted down and the sky was a mass of roiling clouds. The creek flowed wide and fast below, over its banks, washing through picnic tables and climbing the grassy hills. Behind and below her the ground was a tangle of railroad ties, fallen junipers, and concrete chunks from the destroyed sidewalk. There was the sound of straining wood, as if the shed was tearing itself apart.

52.

JERRY YANKED OFF his muddy boots and ran into the house through the back door, thinking hard while he put on dry clothing. He had badly misunderstood Phibbs, and in about six different ways. So had Jane, but he had brought this on both of them: Jane hadn't known what he knew. Last night's disclosures were too little, too late.

He drove to the corner, where Chapman Avenue was running axle-deep, and he slowed down to a crawl in order to cross it and get to higher ground. Maple Street was passable, and he turned east in the direction of downtown, considering what he could possibly say to the cops: *So Phibbs kidnapped my wife, stole my gold, a sack of bones, and a jar with a ghost in it, and then drove away in an old Honda Accord with unknown license plates in an unknown direction.*

The conversation would be like digging a hole with a teaspoon. He could catch their attention by saying that Phibbs had almost certainly murdered Peter Carmody out in Tustin last night, but they'd wonder exactly how he knew that.

He reached the train station and turned down past Ruby's Diner, intending to circle around to Jane's office. There were lights on inside and three cars in the lot, but of course none of them were Jane's—a useless hope. Phibbs would already have had Jane's phone when he had made the call. He slowed down to maneuver through high water on Chapman Avenue and was forced to detour up Lemon Street at the post office to avoid the river flowing downhill from the Plaza. Two or three cars were stuck in the flood, haphazardly parked near Rod's Liquors.

Almond Street was in better shape, and he finally turned into the parking lot behind PJ's Abbey, where he saw Jane's car parked in her usual spot. It meant nothing, of course. And yet for all he knew she might be tied up in her chair, or worse. He leapt out of the car and high-stepped it through the flood to the parking lot door, sprinting up the stairs and through the open office door. No Jane. Then he saw that her purse sat on the desk. Phibbs had taken her.

Where? He descended the stairs two at a time, out into the rain again and climbing into his truck, thinking through his conversation with Phibbs this morning, and saw what he had been too addled to see then. She had pulled the old phrase out of her hat: "God willing and the creeks don't rise,"—her usual nonsense, but apparently hilarious to her. Clearly it wasn't nonsense, she was being literal. Jerry headed south toward the park, stop-and-go through flooded streets, the windshield wipers working overtime.

He knew why Phibbs had put on that wig and spied on them at Hart Park—dead obvious now. She had been putting together a plan, figuring it all out in advance. She had come to the house with Bob Hovel yesterday to give him a last chance. Probably she had planned to murder Carmody all along . . .

He parked the car at the bottom of Shaffer Street, jumped out into the staggering wind and rain, and waded across the river that flowed down Shaffer Street into the park. When he reached the walkway to the Co-op garden he could see that the hillside had slipped, taking down trees and dismantling the railroad-tie stairs and terracing. What was left of the broken walkway was ankle-deep in mud and water. Then abruptly there was no walkway at all, just tilted chunks of broken concrete that had mowed down the forest of junipers.

A hundred feet below, the garden shed was half-off its foundation and skewed around. A big orange tree, caught in the mudflow, had plowed into it, its limbs grappling the shed, either holding it in place or pushing it down the hill; it was impossible to say. A heavy layer of lava-like mud crept downward, heaping up onto itself as the ground leveled in front of the shed.

Something moved in the orange tree, and as if by magic Jane appeared, climbing up onto a limb, a dark figure veiled by rain and leaves. Lightning flashed in the sky, illuminating the scene, and when she looked up, she saw him and waved wildly.

The path downward was buried under mud, deep enough to suck the shoes from his feet. He turned and ran back down the path the way he had come, one hand holding onto his rain hood, which was billowing in the wind, the rain driving in underneath. He leapt out into the knee-deep water, which drove hard against the back of his legs. The gale blew him sideways, and he leaned against the pressure, wading downward along the wall that bordered the entryway to the parking lot.

His foot went into a hole and he fell, the current spinning him around, bearing him along toward the creek. He made a wild grab for the long, triangular swing-gate that closed off the lot, managing to catch his foot in the angle where two pipes were welded together. The current jammed him against it, and he grappled his way hand-over-hand along the pipe, hauling himself out of the stream and crawling up onto a grassy knoll, where he climbed to his feet.

He could see the shed now, pushed halfway around on its axis by the wall of mud, but he couldn't see Jane. He put his head down and ran across the wet grass, looping around a wide swath of mud and debris, uselessly shouting her name, his voice blown away by the storm.

And then suddenly there she was, pushing through a tangle of limbs. She leapt the last three feet onto a clear patch of lawn, catching herself as she fell forward and then picking herself up again. She headed toward him, leaving the shed and the mud-flow behind her, and they met in the pouring rain, thunder booming around them.

"You were so graceful," Jane shouted, and then started to laugh, which turned into crying.

Jerry hugged her to him, realizing that he was crying, too, which he hoped would be hidden by the rain . . . He let the senseless thought go, held her shoulders, swallowed hard, and said, "I'm glad I got here in time to save you," except that his voice sounded as if he'd swallowed gravel, which set off Jane's laughter again.

They kissed each other, surveyed the surroundings, and headed east toward the footbridge, which was perilously close to being inundated. They crossed to the far side where the elevated road that led east out of the park was still passable, and headed north in order to loop around through the neighborhood to retrieve Jerry's truck.

53.

AFTER LEAVING Jerry gawking in the driveway, Lettie made two left-turns and then pulled over to the curb near the Water Department to yank the tape off the car's license plates. She threw the balled-up tape, her wig, her pistol, and Jane's cell phone, into the water flooding down a storm drain—one of three that she had mapped out when driving around the neighborhood yesterday. As soon as she saw the phone vanish, she pulled off her yellow rain-suit and samurai hat and crammed them into the trunk with her two suitcases. Within half a minute she was heading east up Chapman Avenue toward the foothills, the heater going full blast.

The intersections were flooded, and the rain was steady, but nothing the wipers couldn't handle. The brakes and the tires were good, the gas tank was full, and the street behind her was empty for half a mile. She was comfortably toasty and dry, the rain gear having done its job.

"Mad dogs and librarians," she said aloud, "go out in the morning rain!" and she hooted three times to blow off energy. She wished she could have kept the pistol, but it would condemn her outright if she was caught with it.

After a nearly sleepless night and a long damned morning, she had done it, by God. It had almost been too easy, Jane waiting like a good girl to be plucked out of her office, and Jerry having gotten everything into a tidy pile, not knowing that his destiny was driving toward him through the storm.

She glanced at the dashboard clock. The entire caper had taken fifty-two minutes since she had walked into the Co-op office. It would qualify as record time, if anyone had ever done such a thing before, which they hadn't—not in the history of the world. That *meant* something. She would have plenty of time to contemplate what it meant when her Honolulu-bound flight was airborne out of San Diego International and she had a Malibu Rum cocktail in her hand.

She drove through yet another green light at Crawford Canyon Road—green lights all the way so far—and wound her way up Orange Hill. The rain had picked up, and even with the wipers at high speed, she had an off-and-on view of the world through the windshield. Water poured down the roadside ditches, and the street was sheeted with flowing water, but nothing the Honda couldn't handle.

She passed the entrance to Orange Hill Restaurant now, where Peter Carmody had given her the pashmina at her birthday happy hour. His treachery had led him to an early grave, that and his own stupidity. He had turned out to be a hollow man in the end, a husk, but for those few years that he had worked for her, he had been her sole companion.

Her breath caught in her throat, and she swallowed to keep down her emotions. What was done was done, she told herself—spilt milk. So much—so *much*—had happened in the past few days. The storm had carried on it the winds of change. Ironically, the storm had become her only ally, working for her like . . . like a cloak of invisibility.

She lost track of the thought when she braked for the light at Jamboree Road—the point at which Chapman Avenue became Santiago Canyon Road. The suburbs had vanished behind her, and the wilderness widened out ahead. The canyon road would take her the back way into San Juan Capistrano, where she would emerge onto the San Diego Freeway for the 45-minute south-bound run to the airport. She should make it with four hours to spare—plenty of time to find a secluded, dry place in the parking garage, where she could pick through the goodies she had taken away from Jerry, repack them, abandon the car, and get through security in time to find a hot lunch and a glass of wine.

She was alone on her side of the intersection. Across the road, aimed toward the flatlands, a big SUV sat waiting for the light, splashed up the fenders with rain-streaked mud and packed with boxes and bins. She made out two adults up front and children in the back seat, probably a family from Silverado or Modjeska, evacuating their home.

The light changed and she drove past them, alone on the now-deserted highway, passing the turnoff for the toll roads, the elevation rising. Irvine Lake, visible on her left, stretched up into the grasslands and chaparral like an inland sea. She thought of Jane, locked into the old shed, and wondered if the flood had already taken her. Would Jerry have been stupid enough to wait for his phone call? That had been an IQ test.

For the first time she wondered if it might have been smarter to take the high-riding Escalade despite its being so easy to identify. There was literally no one on the road to identify it, but how could she have known that? The morning was going as planned, but what if the plan was faulty? What if the canyon was flooded and she couldn't get through in the low-riding Honda?

She had those four hours on her side. She could turn back and take her chances with the toll road if it came down to it. Irvine Lake passed out of sight, and a wooded area lay along the right-hand side, live-oaks and sycamore trees and dense scrub, dark green and obscured by the curtain of rain. Lightning flashed, and the crack of thunder boomed out, rolling across the sky. The rain redoubled, banging on the roof of the car and streaming down the windshield, obscuring the view, the wipers nearly useless. She slowed even further. Better to take it easy than rush along needlessly. Cloudbursts didn't last long, although God knew she'd never seen anything like this. Pulling over was a bad idea, though, unless she wanted to get mired in the roadside mud.

The road steepened, and dark water moved fast down both sides of the highway, pushing rocks onto the asphalt, rills and waterfalls flowing down out of the trees and feeding the flood. Santiago Creek itself appeared on the left, close to the highway. She saw it clearly through a gap in the hilly verge of the road, its waters raging and boiling along.

The car banged over something, and the steering wheel jerked to the left—a rock probably, although she could see nothing in the rearview mirror but pelting rain. She backed off on the accelerator a little more and held her breath, creeping along, waiting for the grinding sound of a broken axle or the pull of a blown-out tire, but there was nothing—no hint of damage.

She edged to the center of the road and held the car at a steady fifteen miles an hour, catching sight of a road sign for the left-turn into Black Star and Silverado Canyons up ahead, past where the creek flowed under the road. In a pinch she could wait out the worst of the storm at the Silverado Café, given that it was open. In the parking lot if it wasn't. But if the storm didn't let up, conditions would only get worse, and she would find herself waiting in vain, maybe trapped.

She remembered the wide spot along the highway at the Silverado turnoff, where she had U-turned when she made the run yesterday in better weather. She could do it again if she had to and head back down. She probably should have taken the damned toll road when she'd had the chance—when it was apparent that she was the only one heading into the canyon. She had chosen stealth over common sense. Still, if Jerry had called the police, they would never assume she would chance the canyon.

The air smelled strange, a musty odor, like mold, or a mummified rat, along with something sweet and . . . grapey. She bent forward and breathed in the air coming out of the heater vent, but it wasn't the heater, which was doing its job nicely, keeping the windshield clear and the car warm. She glanced back over her shoulder, realizing that the smell must be emanating from the stuff in the back seat. The dirty canvas bag might account for it, and it dawned on her what might be inside—why Jerry was digging that grave in his back yard.

She reached back and grabbed the bag by its straps, pulling it into the passenger seat before checking the road again. It was still raining hard, but not a deluge at the moment, and she sped up. Too much caution might strand her. The smell had heightened, and it had a sagebrush odor to it, like the evening smell of a Santa Ana wind. There was a cow pasture smell, too, maybe from the grazing land near Silverado.

She jerked at the zipper that closed the canvas sack and managed to slide it open. A big coffee-can sat in the middle of dried bones that the liar Jerry Larkin had dug up from his cellar. She tilted it toward her, puzzled to see that it was apparently filled with what looked like dirty salt. The car jolted over another rock, the heavy bag toppling sideways, the can spilling its salt onto the floor of the car, followed by a human skull, the Yenshing charm coin clamped in its teeth. A litter of bones tumbled down on top of it. She couldn't force the bag's zipper closed without two hands, and she didn't dare let go of the wheel, so she picked up the bag and what was left inside and dropped it behind the seat.

When she looked at the road again, she was too close to the flooded culvert along the edge, and she pulled the steering wheel hard to the left, the car swerving sharply back toward the center line. A creaking noise sounded, and she thought about the axle again, although, weirdly, it seemed to have come from within the car.

Once again she glanced back, looking at the big, square Mason jar and what lay inside it. She could make out a pocket-knife, a burned-down candle in a holder, and a couple of smaller items—jewelry, probably. There was a puddle of something on the bottom of the jar that had a greenish, lightning-bug glow to it. She looked up at the ceiling, thinking that it might be the reflection of the dome light, but the light wasn't on.

She topped a rise now, the road curving steeply downhill, the swollen creek appearing and disappearing behind sandstone hillocks. There was a high, keening sound right at the threshold of her hearing, and a banging noise like a door shutting that made her wonder if she had knocked loose a fender. A sudden drop in air pressure blocked her ears.

Through the rain she saw a heavy tree limb on the road, dead ahead, and she hit the brakes, the back wheels skidding on slick mud. She fought to control the skid, but her vision was obscured by suddenly appearing willow trees superimposed on the window glass. She wrenched the wheel again, and the car slewed, but the willow trees still stood dead ahead, and she was confused by the sight of the moon in the sky above them.

She heard a mewling sound and realized that it was coming from her own throat, and saw too late that the roiling waters of Santiago Creek had flooded out of the culvert where it flowed under the road. She felt the presence of something horrible behind her, as if she had fallen into a nightmare, and the impossible reflection of the willow trees on the windshield metamorphosed into the shape of a man, rushing toward her, a shovel upraised in his hand, murder on his face.

She threw her right hand up to block the blow from the shovel, yanking the wheel to the left. She stomped her foot down onto the brake just as her car tilted forward, the front end slamming down into the flood, the car slewing sideways. A sandstone outcropping appeared dead ahead, and she heard herself scream as the car slammed through a cleft in the rocks, jolting her sideways, her head banging against the side window, debris flying out of the back seat. The Honda was held tightly for a moment, nose down, beaten by the flood waters. Then it broke loose and tumbled into the ravine, smashing down onto its top in the creek, the passenger-side door torn off and cold water pouring in.

Lettie fumbled groggily with her seat belt, jiggling it uselessly, her thoughts astray, panic rising within her. She was confused by the big boulder jammed against the door and the litter of floating bones swirling in the thundering water. The skull with the laid-to-rest charm in its teeth bumped past, and the sight of it focused her thoughts. She knew that if she opened her mouth she would drown, and in that moment she released the seatbelt and fell, only then realizing that she had been hanging upside-down and was now on the ceiling.

The car wrenched loose and swung around, bumping and lurching down the creek, the rending and scraping of the rocks shrieking in her ears. Driving water hammered the car, shaking it, pouring in through the open door and engulfing her. She latched onto the steering wheel and struggled to right herself, her lungs burning, fighting against the urge to gasp creek water into her throat, knowing that death was only a breath away. When she was at the very edge of darkness, the thought drifted into her mind that she should have taken a different route.

Epilogue

After the flood

JANE STEPPED OUT onto the front porch carrying the second bottle of anniversary champagne in an ice bucket, which she set on the table alongside two champagne flutes and a dish of crab dip and crackers. The air was perfumed with the last bloom of fall roses, and the clouds in the western sky were salmon pink, outlined with crimson on the bottom. The temperature was balmy—an Indian summer evening.

Peewee sat on his bed in his usual spot, watching the street and sidewalk through the rose trellis. Mrs. Collins came out to fetch her mail from the box, and she waved at Jane and shouted, "How about this weather!" before going back in. Two skateboarders cruised past on the sidewalk, and children played on a front lawn at the end of the block while their father trimmed a hedge. An unseen parrot flock was shouting nonsense somewhere nearby, and she heard the music of the reggae ice-cream truck a few blocks away, back in business now that the storm had passed.

Jerry was on his way home from a trip to the park, carrying the news about the shed and the damage to the gardens. Jane hadn't had the heart to go along with him, and in fact it had been a do-nothing day for both of them. His pickup appeared down the block, and he beeped the horn twice when he pulled into the driveway, which sounded like good news.

"Shed's still there!" he shouted through the open window, waving a newspaper at her.

She was stunned by this revelation, and she realized that she was perilously close to crying as he crossed the grass and climbed the porch steps. She stood up and kissed him, and then poured two glasses of champagne. "Tell me about it," she said, the two of them clinking glasses.

"The damned thing is sitting right there on the slope where we left it. We'll have to cut that orange tree up with a chainsaw when the mud dries out. And it'll take some digging, but we should be able to dismantle the walls and the foundation and save most of the siding and the rock. We might even be able to talk Peabody into removing the roof in one piece, if he can get a crane in there."

"Sounds like a miracle. What's the creek doing?"

"Still flowing wall to wall, and there's some ponds on the grass, but I didn't see any real damage besides mud. I came home through the Plaza. Stores and cafés are reopening, and a lot of the sandbags and debris are already cleaned up. It's amazing."

"You bought a newspaper."

"Yeah, from the bin at Snack Shop."

Jane smeared crab dip and cocktail sauce on crackers and squeezed lemon wedges over them. She passed the tray to Jerry, who helped himself to two.

"Check this out," Jerry said, holding up the front page of *The Register*. SILVERADO GOLD, the headline read. Below it were two photos: one of a wrecked car upside-down in Santiago Creek, and the other of a boy who looked to be about ten or eleven, standing on a creek-side rock and holding up a coin, a wide grin on his face.

"If you've already read it, give me the gist of it while I drink my champagne," Jane told him.

"Okay, so this car in the photo was swept into Santiago Creek yesterday when the creek washed out the road up near Silverado. Guess whose car it is. It's not your friend Needlekin's."

"Here we go again," she said. "Was it Elvis Presley's?"

"Close. It belonged to Lettie Phibbs."

"You're *kidding*," she said, and looked more carefully at the photo. It could easily be the car Lettie was driving yesterday, although there was no way to be certain by looking at the undercarriage. "How do they know it's hers?"

"Her stuff was in it."

"My God. She was running away."

"Apparently so. Sneaking out through the canyon—the wrong place at the wrong moment. Or the opposite of that, depending on your opinion of Phibbs. She was the only reported death from the storm. And get this: the newspaper lists her name as Tilda Lambert."

"Why do you say it was Lettie?"

"I got the inside information from Paul, which he got from a friend on the Tustin PD. They recovered her purse from the car, jammed under the seat. There were two sets of IDs and credit cards, one in a wallet and the other in an envelope. Tilda Lambert's wallet contained a Hawaiian driver's license with a Molokai address, but the cards in the envelope belonged to Lettie Phibbs. Tilda had a one-way ticket for a Honolulu flight and another for an island hopper to Molokai. The license plates on the car were stolen. *And* there was close to $30,000 crammed into the purse."

"So she was living two lives?"

"Looks like she was. Paul said they suspect her of shooting Peter Carmody. Some guy out walking his dog got a look at her on the night of the murder. They didn't find her pistol, though, so that'll turn into a dead end."

"Shouldn't *we* weigh in on this subject? We might know more than the guy walking his dog."

"I asked Paul and he advised against it strongly. The police already have it pieced together. There's nothing we can add that makes a difference. We don't know that she killed Carmody or anyone else."

"She told me she did."

"She told me, too, but we've got no proof, and both of them are dead. I was worried about your phone, but they didn't find it, either. Paul was particular about that, since it was the only link to us. Long story short, Phibbs is dead, so what we think we know is pretty much moot."

Jane shook her head, trying to cram all of this into her understanding of the creature who was Lettie Phibbs. She sipped champagne, thinking about what might have happened if things had gone differently. The irony was that she had thought the storm was the problem, when the real problem had been Lettie, who could not have known that the storm would seal her own fate rather than Jane's.

Jerry held up a penny between his finger and thumb. "A penny for your thoughts," he said. "Zinc plated, 1943. I found it at the park. The rain washed all kinds of stuff down the hill. It's yours, but only if you tell me what's on your mind."

"I'm thinking that Lettie was Dr. Jekyll and Mr. Hyde, and I didn't see it. I'm still having a hard time with it."

"I didn't see it either. Not really. Nobody saw it." He handed her the penny.

"Thanks," she said. The coin looked new—almost no corrosion at all. How do you know it washed down the hill? Maybe it fell out of the sky."

"Sure, that's entirely likely, just like in this other photo." He held the paper up again. "This kid found one of the Adobe Slugs—the ingots—a hundred yards down the creek. He doesn't have any idea it's worth half a million bucks. The treasure box was apparently thrown out and smashed apart, so no one knows how many coins were in the box or whether they're hidden under the rocks or washed downstream. People will be searching the creek for years—another gold rush."

"*You* know something about it."

Jerry shrugged and took another cracker from her. "I know nothing." He shoved the cracker into his mouth and made a zipping gesture across his lips.

"And what about your coin man? He must have some idea."

"My pal Dutch? I called him this afternoon, and asked him not to submit an insurance claim for the two slugs that Carmody stole. He said that was eminently sensible—his very words. The slugs might easily have been counterfeit. He never had a chance to find out."

"And now that they've disappeared we'll never know."

Jerry shrugged. "The whole thing's hypothetical."

"So we lost the treasure and the skeleton and the ghost, all in one fell swoop."

"Don't forget Phibbs," Jerry said. "Easy come, easy go."

"It wasn't all that easy. What *did* happen to Lettie? They found her purse under the seat, but how about her body? You told me she was dead."

Jerry looked at her for a long moment and then said, "There was no body in the car, but the passenger door was torn off, so they figure she washed out and tumbled downstream all the way to Irvine Lake. They're dragging the lake now, fishing for Phibbs and hauling up boats and debris. I figure that those big lake catfish are eating the evidence as we speak."

"So you were *speculating* when you said she died?"

Jerry held out his glass for more champagne. "The official assumption is that she either drowned or died of injuries or both."

"That's the assumption? Sounds biblical. Do *you* believe she's dead?"

"Well . . .," Jerry said, sipping his champagne and giving Jane a shrewd look. "She never got onto that plane for Honolulu, and she left a big pile of money behind, behind. So, yeah, I think she's dead."

"Then so do I," Jane told him after a moment. "By tomorrow she'll be yesterday's news."

The sun had gone down somewhere beyond the Plaza, and the twilight sky was dark blue. A cool breeze wafted through, smelling like the ocean. Jane thought about going in after a flannel shirt, but she poured them each a last glass of champagne instead. With autumn settling in, they would run out of balmy, front-porch evenings until spring came around again.

Jane looked at the penny, polishing it with her thumb. "I want to put it on a chain and wear it as a necklace," she said.

"Good idea. It might be worth a fortune."

"Could be," she said, smiling at him. "But I wouldn't sell it. I know a lucky penny when I see one."

JAMES P. BLAYLOCK, twice winner of the World Fantasy Award, is a southern California writer whose short stories, novels, and collections have been published around the world. He was one of the literary pioneers of the Steampunk movement along with Tim Powers and K.W. Jeter. His short story "Unidentified Objects" was nominated for an O. Henry Award in 1990. Despite his close association with Steampunk, most of his work is contemporary, realistic fantasy set in southern California. His novel *The Rainy Season* was chosen by Orange Coast Magazine as one of the ten quintessential Orange County novels.